THE FAT WOMAN NEXT DOOR
IS PREGNANT

CANADIAN LITERATURE

→ existance of
a community as/in
a community.

→ essentially a colonial
nature. w/in that
colony is French-Canadian
colony.

" I Remember "

THE FAT WOMAN NEXT DOOR IS PREGNANT

MICHEL TREMBLAY

Translated by Sheila Fischman

SERPENT'S
TAIL

British Library Cataloguing in Publication Data
Tremblay, Michel, *1943-*
The fat woman next door is pregnant.
I. Title II. Series
813.54 [F]
ISBN 1–85242–198–3

First published 1978 as
La grosse femme d'à côté est enceinte
by Les
Editions Leméac, Montreal.
Copyright © 1978 by Les Editions Leméac

First published in English 1981 by Talonbooks,
Vancouver. Translation copyright © 1981 by Sheila
Fischman

This revised edition first published 1991 by
Serpent's Tail, 4 Blackstock Mews, London N4

Typeset in 10/12 Plantin by
Selectmove Ltd, London
Printed on acid-free paper by
Nørhaven A/S, Viborg, Denmark

to Hélène,
who rebelled twenty years before everyone else
and had to suffer the consequences

to Louise Jobin and Jacqueline Rousseau,
with all my affection and gratitude

E pur si muove
Galileo

Multiple Relationships

Victoire
Edward
Paul ∞ Albertine
/ Therese
Marcel

Fat lady
∞ Gabriel
Richard
Phillipe

Mercedes, Beatrice
- prost.

→ They seem to know the whole history of the street.

⇒ reminiscent of the 3 Fates

→ how much control do these women have?

[handwritten annotations: omniscience? is this an all-knowing author?]

[handwritten annotations: organization of novel: no hierarchy]

*[handwritten annotations: * each characters thoughts + perceptions have equal billing → why? — no diff btw kids + adults + cats + prost. — lack of focalizer]*

[handwritten annotation: Florence = mother]

May 2, 1942

Rose, Violette and Mauve were knitting. From time to time, Rose (or Violette or Mauve) would put her knitting on her lap, cast a half-amused, half-severe glance at her sisters' work and say: 'You're knitting too loose' or: 'I'm glad Mama didn't give *me* that colour wool!' or then again, she might say nothing at all. If she was inactive for too long, one of her sisters would look at her. 'Finish your bootie, then you can daydream.' And Rose (or Violette or Mauve) would sigh discreetly and take up her work again. Silence settled in. Comfortably. But after a few minutes: 'Not often you can sit outside on the second of May, eh?' 'Mmm. . . yes. . . . This is the first time, I think.' 'Come on, you're kidding! What about. . .' 'That's true, you're right. . . . I remember the year Victoire had Gabriel. . .' 'Not the year she had Gabriel, the year she had Edouard, her second. . .' 'Whatever you say.' 'It isn't whatever I say, that's the way it is. It was the year she had Edouard.' Silence again. The triple clicking of knitting needles. 'Well, anyway, it was the second of May.' Rose, Violette and Mauve were sitting on straight-back chairs. Rocking chairs encouraged laziness. Backs stiff, elbows at their sides, eyes lowered on their wool. Blue. Or pink. Or yellow. Or some other colour. In the morning, before they brought out the chairs, they had washed the balcony. As they would every day until the beginning of September. A pail of water, lots of detergent, three brushes. The tiger cat that had spent the night under the balcony, exhausted after three days of fasting and violent love, has awakened, spitting foul-tempered 'phhttt's' and cleared out, cursing the smell of fanatical cleanliness. 'That cat this morning, was it Marie-Sylvia's?' 'Yes.' The door behind them opened softly. Meekly, they went on with their work. In the motionless tableau, only their hands moved. And the door that was opening. The house across the street slid to the left in the doorpane, then the house next door to it, then the others. And finally, Marie-Sylvia's restaurant at the corner of the lane. With a bit of sky this time, because Marie-Sylvia's restaurant, pretentiously baptized Rainbow Restaurant, was on the ground floor of a two-storey house, the only one on the street — a luxury in this neighbourhood where only three- or four-storey houses had been built, to save space. And money. 'When you're done, bring them inside instead of leaving them out on the balcony. It looks sloppy.' Florence, their mother, glided out of the house and bent over the work of her three daughters. 'You're knitting too loose.' 'I'm making summer booties!' The other two laughed. Florence smiled. 'There's no season for babies.' Florence straightened up, turned and went inside. The door was ajar. 'I think she's going to come out and sit with us.' Rose, Violette and Mauve got up, moved their chairs and made room for their mother. Before they were seated again, Florence appeared in the door with a rocking chair. She put it down on the clean floor. They all sat down. The creaking of Florence's chair blended with the clicking of her daughters' needles. Rose, Violette and Mauve were knitting booties. For the fat woman next door who was pregnant. 'Tomorrow, we'll start on Madame Jodoin's.' And Florence, their mother, began to rock.

'Duplessis! Duplessis!' All dolled up, though it was early in the day, Marie-Sylvia was standing on the first of the three cement steps that went up to her restaurant. 'Duplessis!' Summer and winter, beginning at 7 a.m., on St John the Baptist's Day as well as Epiphany, and even on Good Friday, Marie-Sylvia wore rhinestones in her ears and glass beads around her neck. Her lipstick, which stained her teeth and made her breath smell sugary, was famous on the whole street. The children said Marie-Sylvia smelled of candy. The women said Marie-Sylvia smelled. 'Duplessis!' She was wearing her Saturday dress. Yes, she had a dress for every day of the week. Just one. They never varied. You could tell what day it was by Marie-Sylvia's dress. Some people did just that. If Marie-Sylvia had bought a new dress, not only would the whole street have known about it, some of the residents wouldn't have been able to tell what day it was. Marie-Sylvia went back into her restaurant, peeved, dragging her tired bedroom slippers along the hardwood floor. For Marie-Sylvia was stylish only above the knees. She'd never been able to tolerate shoes, which she called 'foot-killers.' 'Shoes? Who needs them behind a counter? What people can't see won't hurt them! Why should I suffer like a martyr day in, day out, just to sell one-cent candies to dirty-faced brats!' She walked behind the glass counter that faced the door, and slipped into the back of the shop. Her kingdom. A veritable Aladdin's cave piled up to the ceiling with cases of soft-drink bottles, statues made of plaster or of salt, in a full range of sizes (phosphorescent or not, painted or plain), most of them depicting the Blessed Virgin or St Joseph, as the other saints of the calendar were not very popular in the neighbourhood, odds and ends that spilled out of bashed-in cartons, from which packages of hair pins and tangles of shoelaces escaped, and an armchair so old that even Marie-Sylvia, who knew the origin of every article in her restaurant by heart, even the most insignificant, called it 'the mysterious armchair.' As a matter of fact, the chair had already been there when she had taken on the premises, but Marie-Sylvia claimed she'd found it in the lane with a note addressed to her. 'It's a present. A mysterious present. I never found out who it was from. Maybe a secret admirer. . .' Marie-Sylvia wasn't known to have any admirers, secret or not, so people let her go on about the chair, the note, the bashful lover, nodding discreetly as they took out

the change for an ice-cream cone or a bag of peanuts. Sitting
in her mysterious armchair, Marie-Sylvia saw everything that
went on in the restaurant and, especially, everybody who
walked past it. She'd never been seen to read or knit or even
sleep in her armchair. No. Neck craned, she watched intently.
She saw everything, and according to the neighbours' comings
and goings, she could interpret their moods, their days, their
lives. If they were looking for someone in the neighbourhood, a
lost child or a pie-eyed husband, Marie-Sylvia would say: 'I saw
him at such-and-such a time. He was going in such-and-such
a direction, wearing such-and-such, and he looked as if he
was thinking about so-and-so.' Hence, the nickname, 'the
neighbourhood newshen,' that the fat woman had given her.
Marie-Sylvia walked past her armchair without even looking
at it and into the short hallway that led to the back of the
house. She came into the tiny kitchen that still had the lovely
smell of fresh coffee. 'I'll kill him! Three days now, he's been
gone! Three days!' She opened the door that gave on to the
lane. 'Duplessis! Duplessis!' She looked in every direction,
her tongue travelling along her upper teeth to erase any trace
of lipstick. And to taste again its sweetness, which made her
feel so secure. She closed the door abruptly, sighed and poured
herself another cup of coffee. 'Never trust anybody! Never!'
Her hand trembled slightly. A tear sparkled through the lashes
of her left eye. 'Comes as no surprise. . . .' She returned to
her cave and slumped into her mysterious armchair. Her head
turned automatically towards the restaurant. Towards the door.
Towards the glass, always clean. The chair was placed in such
a way that Marie-Sylvia could spy at ease, without being seen,
and drown herself completely in other people's lives. Between
the two counters with their candies, chips, cupcakes and ice-
cream, a breach opened on to the world.

His dream was filled with biting and screaming. Vague images,
just precise enough to excite him, appeared in his mind and all
his muscles tensed, allowing him to pounce on his fantasies,

lacerate them, tear them, plough them, rip them to shreds that were easy to chew, swallow, digest, forget. But he couldn't move. Other images, more provocative, replaced the first ones and he snapped his jaw at them. The voice, his own perhaps, or that of a squirming victim he hadn't yet managed to fell with a single blow, seemed to blossom from his own throat, then suddenly move away and come back so powerfully his skull exploded and he cursed because it prevented him from leaping and overpowering the wild dreams that assailed him, that voice was suddenly silent. The phatoms vanished. He opened his eyes. He saw the old woman shut the door. He stretched, yawned, sighed and curled up again. Later, caresses. First, he must destroy the shape over there that was running away, crawling (Crawling? No, it was floating, but where was the sky? Where was the ground?), that he thought for a moment he recognized, but then it was transformed before his eyes, goddamn it, and it charged, almost crushing him beneath a huge padded paw. 'I'm suffocating! Death is coming for me! That's it, that's it, it's death.' Then a rain of heads began to fall. Identical heads. 'I know them all! Every one of those heads is known to me! And I must destroy them all!' That cry again. That voice. A shadow drew near. Hands grasped him. He whistled, bit, clawed. Louder, he heard the cry. His name. He decided then to deal the final blow, and, digging his claws into the substance that was, however, impalpable, he heaved obscenely, rubbing himself against the shadow, which was immediately subdued. And his dream ended with two convulsive moments of deliverance. Duplessis was well and truly awake now, and he began to wash himself.

Béatrice remembered him well. 'The old soldier?' Mercedes dragged on her cigarette, squinting because of the smoke. 'Soldiers, that's all we had yesterday, Betty!' 'I know who, anyway. The one with the dyed hair. Is that the one?' 'That's the one.' 'I'm surprised he complained. He didn't do anything!' 'That's just it!' Mercedes held her cigarette straight between her teeth and managed to speak almost without moving her lips. 'If he *had* done anything, he wouldn't't've squawked!' 'If he'd asked for something, he'd've got it!' 'Maybe he didn't want to ask, Betty. Maybe he wanted you to take the initiative. . .' 'Don't start using those fancy words. Talk simple.' 'Sometimes, when they don't do anything, it's up to you to take care of things.' 'I get fed up when they don't do anything.' 'It doesn't matter if you're fed up or not.' Mercedes' bed was inviting. Warm. Béatrice approached her employer, whose outstretched arm made a cosy shelter. 'That's a nice nightie, Mercedes.' 'I worked for it. I took the initiative.' 'I can't get over these soldiers. I get sick just thinking they're going over to the Old Country to get killed. I feel as if they're already dead.' 'Don't think about it.' And beside, they're so full of themselves, thinking they're going to save France. And England too. I ask you! Both of them at once. Before this war, if they ever saw a Frenchman from France, they'd laugh at the way he talked and call him a fairy; and if they saw an Englishman, they'd say all kinds of stupid things about him because Englishmen are scummy and. . . kind of weird. And now, out of the blue, off they go to get themselves killed, cut into bits, lose part of their arms and legs, because France and England are in danger. . .' 'France has been occupied for two years.' 'It deserves it!' 'You say the craziest things.' 'Mercedes, you've tried to explain what's going on a hundred times, but I still don't get it. What can I do? Maybe I'm dumb, but I can't help it. I just don't see why our men have to go across the Atlantic to defend two countries they've hated all their lives.' Mercedes smiled. 'They don't all want to go.' 'There's one hell of a lot that's gone all the same.' 'If you don't want to understand, Betty don't. But don't spit on the soldiers, they're how you make your living.' 'They'd come here even if they weren't soldiers.' 'If they weren't soldiers, they couldn't afford you.' 'What were you doing before the war anyway, before there was soldiers?' 'There's always been soldiers, Betty, and there always will be. Before the war, I was doing the same thing I'm doing now, but it was assembly-line fucking.' 'And just what does that mean?' Mercedes turned towards Béatrice. She took her cigarette from her mouth, butted it in an ashtray placed between her thighs, coughed and took a deep breath. 'You like it here, Betty?' 'No.' 'You hate it?' 'No.' Béatrice stood up, then sat on the edge of the bed and looked out the window, through the lace curtains. On the other side of the street, Marie-Sylvia's cat was meowing, its nose pressed against the restaurant door. 'Duplessis wants to get in the restaurant and Marie-Sylvia's just standing there looking at him. She's standing behind that door doing nothing. She's nuts.' Mercedes stood up too. 'Ever notice how they yell at each other sometimes?' Mercedes got up. In two strides, she was in the bathroom. 'You know, sometimes you'd think it was a serious fight.' Mercedes looked at herself in the bathroom mirror. 'Take a bath with me?' 'Okay!' 'Heat up some water in the kettle. . . Go in the kitchen and. . .' 'I know what to do, Mercedes. I was taking baths before I met you!' Béatrice smiled. 'A nice hot bath. Come on, move!' 'So what'd you say?' 'To who?' 'The soldier with the dyed hair.' Mercedes stuck her head in the doorway. 'I didn't *say* anything. I just did what you should've done.'

When Duplessis was eating, everything in the restaurant came to a standstill. No matter what she was doing, Marie-Sylvia would leave the store and come and sit next to the plate of liver that Duplessis, indifferent to his mistress's presence, was devouring with his eyes shut, tucked inside a round and perfect happiness where there was room only for him: chew, chew, chew and swallow these soft things, dark, that smelled strong and tasted even stronger, that restored his energy by leaving a trace of blood in his mouth, as though he'd killed a bird, another cat, or even the old woman watching him. Yes, as though he were devouring that woman before whom he had to grovel, rubbing himself against her and sticking his tail up so that she'd feed him. If Marie-Sylvia was unfortunate enough to make some gesture suggesting she was going to caress him or just encourage him, he would suddenly straighten up and spit at her, his claws out. Hatred would make his fur bristle like an electric charge. 'I'm eating! Afterwards, we'll see if I'm in the mood to twist around in your apron and pretend I'm enjoying it! We'll see!' He stuck his face back in his dish as though nothing had happened. 'Ah! There's some left. . . . Oh oh! Not much though. . .' Marie-Sylvia would wait for him to finish, then unfailingly ask: 'Did Mummy's big pussycat have a yummy lunch?' Duplessis would give her a contemptuous look which she interpreted as gratitude. Then she'd pick up the empty dish while the cat went out of the kitchen, heading for his box of clean sand. Conscientiously, she would wash the wooden dish. 'Cats are clean, so we have to be clean with them too.' Then she would return to her customers, who'd been left high and dry, or to her empty store. As she walked past Duplessis's box in the corridor, she heard the sand fly and she smiled. 'Health.' But that morning, as Duplessis was devouring a larger quantity of liver than usual, clicking his tongue and struggling a little with the pieces that were too big, Marie-Sylvia didn't admire his slender form, his striped fur, his long ears and striped muzzle. She gave him hell.

Mercedes had met Béatrice on the number 52 streetcar that started from the corner of Mont-Royal and Fullum, then went down to Atwater and Saint-Catherine, by way of Saint-Laurent. It was the longest ride in town and the housewives from Plateau Mont-Royal took great advantage of it. They would set off in a group on Friday or Saturday, noisy, laughing, tearing open penny bags of candy or chewing enormous wads of gum. As long as the streetcar was going down Mont-Royal, they were fine, giving each other slaps on the back if they choked, calling out to other women they knew; sometimes they'd even ask the driver how come he wasn't in the army. But when the streetcar turned south down Saint-Laurent suddenly they'd calm down and sink back into the straw seats: all of them, without exception, owed money to the Jews on Saint-Laurent, especially to the merchants who sold furniture and clothes; and for them, the long street separating Mont-Royal from Saint-Catherine was a very tricky one to cross. 'Hope Sam doesn't see me! I'm two months behind!' When the streetcar passed certain stores, heads would turn away abruptly or dive into shopping bags. 'You're awful quiet all of a sudden, Madame Jodoin. You scared of Sam Katz? How about that — there he is right now!' The woman would turn or bend down, pretending to tie her shoelaces. The other women burst out laughing. 'You always fall for that one, Madame Jodoin. And we do it every week!' But usually, when they were really too far behind in their payments, they sat there silent, musing. They didn't even dare to look outside; they told themselves it was harder to recognize a face seen in profile than head on. Some, but really just a few, even took out their rosaries. They'd scarcely pretend to hold their noses when an old Jewish woman got on the streetcar, laden down with bags of groceries with carrots or leeks sticking out. 'She's gonna make herself a dandelion salad!' they would snicker. 'What do you think stinks so bad, the garlic she ate yesterday or the clothes she's going to wash next month?' They pursed their lips. 'I hear they keep their transfers for toilet paper!' Madame Jodoin, the biggest giggler of the lot, was moaning like a cat on heat, about to explode with laughter. But as soon as they turned the corner of Saint-Laurent and Saint-Catherine and headed west, they were more jubilant, filling the streetcar with loud shouts and heartfelt laughter. 'You nearly killed me, you nut!' 'You were as red as a banana — I mean, a poppy, Madame Jodoin!' 'All of a sudden, the Jew understands French!' 'No, she doesn't, she doesn't want to sell us anything!' The old Jewish woman, aware they were talking about her, would look down at her bag of groceries. All along Saint-Catherine going west, noses were pressed to the windows in winter, arms rested on the windowsills in summer. 'Tell us who's playing at the Gaiety, Madame Chose, you're on the right side?' 'Woodhouse! My Lord, here's where I get off!' 'Oh, come with us till Eaton's, Madame Lemieux!' 'Not on your life, they're a pack of thieves!' 'So what? You never buy anything.' 'If all the women that never buy anything never went to Eaton's, there wouldn't be anybody there at all and

they'd have to close down, the goddamn thieves!' 'As far as
that's concerned. . .' 'Come to Woodhouse with me, Madame
Guérin.' 'No, it's as dull as dishwater. I like a thief that's fun
better than an honest man that puts me to sleep!' The last
women got off at Eaton's, at the corner of University. Never
had anyone in their group gone any farther than Eaton's. West
of the big store was the great unknown: English, money,
Simpson's, Ogilvy's, Peel Street, Guy Street — after Atwater,
they started feeling at home again, because of the nearby
Saint-Henri district and the smell of the harbour. But no one
had ever gone to Saint-Henri and no one from Saint-Henri
had ever come to Plateau Mont-Royal. They met halfway, in
the aisles at Eaton's, and they'd fraternize over a chocolate
sundae or an ice-cream soda. The women from Saint-Henri
spoke with pride of Place Georges-Etienne Cartier, while those
from Plateau Mont-Royal talked about boulevard Saint-Joseph.
Be that as it may, one Saturday morning, very early, Mercedes
was returning home after an active but disappointing night with
a dentist from Sherbrooke Street and Béatrice was coming back
from spending the night at a girlfriend's. Mercedes had already
noticed the plump young woman, a sales clerk in a store, who
lived in the same building as she did, at the corner of Fabre
and Gilford. She always said hello when they met on the stairs
or the landing, but never looked her in the eyes. 'She's judging
me.' Unlike the other tenants, though, who went so far as to
pound on her door and yell insults, little Béatrice was always
very polite. And said hello. Always. She'd even refused to sign
a certain petition. . . So, Mercedes came up to Béatrice on the
number 52 streetcar. 'You got shadows under your eyes. Didn't
you sleep last night?' 'Just because you don't sleep, doesn't
mean other people don't!' Mercedes laughed. 'Not working
today?' 'Yes, I'm just on my way.' 'To sell your bits and
pieces?' 'Yes. And what of it?' 'That's what you want to do
for the rest of your life?' 'I can see what's coming, you're going
to stick your big nose. . .' 'You'd rather sell buttons?' 'Don't
know. I've never tried what you do.' Mercedes took her lipstick
from her handbag. A twenty-dollar bill fell to her lap. 'Lots of
work available in my line these days. . .' Béatrice looked at the

money. 'You know, the soldiers. . .' 'Aren't you going to pick
it up?' 'What? Oh, that.' She crumpled the bill nonchalantly.
'How much do you make a week?' Béatrice turned away.
She looked outside, as though she hadn't heard Mercedes's
question. The driver had just got off the streetcar, taking a
long iron rod to fiddle with the rails to make the car turn
east on Mont-Royal. 'What's your name?' 'Béatrice.' Mercedes
was still putting on her lipstick. 'Mine's Mercedes. Mercedes
Benz.' Béatrice looked at her surreptitiously. 'That's not your
real name! Nobody's got a name like that!' Mercedes finally
stuffed the twenty-dollar bill back into her bag. 'No, my real
name's too blah.' Béatrice watched the driver get back inside
the streetcar. He noticed that she was staring and he gave her
a wink of complicity. Under a shower of sparks, the streetcar
slowly turned right. Béatrice smiled, her head leaning against
the window. 'I'd call myself Betty. Betty Bird.' 'Why Bird?'
'Because of my father. Because of you too. My father, he used to
call twenty-dollar bills birds. Maybe because whenever he saw
one, it was always far away, like a bird in a tree, or up in the
sky — always far away.' The two women smiled at one another.
'Betty Bird's a great name. Catchy.' 'Yes. I've been thinking
about it for a long time.' Mercedes yawned. The shadows under
her eyes grew larger. 'You should come over one of these days
and have a good talk about things. . .' 'To tell you the truth,
I'd just as soon come over right away. . .' 'You don't waste any
time, do you?' 'I'm sick of buttons!' 'When could you start?'
For the first time, Béatrice looked Mercedes straight in the
eye, looked into the depths of her soul. 'You know as well
as I do, I've been ready for ages. What else can I do?' And
Mercedes had been afraid. As she rubbed Betty's back in the
tub, she thought about it all again and a broad smile lit up her
face. 'What's the joke?' 'I'm thinking about how scared I was
of you in the beginning. The way you just let things happen to
you.' 'And now, you aren't scared any more?' 'Sometimes, yes;
sometimes, no.' 'Anyway, that was all a long time ago. . .' 'Not
that long, Betty. A year.' 'It's a long time all the same.' Betty
grabbed the sponge which was dripping soap suds. 'Come on,
turn around and I'll do your back.'

Edouard and Thérèse had got up at the same time. Their rooms faced each other, so they'd found themselves face to face when they opened their doors. 'You're up early, uncle Edouard. And today's Saturday!' 'When you gotta go, little girl, it doesn't matter what day it is.' They both ran to the bathroom at the very back of the house, past the dining room and the kitchen. Thérèse got there first, but gave way to her mother's brother. Marcel, Thérèse's brother, who was so small, despite his four years, that people thought he was barely two and a half or three, heard them running and when Thérèse and Edouard passed him, he lisped a shy good morning, which the two runners didn't hear. Marcel slept in the dining room, in a bed converted into a sofa in the daytime. It was far too big for him and he hated it. Marcel witnessed all the comings and goings in the house — and God knows, there were lots. When his uncle Gabriel, who worked nights, came home around two in the morning, Marcel would wave at him. But Gabriel, preoccupied, tired, head drooping, rarely looked in the baby's direction. He would hurry into his own bedroom which opened onto the dining room, where the fat pregnant woman, his wife, was waiting for him. When Albertine, Marcel and Thérèse's mother, got up at night to make tea to calm her nerves, Marcel would slip out of bed and follow her into the kitchen. She would take him in her arms as she waited for the water to boil — and Marcel inevitably would fall asleep, his head resting against his mother's plump shoulder. Albertine would rock her youngest child as she stared at the kettle. Sometimes, she fell asleep on her feet, leaning against the stove, waking with a start just as Marcel was about to fall, or the water began to boil over on the coal stove making an unpleasant sputtering sound. And when old Victoire, the mother of Edouard, Gabriel and Albertine, got up at night to go to the bathroom, Marcel would huddle in a corner of his bed and close his eyes. Marcel was afraid of Victoire. Not that she was mean or nasty. But a strange sickness in her left leg made her limp, made her suffer dreadfully and made her irritable. And so, she was often impatient with her grandchildren. Victoire passed Marcel's bed like a shadow and slipped through the kitchen, then into the back room where she began to produce sounds that would have made Richard or Philippe, the sons of Gabriel and the fat woman, laugh, but which literally terrified the little boy. When she was finished, she would let out a sort of long moan and vigorously pull the chain. The sound of the water flushing drove Marcel almost crazy with fear, because he knew it meant the old woman was about to limp past his bed again. Would she jump into his bed, jump on him with both feet as his cousin Philippe, four years his elder and already a smooth talker and storyteller, had promised? Would she beat him, kill him, eat him up? But Victoire walked past without giving him a thought. Marcel went back to sleep, trembling. 'You been in there a long time, uncle. Let me pee, then you can go back.' Edouard came grumbling out of the bathroom. Immediately, Marcel shot across the dining room and kitchen and threw himself into the arms of his uncle, who tossed him up to the ceiling, as the child shouted and laughed. 'What do you want for breakfast, Marcel? Eggs? Two dozen? And bacon? Two pounds? And toast? Two whole loaves of bread? Coffee? Two coffeepots?' Thérèse shouted from the bathroom. 'You're going to wake up the whole house!' 'Shut up and piss!' 'You know very well he doesn't eat any of that stuff anyway. . .' 'If he doesn't eat any of that stuff, it's because you don't give it to him! I'm sick and tired of seeing him eat pablum. . .' 'He doesn't eat it because it doesn't agree with him.' 'That's your mother's bright idea, Thérèse, that it doesn't agree with him. . .' Thérèse came out of the bathroom, tying her pyjama cord. 'You can go in now.' 'Will you put the coffee on, my sweet?' Edouard rushed into the bathroom as Thérèse bent over her little brother. 'Did you make peepee?' 'No.' 'Do you have to go?' 'Yes.' Thérèse picked Marcel up and took him to the edge of the kitchen sink. 'Go on, or it'll be too late. . .' Pink with pleasure, Marcel took out his little penis and bent his head over the sink. 'Do you always watch yourself when you make peepee?' 'Yes.' 'Why?' ''Cause I like to.' 'Dirty!' 'Diddy? Why, diddy?' 'You'll

find out soon enough!' Thérèse was eleven. The same age as
Richard, the elder son of the fat woman and Gabriel. Thérèse
and Richard had been born two days apart: Thérèse on October
31, and Richard, two days later, on November 2. Thérèse was
a clown, merry, always making faces, like a Hallowe'en party,
while Richard was serious, sad, pale and tedious as a Mass for
the dead. But they were inseparable, Thérèse, having fun as
naturally as breathing, Richard, being glum no matter what.
'You're going to wake up my father with your fooling around
and we'll get hell again!' Tall for his age, Richard was standing
in the kitchen doorway, his ears sticking out, his eyes puffy.
'Your father usually gets up on Saturday, Coco, so we can
make as much noise as we want.' 'But you don't have to start
at eight o'clock in the morning!' 'I see, now you're starting,
eh?' Thérèse put her brother down, went over to her cousin
and kissed him on the neck. Richard wiped the kiss away with
his hand. 'Breakfast ready?' Thérèse gave him a withering look.
'No, I've only had time to make noise!' Edouard came out of the
bathroom just then. 'Thérèse, go and dress your brother. And
Richard, go somewhere else to sulk. I'm making the breakfast
this morning!' The kitchen was vacated in two seconds flat and
Edouard got down to work. He took one of the fat woman's
aprons (he himself was rather corpulent, thank you), tied it
neatly at the back, then opened the door of the icebox.

Richard shared a double room at the front of the house with
Victoire, his grandmother, and his uncle Edouard. He slept
in a folding bed under the archway. Every night, he went to
a dark corner and pulled out the iron bed which was folded
in two, with blankets and sheets hanging out of it, and began
to struggle with two hooks that were too tight and refused to
budge. Of course, the hooks would let go all at once, the bed
would unfold and the slack, worn-out springs would clatter and
twang. And every morning, Richard had to fold up the bed
again, sweating, puffing and wheezing. The hooks would refuse
to go into their spaces, the feet wouldn't fold, the thin mattress

was suddenly too thick — and as his grandmother, who didn't even seem to be enjoying herself, looked on placidly, the boy, dishevelled, red and out of breath, would finally manage to fold up his bed. As he pushed the heap of iron into its corner, Richard would curse the fate that had condemned him to leave his parents' room and end up here, in this hole, that reeked of his grandmother's medicines and his uncle Edouard's cologne — Yardley Lotus. That morning, while his grandmother was still asleep, her mouth wide open, as if she were uttering a final cry of despair, Richard didn't tackle his bed. For lack of anything better to do, he turned his head towards the old woman. He could see her face between two bars of the brass bed. In the five years he'd been sleeping in the same room with her, Richard had spent an incalculable number of hours watching his grandmother die. In fact, every time he examined her in her sleep, grumbling, scarcely breathing, mouth open to reveal bare white gums as sharp as knives, Richard expected to see her expire. She was a flickering candle, a dismantled clock, a motor at the end of the road, a dog grown too old, a servant who had finished serving and was dying of boredom, a useless old woman, a beaten human being, his grandmother. If she wanted to do anything in the house, her daughter-in-law, the fat woman, or her daughter, Albertine, very attentively would anticipate her intentions: 'You just rest. . . you've done enough work in your life. . . sit down, Mama, your leg. . .' The old woman would lay down the dishcloth or the wooden spoon, swallowing so she wouldn't explode. Richard had often seen his grandmother weep with rage, leaning against the window in her room that looked out on the outside staircase. He'd even heard her curse the two women, cast impotent spells on them; he'd seen her stick out her tongue and pretend to be kicking them. From morning to night, she wandered from bedroom to dining room, from dining room to bedroom, a superfluous object in this house where everyone and everything had assigned tasks or at least was of some use — except her. She would have liked to take out the garbage, make supper, wash the fat woman, soak the curtains in the bathtub, wallop Philippe or Thérèse or Richard or Marcel, wallop someone; instead, though, she

invariably ended up in front of the radio, her ear pressed against
Donalda's confidences or fat Georgiana's mercurial moods. In
the very middle of a snore, Victoire opened her glassy eyes and
her hand removed a white lock from her forehead. Richard
immediately looked away. 'What time is it?' Richard didn't
answer. 'What time is it? I know you aren't asleep, Coco.
You're all dressed!' 'Eight o'clock, granny. A little after.'
Victoire cleared her throat, took a small handkerchief from
under her pillow and spat. With gusto. Richard shut his eyes.
Victoire sat up with some difficulty and looked at her grandson.
'Will you stop spying on me, for Heaven's sake!' Richard
quickly turned his head towards his grandmother. 'No.' Long
silence. Victoire, who was very short-sighted, couldn't see her
grandson. But she could feel him looking at her. She could
always feel him looking at her. It was the same look that had
just drawn her from her sleep. 'Someday when you're asleep,
granny's going to get up and come and wring your little neck.
Like a chicken.' 'No. You love me too much.' The woman
smiled. 'You think so?' 'Yes.' In turn, Richard smiled. 'I like
it better when you're awake.' 'Me too!'

Dragging Marcel behind her, Thérèse burst into the other large
room that was both the bedroom of her mother, Albertine,
and the living room where she and her cousin Philippe had
been sleeping for several years. Thérèse and Philippe shared
the same sofa in a succession of laughing, slapping, jumping,
tickling and ill-concealed modesty. Misunderstood modesty,
too. Philippe was only eight, but already he knew where to
fumble and how to avoid slaps by assuming an innocent or a
guileless attitude. Thérèse and Philippe's sofa was a constant
source of amused murmuring, an oasis of gaiety in the midst
of the desert of extinguished passions and unappeased desires
that inhabited the four corners of the house. Albertine slept at
the back of the large room, in a sort of boat, black in colour and
black in mien, that her husband, Paul, now off at war, thank
God, had brought as a wedding present twelve years earlier

from the wilds of his native Laurentians. Albertine had always hated that rancid-smelling box where the worst experiences of her life had caught her by surprise when she was scarcely more than an adolescent, when she was ignorant and pure beyond common measure. She had been, and was still, subjected to this bed as to some inevitable catastrophe that might occur long after it has been announced and then go on to mark and direct an entire lifetime. The whole existence of this rather fat but very beautiful woman was contained between the painted planks, on the worn-out mattress, in the thin, frayed linen sheets: disillusion at the small amount of pleasure — when she had been promised paradise — was there just beneath the surface. Albertine was waking up as her children rushed past the door like a whirlwind. Immediately, she sat up in bed, her head bristling with curlers, arms bare, in a pale pink cotton nightdress. 'How come you're tearing the house apart so early in the morning? Isn't the baby dressed yet? Did he eat? Did he wet the bed again?' Thérèse looked at her mother with a broad smile, as Marcel hid behind her. She spoke softly, as though she were awakening her mother after a very peaceful night. 'Hello, Mama. How are you this morning? Sleep alright?' Visibly disconcerted, Albertine stared at her daughter, her arm still raised accusingly, but not so sure of herself now. 'Okay. I get it.' She threw back the covers and swung her legs out of the bed. 'Bring in the baby.' Thérèse picked up her brother and brought him to their mother. Amazed to see her suddenly so gentle, Marcel looked at her as though seeing her for the first time: he was torn between a desire to cry, brought on by Albertine's anger, and a need to snuggle in her arms, because he loved her beyond reason — even beyond his fear. Sensing the baby's hesitation, Albertine decided to smile. Marcel opened his eyes wide, eyes that were wild with happiness, and began to laugh uncontrollably, so that his stomach quivered and his shoulders shook. 'There's one you don't even have to tickle!' Albertine tossed Marcel onto his back on the bed. 'Good thing I've got you!' Thérèse, who couldn't explain the mixture of delight and jealousy that stirred inside her, moved away from the enormous bed from which Marcel's laughter burst out in bubbles of joy.

Thérèse and Albertine had had a serious conversation the night before. Or rather, Thérèse had tried to talk with her mother the night before. Wild with fear, but with her mind made up, she had come right out and asked her mother to stop shouting all the time when Marcel was around. The only answer the little girl received was a slap behind her ear, but all the same, she felt that she'd made her point. And here was the proof. Seeing her mother smile and play with Marcel, stroking the soles of his feet and nibbling at him, was a rare and brand new experience, too new, perhaps, for Thérèse to be able to relish it completely. And she knew very well that, in any case, her brother would be the only one to benefit from it. Hadn't she done it all for him? So as not to see him go from laughter to tears whenever Albertine's frustrations exploded in rude words and hysterical cries? Her mother hadn't frightened her for a long time now and her abrupt changes of mood left Thérèse indifferent; no, not completely — her mother's changes of mood were beginning to awaken in her a brand new feeling that she didn't understand yet, but which filled her with a doleful joy that was ill-defined, almost unhealthy: contempt. She couldn't name this feeling, but she knew instinctively that she must bury it deep inside her, in that place where you are alone, always alone, to savour the cold dish that leaves a sickly sweet taste in the mouth. Thérèse sat on the edge of the sofa. Philippe was pretending to be asleep. Thérèse lifted the covers, lay down beside her cousin and huddled against the little boy's plump, soft body. She pressed her mouth against her cousin's ear: 'If you sleep so much, your little thing won't get stiff!' Philippe laughed so loud everyone in the house was startled.

'The bay isn't an open bay. It doesn't open onto the ocean. No. . .it's an enclosed bay. When you look straight ahead, you don't see the open sea. The two arms of the bay close in. . .they practically touch. If you want to get there by boat, you have to go in between the two closed arms. It's the calmest

bay in the world because the waves from the open sea don't
reach the beach. The waves are still. Always. And behind
you, there's the mountains. So high the clouds get stuck
on them and never come out to the bay. It never rains on
the bay in the winter because the mountains hold back the
clouds. It's never ever rained in the winter.' Arms folded
over her enormous bosom, head against the back of the chair
she hadn't left for almost two months now, the fat woman
spoke in a soft, even voice. The emphasis came from her
eyes. Her eyes saw the bay, the waves, the rocks, sensed
the clouds clinging to the mountains, like angel's hair on
the branches of a Christmas tree. When the vision was too
beautiful, the fat woman's eyes filled with tears which she
let fall to her chin, to her neck. 'I could sit in the water,
just on the edge of the shore and feel myself sinking into
the sand. Because when you sit in the sand on the edge of
the water, the waves hollow out a hole underneath you. I'd
put on a housedress with every colour of the rainbow in it
and people would point to me and say: "See how happy that
fat woman is!" I'd lie on my back at the edge of the water
and the waves would come and spread their foam around
my head. The whole month of January. The whole month
of February. The whole month of March. We wouldn't hear
a word about the war and we wouldn't know who'd died or
disappeared or been maimed for life. You'd read *Notre-Dame
de Paris* or *Eugénie Grandet* out loud, and when the waves
weren't filling my ears, I'd listen. . . . I'd stay there, pinned
down by the sun, and fondled by the ocean. And I could
have as many babies as I wanted!' Lulled by the sound of
his wife's voice, Gabriel had fallen asleep. He began to snore,
gently, as though not to disturb the fat woman. She looked
at him for a few seconds, then went on with her story, as
though he were still awake. 'At noon, you'd go and pick
pineapples and coconuts. We'd eat under the palm trees,
laughing and kissing. All the children I'd had would be at
our feet, all the time, and we'd love it!' The door opened
and Albertine, carrying a basin, burst in. 'Sleep well?' 'Not
a wink.' 'Do you have to. . .?' 'Of course.' Albertine slipped

the basin between the fat woman's legs. 'It gets more and more complicated. Seems like you're getting fatter and fatter.' 'I *am* getting fatter, it's normal. . . . I've got another two months.' 'If you hadn't decided to have a baby at your age. . .' 'Now don't start that again, Bartine!' Marcel had followed his mother into the bedroom, but he didn't dare come up to the armchair. 'Hello, Marcel. . . I heard you crying last night. Did you have a bad dream?' The little boy scampered off like a frightened squirrel. 'The coffee smells good.' 'I'll bring you some in a while, but I don't know how good it'll be. Edouard's making it!' The fat woman smiled. 'Edouard! Edouard lifting a finger in the house? Now I've heard everything!' Albertine took the basin from between the fat woman's legs. 'I'll come and change you after breakfast. You must be sweltering in here. . .' The fat woman frowned. 'You're so nice this morning, Bartine.' 'I'll explain everything. . .' Albertine walked away from the armchair. 'Wake up my husband. He has to eat.' Albertine bent over her brother and gave him a gentle push. Gabriel opened his eyes. Albertine withdrew without a word, closing the door behind her. 'Sorry. I fell asleep while you were talking. I had a hard day yesterday. . .' 'Doesn't matter. Anyway, I think I dream more for myself than for you.' 'No. I like listening to you. It's as if we were there.' 'Go and eat.' Gabriel got up and kissed his wife on her forehead. Her forehead was damp with sweat. 'Want to try and get up this morning?' 'You know very well I'm not supposed to.' When the door had closed behind her husband, the fat woman turned to the window of their bedroom. She could see the shed at the end of the wooden gallery, part of the third floor of the house and a scrap of blue sky the size of a handkerchief. The rebellion she'd kept inside her for so long, that she'd managed to subdue at the bottom of her belly — a wild animal that refused to be tamed, which she had nourished with dreams and lies — suddenly awoke in her throat and the fat woman opened her mouth to scream. A single word came out, like an admission of defeat or an accusation: 'Acapulco!'

Three times a day, they laid the big table in the dining room:
the morning meal took place almost in silence, with only
Albertine's shouts sometimes flying through the house like
butcher's knives, but no one listened. Their noses stayed in
their plates and Victoire's head, dishevelled by sleep, continued
to nod. The midday meal, more animated, was the particular
domain of the children, home from school or from their noisy
city kids' games, a quick bowl of soup, a quick sandwich and
it was over. As for the evening meal, it was something between
a total free-for-all and 'The Garden of Earthly Delights' by
Hieronymus Bosch, each family going into it kicking and
screaming — 'Ham again?' 'There's no salt in the soup!'
'The soup's too salty!' — highly indignant because the others
didn't know how to behave. Victoire was always enthroned
in the same place, in the very middle of the table, 'on the
crack,' as Albertine put it, the ends being reserved for the
two fathers of the household: Gabriel and Paul. Since Paul
had gone off to the war, his wife, Albertine, had taken over
his place in such an imperious way that Richard started calling
her 'uncle Albertine.' The children were scattered around the
table according to their rank: Richard and Thérèse, the two
oldest, sat on either side of their grandmother, 'to keep her
from drowning in the gravy,' and Marcel and Philippe sat
with their mothers on the other side. As for Edouard, his
official place was across from his mother, but he enjoyed
changing, passing from Albertine's camp to the fat woman's,
and sometimes even taking Paul's place — to the great dismay
of his sister who would shout at him: 'When you've got a wife
and kids, you'll have the right to sit at the end! In the meantime,
you can share the crack with Mama!' Ever since the fat woman
had been sentenced to her bedroom, Edouard, perhaps as a
joke on Albertine, who took herself for her husband, had sat
in his sister-in-law's place, where he enjoyed imitating her,
exaggerating the way she sighed and her way of threatening the
children in a gentle, even voice. Slowly, he would say, without
even looking at the child he was addressing: 'Richard, you've
got ears like a monkey now, but if you don't stop fidgeting,

I'll do something about it and you'll look more like a jackass!'
The imitation was so perfect the whole household burst out
laughing, even the fat woman who had asked that the door to
her room be kept open and who heard everything from the
depths of her prison. But when he went so far as to call Gabriel
'my husband,' gently placing his hand on his brother's shoulder
as his sister-in-law always did, Albertine would knit her brows
and cast a reproving glance at her mother, who, to provoke her
even more, would say to Edouard: 'Again! Again! Sounds just
like her!' When the evening meal was over, when Hieronymus
Bosch really took hold of the children and they started hurling
glasses of water and pieces of bread back and forth, when the
real foolishness started, the adults would get really fed up and
inevitably there would be trouble. Every night. On slack days,
Marcel would get a cuff on the head and everyone would be
disappointed; on good days, anything could happen. Once, for
example, Edouard, pissed to the gills, threw what was left of
his steak in his mother's face, rendering her speechless for a
good three days, but that was before the war when 'steak grew
plentifully in the garden of the cows,' as Gabriel said (now if
you found a piece of boiled beef in your soup, you thought
you were dreaming); once, too, Paul had taken Marcel in his
arms because he was crying so loud, then sat him down in
the spaghetti bowl, in the midst of congealed noodles and cold
pork chops; but that, too, had been before the war; it had even
happened — and this was the most heroic deed in the history
of the three families — it even happened that Victoire got up,
limped around the table and poured a cup of boiling tea over the
Brylcreemed head of Edouard, her beloved son, the last born,
the pride and joy of her accursed soul. Why? No one ever knew.
Was it after one of their numerous rows from which they always
emerged humiliated and happy? Was it because of something
one of them hadn't said that, according to a prearranged plan,
should have been? Or was it just the end of a too peaceful meal
when no one had paid any attention to the old woman so that
she'd felt excluded and abandoned? The fact is that her scalded
son had dared to answer back and Victoire found herself on the
floor, skirt above her waist, one eye changing colour and size

from one second to the next. They still talked about it. And they'd go on talking about it until the end of time. It was the most precious jewel in the crown of their daily crises — and when they referred to it, they almost fell to their knees. From laughing. That morning, then, Edouard had worked like a truly accomplished and happy mistress of the household, singing at the top of his lungs, 'Happy as a King,' in a perfect imitation of Robert L'Herbier, his mother's idol, and therefore, his rival, a sworm enemy, his favourite whipping boy, his nightmare, his death. When Victoire talked about Robert L'Herbier, Edouard would puff up like a red balloon, and when the balloon burst, the poor singer would be spattered with shit, white secretions and gastric acid. But, for once, Edouard hadn't changed the words, he hadn't sung, 'Happy as a Queen,' swaying his hips and raising his arms to the ceiling like some bloated Mistinguette coming down a too-steep staircase on too-high heels. His mother didn't abuse him this time; she was content to listen to her idol's voice blossom from the mouth of her god. Because Edouard was working, Albertine found herself with time on her hands. She'd done her best to stick her nose in the kitchen, but her brother made as if he were going to unbutton his fly and Albertine vanished like a charm. What she called her brother wasn't exactly charming, but in any case, Edouard preferred Albertine's absence, with the sound of her voice in the background, to her presence, with her voice in the foreground, because Albertine was never silent. Sometimes, Edouard would say: 'You can hear Albertine talking even when she's gone shopping at the other end of town' or: 'Albertine? She was vaccinated with a gramophone needle. They hired her to record His Master's Voice, but the dog got scared!' For half an hour, the feverish atmosphere in the house kept mounting: all the children were sitting on Marcel's sofa in the dining room, silent, craning their necks towards the kitchen, anxious. Albertine had made the beds, shaking the mattresses a little harder than usual. And Victoire hadn't turned on the radio to listen to 'the news from overseas.' Richard murmured in Thérèse's ear: 'If you ask me, it'll be so awful we'll all get sick!' Richard clearly didn't like his uncle. Didn't he act as a

buffer between his grandmother and Edouard when the latter
came home late (which happened rather often), drunk and
smelling of cheap liquor? And even cheaper perfume! Richard
maintained that his uncle drank perfume because liquor wasn't
strong enough for him. Thérèse watched him for two seconds,
then shrugged. 'Even if it's awful, at least it'll be a change!'
But it was a complete surprise. Never in living memory had
they eaten so well in time of war. In spite of rationing, the
shortage of sugar, 'the shortage of everything,' as Victoire said,
Edouard had managed to create a breakfast that not only had
some taste, but also looked like something: the oranges were
cut in quarters, the toast was nicely toasted, the eggs (all the
eggs for the week!) were perfect, and the coffee. . . sublime.
Everything was so good that morning, no one slept during the
meal. And the silence that settled on the dining room was
appreciative. Only Edouard allowed himself a few asides. For
example, he walked around the table carrying the coffeepot,
declaring in an affected French accent: 'I'm the Star Fairy and
all my supplies come from Father Christmas!' Victoire looked
at him lovingly; his sister gave him the dirtiest of looks, the
children gazed at him flabbergasted. He made such an effort
that at one point Gabriel, his brother, asked him slyly: 'You
sure the army turned you down because you got flat feet? If
you ask me, those flat feet stir up a hell of a wind!' Edouard
stopped smack in the middle of the doorway and answered
without turning around: 'Gabriel, are you sure you didn't
get your wife pregnant just to stay out of the war?' And
that was that. Once more, the two brothers had shown their
true colours and the rest of the house pretended not to hear.
Edouard opened the fridge in search of some milk, muttering
to himself: 'I'd rather have flat feet than a brain on the skids!'
He took out a quart of milk and came back to the table: 'I'm the
Star Fairy and Father Christmas supplies all my eggs, cream,
bread, sugar and meat. But don't ask me what I do for him or
you won't keep your breakfast down!'

Edouard tiptoed into the fat woman's bedroom. She was dozing, or rather, she was pretending to doze as she didn't want Richard or Philippe to come and see her before she was washed. Quietly, Edouard picked up the tray with the remains of his sister-in-law's breakfast. 'Are you asleep?' She turned her smiling face to him, somewhat relieved. 'Ah, it's you.' Putting on his French accent again, Edouard murmured conspiratorially: 'Did you think it was the drrreadful Alberrrtine?' The fat woman laughed. She pointed to the tray. 'That was good.' 'Thank you.' Edouard looked around. Aside from the fat woman's armchair, the bedroom was furnished with only a bed and a chest of drawers, so large that they took over the room and made it look small, even though it was the biggest bedroom in the house. The chest of drawers in particular, a sort of brown dinosaur with many drawers and massive, crooked feet, surmounted by an oval mirror that distorted everything, seemed to want to pounce on anyone who entered the room. This piece of furniture fascinated the children, who had been told that they had been found in various drawers the day they were born: at the very top were the twin drawers of Thérèse and Richard, bigger than the others and blacker too; then came those of Philippe and Marcel, wedged into the interlacings of carved wood; and finally, a little lower still, the one for the baby to come. It was tiny, a glove-drawer, in fact, plain, somewhat lost. Marcel would often be seen gazing at this secret drawer. He didn't dare to touch it and if anyone asked what he was doing there, he said: 'I'm waiting for the mail!' The fat woman pulled down her nightgown, which had a tendency to creep up. 'Sit down a minute, let's talk.' 'I haven't really got time. . . . Albertine's waiting for me to do the dishes. . . . I wanted to cook, so I have to finish the job.' 'But you aren't usually so scared of her.' 'I'm not scared, but she's acting so nice this morning, I don't want to do anything to get on her nerves. I want to enjoy it while it lasts!' All the same, Edouard sat on the edge of the iron bed, the tray on his knees. 'You must be sick and tired, eh?' 'And how! I'm telling you, if I'd known. . . I say that, but it isn't true. . . I want this baby so badly! Anyway, it will be good-looking — and clever!' Edouard smiled. 'That, I

don't doubt. We'll spoil it and show it how to live, eh?' 'But
the two things don't go together.' She looked at the little scrap
of blue sky. 'You came in at four in the morning again. . .'
'You heard me? I'm sorry, I tried not to make any noise.'
'I wasn't asleep. And I'm not scolding you. That isn't what
bothers me. . . You know, I don't want to preach, Edouard,
you're old enough to live your own life. . .' 'But, there's a "but"
coming. . .' This time, she looked him straight in the eye. 'I
always think of Richard sleeping in between you and your
mother. . . Those fights you have just about every night are
bad for him. . . He hears things he shouldn't hear and maybe
it upsets him. . . You know, he's really. . .' Richard's voice,
which hadn't changed yet, but in which you could already hear
the severity and intolerance that would become the two poles
of his existence, rang through the bedroom, startling the two
adults. 'Don't worry, Mama, I haven't bothered listening to
them for ages. . . Anyway, they always say the same things!'
Richard had already disappeared, frustrated at finding his
mother, whom he venerated like a saint, in conversation with
his uncle whom he despised. Edouard and the fat woman were
silent for several moments. A huge fly buzzed around the cup
of coffee in which the fat woman had put too much sugar.
Edouard shooed it away. 'That's what they call getting caught
with your pants down, eh?' 'He's always sticking his nose into
everything. I don't know what to do with him. . . It's as if he
could smell when something's going on — and he's always there
when you don't need him. . . There's a good reason why he's
got such big ears!' She pursed her lips. 'I just mentioned his ears
again. It's a real sickness that I've got. I have to stop, it doesn't
make sense. That child's so complicated, I can't help thinking
about the only thing about him that's simple!' She took refuge
again in the view from her window. 'Ask Albertine to come
and see me — after the dishes.' Edouard got up and walked
towards the door, his head down. 'Edouard!' He stopped in his
tracks, one foot already outside the room. 'What?' She gestured
to him to come back and sit down again. 'I'm not done yet.' He
came back to the bed, but remained standing. She took a deep
breath before she spoke. 'Sometime. . . Sometime, when you

haven't got anything to do. . . come and tell me what you do when you go out! Come and tell me about your nights on the town. You're the only one that goes out and sees people. . . I don't really know how to tell you. . . I feel all mixed up. . . You know what I mean. I'm stuck in here and you're always gadding around. . . You know how much I like people. . . Come and tell me about the shows you see and the people you meet and what you do. . . if you want, I mean. You don't have to.' Edouard took one of her hands. 'You don't have to say any more. I understand.' The fat woman was so moved that she could say no more. 'You should have asked me before. I never thought you'd be interested. Albertine and my mother shut me up whenever I start to talk about it. . .' Just before he went out, Edouard said, without turning around: 'But I'll tell you everything, and I mean *every* thing! I won't keep anything back. And if you're shocked, it'll be your own fault!' He crossed the dining room, smiling. The fat woman closed her eyes. She was off to Mexico again.

'Big Ears seems to be in a bad mood!' After their mother, Florence, made this observation, Rose, Violette and Mauve put down their coffee cups and cakes and burst out laughing. Rose (or Violette or Mauve) even dropped her little silver spoon onto her dress, catching it just before it fell to the balcony floor. 'You sound just like his mother, Mama!' Florence stared at her daughter (Rose or. . .) before replying: 'God forbid! His mother was brought up in the wilds of Saskatchewan by Cree Indians who'd never seen a mountain in their life and thought the world was somewhere in the hollow of the Great Manitou's hand. For a long time the fat woman's own mother even thought the Saskatchewan River was the Great Manitou's lifeline and that's no joke!' 'I think that's beautiful.' 'And I think it's ignorant, my girl! Maybe I sometimes use the same expressions as that woman, but don't tell me I talk like her!' 'But she's the one we're knitting for. . .' 'We haven't got any choice, it's part of. . . our arrangements!' Richard, unaware of the presence of the four knitting women, was sitting on the second step of the outside staircase that went up to his place on the second floor. He folded his arms and bent over, like someone with a stomach ache. All through the meal, he'd been thinking of the happy moment when he would finally be allowed to go and kiss his mother before he was sent outdoors ('Go out and play, children, it's Saturday and it's a lovely day! Richard, Thérèse, take the little ones to Lafontaine Park, it'll do them good!') for the rest of the day. Ever since he'd seen his mother become fatter, almost as he watched, looking less and less like the soft, enveloping woman who had delighted his tender childhood, and more and more like a mound of soft fat with no personality or character, Richard, for the first time in his life, felt the need to talk to her, perhaps to tell her that he loved her, in spite of her sickness, in spite of what he heard about her, in spite of what he heard at night, when everyone was going to bed and the fat woman would burst out sobbing as she accused each and every one of them of hating her, of passing judgment on her, of blaming her. But not once in the three months his mother had been glued to her armchair, had he had the courage to really talk to her. Every morning, he would say the platitudes one used with the chronically ill, a language from which certain expressions and, in particular, any feelings are excluded, as he'd been told to do. He had been told to be impersonal with his mother: 'Your mother's very sick so don't bug her with your kisses and your sweet talk. It'll wear her out. So, just say good morning and make sure you don't say anything about your trouble at school or her trouble here.' What was left for an eleven-year-old boy to say to his sick mother? At times, he felt that the fat woman would have liked to chat with him, laugh, and perhaps even cry as she held him in her arms, but Albertine or Victoire would always turn up with his school-bag and hurry him on his way. Today was Saturday, though, there was no school and Richard had something important to say to his mother. About his uncle Edouard. About what Edouard had said during the night. And about what Edouard had done. He was sure Victoire had seen and heard everything, but could he talk about such

things with a grandmother who was half-lame and half a witch
and who was increasingly suspected of being dotty about her
son? His uncle had told him things he didn't know, confessed
offences he didn't understand, and asked absolution for sins
that seemed to be complete fabrications invented to disturb
the child's mind. But wasn't it just drunken raving in the
early hours of the morning to exorcise ghosts grown too big
for him? That's what he wanted to ask his mother: to confirm
that none of what Edouard said really existed and that he could
forget everything, as he usually did. Instead, he had found the
drunk 'cured,' fresh as a daisy, amnesiac as far as his blunders
were concerned — as usual (but had Edouard really forgotten
last night, hadn't he put on his show at breakfast to try and
make Richard smile and perhaps even, yes, why not, forgive
him?), and on top of everything else, deep in conversation with
his mother, to whom Richard wished he could shout: 'Plug
your ears, Mama. He's starting again!' But all he said was that
he wasn't listening to anything; that he knew nothing. As he
did every time a scene was brooding in the house, or actually
blowing up, Richard took refuge outside. Outside was the only
place where anyone who wasn't in the mood to take part in
the roller-coaster of shouts and blows could find shelter. To
keep from crying, the little boy squeezed his stomach with his
folded arms and pressed his lips together, imprisoning them
with his teeth. Seeing that he hadn't moved for a good five
minutes, Rose, Violette and Mauve got up, walked down the
two steps and over to the staircase between the two houses.
Rose (or Violette or Mauve) said: 'Mama, I think somebody's
really unhappy!' Florence put down her cup, which clattered
against her saucer: 'You know very well we can't do anything
for them. Now come back and work. He doesn't even know
you're there.'

Thérèse crossed Mont-Royal, heading south, dragging Marcel
by the hand, and she thought about the great day of freedom
waiting for them — for her, her brother and her cousins — at

Lafontaine Park. Her mother had told her: 'Now be sure you don't come back before supper. I have to wash your aunt's room and I have to wash her too, so I don't want you kids underfoot!' Thérèse had thrown together some salami sandwiches and taken a big bottle of Coke from the icebox. Richard, of course, turned his nose up at the sandwiches. 'I heard salami's made out of garbage. Some people even found rat hair in it!' 'Not in salami, creep, in hotdogs! Anyway, that's silly talk. If you don't like it, you can eat your toenails!' As for Philippe, he was delighted. As long as he had bread to eat, he didn't care what was on it. He would often remove the filling from a sandwich and eat only the slices of buttered bread. A few paces behind Thérèse, Philippe and Richard were arguing over who would carry the food — or rather, who wouldn't. For the moment, Philippe claimed his arms were tired and he was crying, so his brother would have to carry the bag. 'If you don't take it this minute, I'll drop it and the Coke'll bust and the sandwiches'll get wet and it'll all be your fault!' 'I couldn't care less. I hate sandwiches and I can't stand Coke! Go ahead, drop it. Thérèse'll get you, you'll see!' Richard couldn't intimidate his brother because he knew very well how much Philippe hated violence,but he still threatened him with a thrashing by Thérèse. Philippe, though, knew his cousin too well to be afraid of her. He just had to make his eyes all soft or put on his sweetest smile and Thérèse's vague desires for a squabble would disappear completely and be replaced by a sort of uncontrolled admiration which he couldn't explain, but which he took great advantage of. So, he just made a face at his brother as he pretended to drop the bag of provisions. Richard hollered. Thérèse turned around. Immediately, Philippe assumed a guilty expression. 'I tripped!' Thérèse shrugged and lit into Richard. 'You're always yelling for nothing! Lord in Heaven, is your head screwed on right?' She turned away and continued on her way, walking a little faster. They came to the corner of Marie-Anne Street and Thérèse could already smell the manure from the stable behind the grocery store at the corner of Fabre and Rachel. 'The smell comes all the way down here today.' She laughed. 'The neighbours'll be complaining again, for sure!' 'I smell horse-poo!' Every time he walked past the grocery store, Marcel took advantage of the occasion to say this sentence he'd been thinking of ever since he left the house, because it was the only time he was allowed to use the word 'poo.' He would savour the word for several minutes before saying it, and then for several minutes after, as it was too short for him to savour while he said it. Sometimes, before he went to sleep in the dark dining room, he would repeat it several times, trying to recapture the delightful sensation in the bottom of his mouth: 'Poo, poo, poo, poo, poo. . .' But taken out of context, it was a word with no taste at all, a meaningless sound, and Marcel fell asleep without enjoying it. Here, though, surrounded by the very odour of 'horse,' and supported by big greasy splotches or trails of yellowish dried paste barely concealed by layers of straw, the word 'poo' regained all the importance of something secret, forbidden, unnamable — all qualities that made it fascinating; and Marcel, excited, repeated tirelessly: 'I smell horse poo! I smell horse poo!' until he was silenced by a clip on the ear or a threatening frown. This time, though, his disappointment was great: the smell was there, persistent and pervasive, but the horses and manure had disappeared after the Saturday morning cleaning — the horses, out delivering orders; the manure, rotting at the bottom of the drains, where it still smelled, but invisibly. Marcel couldn't get over it. 'There's no horse and no poo, but you can smell it anyway!' He looked everywhere; he even wanted to go over the fence to see for himself if the horses were playing a trick on him, hiding in a shed or behind the barrels of pickles, but Thérèse held him back with a firm hand. 'If you get too close to the horses, they'll eat you!' As Marcel had once seen a horse eat an apple and been so frightened that he dreamed about it for a whole week, he was content to climb up on the fence and shout: 'Horsey! Horsey! Where'd you put your poo?' At that moment, a Rachel streetcar crossed Fabre, shedding a shower of sparks on the pavement, changing the course of Marcel's thoughts, so he exclaimed with no transition: 'It's raining fire!' as he clapped his hands. Richard, though he was eleven years old, was still afraid of the streetcar's sparks and he stood there, frozen, under the

amused look of his brother, who took advantage of the moment
to call him a scaredy-cat. Thérèse, Marcel and Philippe ran
across Rachel and rushed into Lafontaine Park, howling with
delight. Richard remained behind, leaning against a grocery
store window. His heart was beating like a watch. 'He's right, I
am a scaredy-cat.' His brother's voice came to him, dimmed by
the sound of another streetcar coming in the opposite direction:
'Stop bawling, fathead, then you can come and play with
us.'

Mercedes had told her: 'Be sure you're back by two, it's
Saturday!' Béatrice kissed her forehead and left. 'You're a
doll, Mercedes. I'll work harder tonight.' On her way down
she ran into the first clients of the day: three tipsy soldiers,
besotted by cheap drink, who obviously hadn't slept all night.
They must have been on a blinder from club to club, from one
illegal gambling joint to the next, shamelessly spending the
meagre pay they got as second-class soldiers, and shouting:
'We're gonna conquer the world!'or: 'We'll get them Germans!
We'll show them English!' as they raised their arms to Heaven
in a sign of victory, unaware that their flies were unbuttoned
or their trousers were stained with vomit. At 10 a.m. then,
they were heading for Mercedes's place, half asleep, driven by
desire that the dancers at the Casino Bellevue, the girls in the
clubs, hadn't been able to appease, caught between their need to
sleep and their need to come. They were clean-shaven, red-eyed,
cold-handed and mirthful for a few seconds, stiff-necked and
irascible for the rest of the time. 'Hey, cutey-pants, where
you going all dolled up?' Béatrice made her way through
their arms, which wanted to give her a feel, and their legs,
which wanted to hold her back, squealing like a squeamish
teenager. But they weren't to be fooled. 'This a whorehouse
or not, goddammit?' Béatrice handed out a few slaps; she even
bit an ear and managed to get past them. 'She don't work here,
that's for sure! She'd ruin the customers!' The soldiers laughed
till their guts ached and Béatrice thought: 'That's it. Now the

neighbours'll complain again! We'll have to move out, and fast, if this keeps on!' She left the soldiers to their delights and hurried past the janitor's apartment, its door always ajar, even at night, even in winter. By chance, he wasn't in, and for once, Béatrice didn't catch his sarcasm and coarse laughter. She slipped out into the first grand day of spring with a light heart, her head held high, her chest straight, a winning smile on her lips. For a few moments, she stood on the doorstep, deeply breathing in the aromas of spring that were settling into the big city: the lilac, early for once, because of the exceptional mildness; the lily-of-the-valley that for several days now had been invading the gardens where winter's last traces were still visible; and even the cold, still present behind the mild air that, in May, would become fragrant before it disappeared for good. The three poplar trees in the street were overloaded with plump glossy buds, but so far, not a single leaf had succeeded in breaking out. The rain that had fallen the night before had washed the streets clean and there was a smell of water in the air. Taking short steps, Béatrice crossed the street, swinging her handbag. She opened the door of Marie-Sylvia's restaurant, humming one of those hymns for the month of May that we learn in school and that, for the rest of our lives, become symbols of spring, of renewal, of grace, even if we lose our faith or forget everything else about our childhood. Marie-Sylvia was serving a fat man in his thirties, whom Béatrice often saw rocking on the balcony of the second house on the left, on the other side of the lane, the overpopulated house from where you frequently heard shouting and squabbling, or howls of joy, which Mercedes called 'the haunted house,' because of the old squint-eyed grandmother who looked at everyone with the evil expression of a frustrated witch. 'Like a witch locked up in a bottle! And let me tell you, I don't want to be around when they take out the cork!' Béatrice leaned on the candy counter, jauntily exclaiming, 'Hi, Marie!' The fat man turned towards her and asked her straight out: 'And how's your little business going, Mam'zelle Betty?' Not a hint of aggression in his voice, no criticism or even irony: he'd asked as you would a butcher how his business was going, or a shoemaker if his customers were

wearing out their shoes. Accustomed to being laughed at and
insulted, Béatrice just stood there, unable to reply. She stared
at the fat man, but she couldn't move a muscle. The fat man
picked up his change and winked at Marie-Sylvia. 'She knows
how to use everything but her head!' The man said goodbye to
both women and walked out of the store without a sound, as
though he were skating across the hardwood floor. Marie-Sylvia
frowned, without speaking to Béatrice. She'd often been heard
to say: 'If they weren't such good customers, I'd have locked
my door to those floozies a long time ago!' She still spoke to
Betty without looking at her, as if the mere sight of her would
be a sin. 'One or two this morning, Betty?' 'Five, this morning,
Marie. I'm going to see my aunt!' 'But it isn't Sunday.' 'I know,
but I got the morning off.' Marie-Sylvia's frown deepened.
She didn't like Béatrice to allude to her profession, not even
remotely. She removed five 'surprise packages' from a metal
stand and placed them in front of Béatrice. The girl took a nickel
from her purse and sent it clattering across the scratched glass.
Marie-Sylvia's 'surprise packages' were a veritable institution
on Fabre Street. Everyone bought them, more out of habit than
desire as a matter of fact. Once a month, Marie-Sylvia would
dig around in the bottom of her candy boxes, pile up the ruins
thus obtained — pieces of liquorice too hard or too short to be
sold, pieces of all-day suckers in every colour, crumbs of sugar
from red-and-white candycanes, pale chocolate dust — and fill
dozens of little brown bags with them, adding a 'surprise,' some
useless trinket or a whole candy, which she then sold for a cent
each. In fact, people bought the surprise packages more to get
rid of their small change than for their contents. Some adults
even tossed them on the sidewalk without opening them. The
children, on the other hand, had a real passion for the stale
candy that tasted of the bottom of a cardboard box, or even,
sometimes, of dust. Was it the word 'surprise' that awakened
their curiosity or just the unhealthy taste for sugar of poor
children? Marie-Sylvia couldn't have said, but whatever the
case, she was interested in getting rid of her scraps and, at
the same time, showing a reasonable profit at the end of the
month. All the money that she made from these left-overs was

put in a jar beside the cash register: she used it to buy food for Duplessis who was thus fed by the whole street. 'Your aunt still living on Saint-Joseph?' 'Well, yes. You know she can't move now that she can't get around any more!' 'Tell her hello from me. . .' 'Sure.' 'Goodbye, then.' 'Goodbye.' After Béatrice had left, Marie-Sylvia watched her crossing Gilford. 'It's a crying shame. Such a pretty girl.'

The three of them were fast asleep in the big double bed, limp, snoring, snorting, sleeping off the cheap alcohol which, for them, distilled bad dreams. The shortest was resting his head against the shoulder of the one with the moustache, abandoned, confident, happy; the third, with the thick head of a common lout, took up half the bed, convinced of his physical superiority, wrapped in the unconditional right bestowed by the best-developed muscles, in a world that has for its horizon only a general's stripes or war medals. He was the one, in fact, who had said to Mercedes: 'We'll start with a little snooze — and you, you wait for us! Afterwards, we'll swing into action. And make sure you're good and ready, because we're really on song!' Mercedes sat by the window which she had just opened and looked outside or, rather, her head was turned that way, but she saw nothing. She was concentrating on her memories of spring in the country, where nature changes abruptly from one day to the next, with no warning, from the motionless white of clean snow to the seething, luxuriant black of the earth at work. She saw again the crows flying over the village graveyard in the middle of April, croaking their eternal question: 'Why? Why? Why?' and her mother who always answered: 'Good grief, because winter's over!' She saw herself again, an ungrateful child whose pigtails were always grubby, running out of school on to the hard-packed dirt road, uttering the cries of an animal set free. It smelled of spring and you could almost hear the sap rising in the trees, letting itself be drawn up by buds about to burst. The dirt on the road was damp, and her footsteps made a sucking sound that her mother called 'April kisses.' And she saw the

house, all lopsided, never painted, flaking, where her mother
bravely raised eight children, between the two markers that set
the limits of her life: morning prayers and evening prayers. She
was religious to excess, more submissive to the priest than to
her husband, trusting the Catholic religion so much that she had
managed to erase any trace of personal character or distinctive
features. She was *la mère* as the Church understood her and
she carried her naïveté to the point of boasting: 'I've never
done anything against the Church or against the good Lord.
And I know for a fact my Guardian Angel dusts off my place
in Heaven every morning!' Mercedes had always dreamed of
destroying this hateful naïveté, but her mother retained it to
the very end. She died saying: 'I see the good Lord! I see
the Blessed Virgin! And I see my Guardian Angel with his
duster!' Mercedes had laughed. Fifty years of misery: eight
births, each more painful than the last — to end up like that!
With no happy old age either. No rest. The woman had never
rested. Ever. Mercedes smiled sadly. 'She's probably dusting
right now. But not for me!' The fat thickheaded soldier let out
a belch and a fart, ridding himself of all his alcoholic gasses at
once. Mercedes closed her eyes. 'I never thought I'd envy that
woman some day!' The fat thickheaded one abruptly turned
over. Mercedes got up, approached the bed, bent down, picked
up the three pairs of trousers that the soldiers had let fall on the
floor and methodically began exploring their pockets.

'If I get soap in your eyes, you tell me, eh? Don't be shy.'
'Don't worry, go ahead and rub. It feels good!' Albertine
had tied a tablecloth around her sister-in-law's neck and put
a basin of warm water on her vast bosom, saying: 'I didn't
make the water too hot, I was afraid I'd scald you.' When
the fat woman could no longer bend over, washing her hair
became very difficult, and Albertine had a tendency these
past few days to turn a deaf ear when her sister-in-law told
her: 'Dammit, Bartine, I itch! I've never had dirty hair in my
life and I don't intend to start at the age of forty-two!' But

this morning, a mysteriously transformed Albertine (Victoire looked at her, her eyes screwed up: 'She's got something up her sleeve, I've never seen her act so nice!') filled with goodwill, awkward because so new, swept into the room. 'Time for a good housecleaning! If the baby's born into a mess like this, he'll be scared silly! So, get ready. I'm going to wash you. Head to foot! Especially the head! I've never seen such a haystack!' Her sister-in-law added timidly: 'It's your fault, you know. I don't know how many times I've asked you!' Albertine abruptly stopped plumping up a pillow. 'That's right, call me a slut.' Then she went on, as if nothing had happened. The fat woman smiled. Albertine had found a book from the Nelson collection under her brother's bed. '*Bug-Jargal*. Lord Almighty, now he's talking Chinese!' She was about to suggest putting the small cream-coloured book on the bedside table, but stopped short when she saw the author's name. 'Victor Hugo!' She looked at her sister-in-law, panic-stricken. 'That book's banned by the Church!' The fat woman sighed. 'I couldn't get to sleep last night. I asked Gabriel to read to me. It's a good book, you know.' 'You didn't answer me! That book's banned!' 'You know, we're just finishing it and I wonder what it is in that book that made the Church ban it.' 'Victor Hugo's made the Church ban it, that's all! The works. We aren't allowed to read him, you know very well! Committing a mortal sin like that in your condition, that takes gall!' 'But it's so beautiful, Bartine, if you only knew!' 'What's so beautiful about it?' 'It happens far away.' Albertine rubbed the fat woman's scalp vigorously and long streams of suds fell on to the white tablecloth. 'Ahh, that feels good. Don't stop!' With relish, Albertine released all the hostility she'd been holding in since morning: the firm flesh of her arms and her double chin bounced in every direction while her sister-in-law moaned softly with pleasure. 'You and my brother, I think you're playing with fire sometimes, reading those books! It's no good, reading too much. They told us that often enough!' 'Bartine, if you don't mind, just be quiet! If you read a little more, maybe you'd understand a little more about life. . .' Albertine cut her off so vigorously that the fat woman almost dropped the basin. 'I'd rather be ignorant and in a state of grace than know about everything and be damned!' Edouard, who was reading a newspaper in the dining room, burst out laughing. 'That's going to get around, little sister. That's going to get around!' Crimson with rage, Albertine plunged her arms into the basin and poured a generous quantity of water over her sister-in-law, who began to laugh as well. 'Tell the whole world, if you want, Edouard. I'm not ashamed! When you're boiling like a stew in the big kettle down there and I'm fanning myself with ostrich feathers up in Heaven at a concert, you'll be sorry about an awful lot of things!' 'Albertine, don't drown me. I'm not in a state of grace!'

Given the proximity of Doctor Sanregret's office, Aunt Ti-Lou's apartment always smelled of medicine, so people expected to find there syringes and flasks, glass cupboards full of jars with vaguely disgusting things inside them, and even the inevitable waiting room, perpetually crammed with all the misfortunes, all the diseases, all the deformations dragged around by a people kept in ignorance and poverty: the little bumps at the base of the neck, detected in childhood and left to develop, that turn out to be tumours; the pimples that appear and disappear at regular intervals, syphilis almost too far gone to be cured; bleeding haemorrhoids too long neglected, the beginnings of cancer. Doctor Sanregret often went across to see Ti-Lou, bringing her sedatives (only one landing separated them and they shared the same entrance), and he sometimes stayed for hours, telling the old woman how he had to flick out his patients, who almost always waited too long before they came to see him, and then howled as they demanded, yes, *demanded* a miracle! Ti-Lou listened patiently to the doctor (it was the price that she had to pay for her sedatives), half-closing her eyes and gently agreeing with him. Then, the old family doctor would limp away, bent over by fatigue, and at last Aunt Ti-Lou could open her box, open her flasks, take the caps off her bottles, trembling, grab a glass half-filled with water and pour into it six, seven, eight drops of a syrupy yellowish liquid: peace, exhilaration, apathy, insouciance — but most of all, insouciance. Béatrice came into the living room where her aunt was waiting, carrying a tray piled with slices of buttered bread (Ti-Lou had real butter, so rare in wartime, but Ti-Lou had connections!), a few slices of ham, a pot of coffee, cups and — the greatest luxury of all — a bit of fudge Ti-Lou had kept just for her. 'Must have taken all your rationing cards to buy that, auntie Gee — butter, cream, ham!' Ti-Lou replied with the vaguely American accent she'd learnt working in Ottawa at the turn of the century and kept ever since: 'Since when does Ti-Lou, the she-wolf of Ottawa, need rationing cards, I'd like to know! They're presents, Béatrice. How many times do I have to tell you, you'll never meet the man who'll shower you with cream and butter and ham during war time if you stay at the back of a rooming house on Fabre or go on selling fly buttons on Mont-Royal!' Béatrice put the tray on a pouffe in front of her aunt's armchair, holding back a smile. She still hadn't admitted to Ti-Lou that the days of tits and tots were over now and that she, little Béatrice, 'auntie's little baby,' as Ti-Lou called her, had taken the great leap that turned a 'potential whore' into a 'a whore with potency,' in the words of the Ottawa wanton. Béatrice thought: 'There's no butter or cream or ham yet, but it sure beats spending Saturday night deciding between a French show at the Passe-Temps or a chocolate sundae at Larivière et Leblanc!' The former wanton of Ottawa picked up her crutches, which were leaning against the piano, and got out of her chair, hopping on her one leg. 'We'll eat beside the window. I'm sick and tired of being in the dark.' Béatrice picked up the tray again and took it to the little table by the window. A bus went along boulevard Saint-Joseph just then and Ti-Lou sighed. 'Soon as you decide you want to sit by the window, a bus comes and fumes in your face!' 'We can shut it.' 'No, it's too nice out. The weather's so warm!' On the other side of boulevard Saint-Joseph stood the Bruchési School, nondescript and brown, which Béatrice remembered attending in the early thirties. The children in the parish went there for their first two years of school; in the third year, the girls went to the Saints-Anges School across from

the church, which Béatrice had left barely five years ago; and
the boys were transferred to Saint-Stanislas, on Gilford Street.
'Whenever you come here, you look at that school. . . You
liked school, didn't you?' 'When I was really young, yes. . .
afterwards. . .' Béatrice bit into a piece of bread and chewed
on it for a long time, staring at the Bruchési School. Suddenly,
Ti-Lou seemed impatient, as if she'd been waiting for something
that hadn't happened. After a few seconds, Béatrice brought
her gaze back to her aunt. 'How about you, auntie, did you
go to school in Ottawa?' Now, the word was spoken. Ti-Lou
smiled a little stiffly. 'Not on your life! I was born right here
in Montreal! Ottawa came a lot later!' Béatrice leaned back in
her chair. She stopped chewing. There was a tacit agreement
between Béatrice and Ti-Lou: when the older woman wanted
to talk about Ottawa, she would send someone, usually a little
boy from the neighbourhood, to invite Béatrice for lunch the
next day. Then, as they ate, Béatrice would ask her aunt a
question about Ottawa. It was simple, it worked and both
women were happy: Ti-Lou to tell of her incredible life
filled with revelling, roaming and scandalous adventures; and
Béatrice to listen, her heart pounding and her imagination in full
flight. Sometimes, hours passed before Ti-Lou felt any fatigue,
which was manifested by imaginary shooting pains in the leg she
no longer had. She would straighten up in her armchair then,
and say to her niece: 'You're tired. That's enough for today.'
And Béatrice would say nothing, kiss her aunt on both cheeks
and leave. In the house on Fabre Street, her first clients would
find her remote, cold: it was because Béatrice was still out on
the Rideau River in a rowing boat, some time in the summer
of 1910, with a cabinet minister or a foreign cardinal visiting
Canada, her dress wrinkled by repeated and insistent caresses,
her mouth tasting of a tobacco-singed moustache. Protected by
her parasol, Béatrice closed her eyes and craned her neck so
the wind could brush against her cheeks. She awoke suddenly,
thirty years later, underneath a potbellied lieutenant on the
verge of apoplexy, who was shouting in her ear: 'Get moving,
do something! I feel like I'm in a swamp of spaghetti!' Ti-Lou
wiped the corners of her mouth with her cotton napkin on which

you could still see, embroidered in blue silk, a wolf. 'When I went to Ottawa, I was around your age — seventeen, to be precise. That was in 1898. Ottawa was a village back then: one church, one tavern, one floozy.' She laughed at her witticism, poured herself a cup of coffee and gazed out the window for a moment. 'Don't worry, there was more than one church. But there was just one whore: me! When I got there, it was the middle of winter and the wolves were prowling the town. . . Somebody even saw one on a street in Hull. He'd hidden under an arcade and they shot him in the head. When I got to the Château Laurier Hotel with my little suitcase and the black dress of a brand-new orphan, and my virtue ready to be sold to the first pig that showed up, the women in Ottawa sized me up right away and all hell broke loose in Parliament. The first night, yes, the first night, in my room at the Château Laurier, 2732, I'll never forget it: three cabinet ministers came to offer me their hearts, their lives, their families and their fortunes. The got down on their knees on the Turkish rug, waving their arms like in the theatre and making their voices tremble like at the opera. Obviously, the only thing they wanted was to rape a poor little seventeen-year-old who wouldn't afterwards go and complain to her father. But they didn't know who they were dealing with! That night, my girl, I lost my innocence three times! But they paid for it — all three of them! I had them thus, by the cheque book and balls! Yes, that's called blackmail — and so what!' She seemed to be replying to some reflection, to some accusation even, but Béatrice said nothing. 'That's how I got them and that's how I hung onto them. And I'm proud of it. I'm the only woman that ever laid down the law in Ottawa! For twenty years, I ruled over Ottawa like Queen Victoria over her empire — except I wasn't treated like any grandmother! When I moved from the Château Laurier to the house on Roberts Street that six cabinet ministers got together to buy me, the women in town followed the carts carrying my baggage, waving placards that accused me of bringing hell into Parliament! That was my triumph! I climbed up on the first cart and I howled at the moon like a she-wolf in heat! Ti-Lou was moving into her new burrow and taking possession of her new

turf. As soon as I got to my new house, I started to sort out my
clientele. I was sick and tired of those provincial ministers on
visits to Ottawa, who nearly always smelled of the stable, the
barnyard or beer. I wasn't provincial meat, I was federal! If I'd
wanted to make money off the French I'd have set myself up in
Quebec City! Okay, the minor politicians from the backwoods
of the province of Quebec were often more generous, but they
weren't nearly as refined as the tall Anglos, so clean and polite,
from Toronto. I skimmed my address book and just kept the
names that floated to the top. And that's how, for twenty
years, I ruled over the biggest fortunes and the most refined
vices in Canada! I went through three Prime Ministers, two
Solicitor-Generals, a few dozen bishops, cardinals, and seven
lowly priests out of generosity. . . The ones that didn't come to
see me, it was either because they were queens or too old. I gave
dinner parties for fifty where I was the only woman and nobody
was bored! When Sarah Bernhardt came to Ottawa, I was the one
they introduced to her because they knew we'd understand each
other! What I didn't know, back then, was that one day I'd lose
a leg too. . .' Ti-Lou was silent. When reality and dream came
together in the midst of her speech, the vision of her amputated
leg intruded like a bite of the present, reminding her of Doctor
Sanregret, the smell of medicine and his patients coughing on
the other side of the wall. Ti-Lou suddenly stopped talking
and Béatrice knew she mustn't dwell on it. Silence settled over
the room like lead. Béatrice waited for her aunt to indicate it
was time for her to leave, but Ti-Lou was lost in the present,
staring at the protuberance that her stump formed beneath her
long dress: the perfect horror, round and smooth as an egg; the
end product of her life. After several minutes, Béatrice took
it upon herself to move a little, to remind her aunt she was
there. Soon, it would be two o'clock and she had promised
Mercedes that she'd be back early. Ti-Lou slowly uttered the
words that broke the spell: 'You're tired. That's enough for
today.'

Suddenly, Duplessis woke up: 'I'm hungry!' He stretched, yawned and jumped up onto Marie-Sylvia's lap. She began to make him purr by stroking his striped fur. Less to make his old mistress happy than to encourage her to feed him again, in spite of all he'd eaten a few hours earlier, Duplessis rubbed against Marie-Sylvia's chest, which she took for a sign of affection. He even went so far as to stretch out on his back on the woman's lap, offering his belly and his fleas to her expert caresses, caresses that verged on the violent and were not unpleasant in the least. 'Let's enjoy it while we may. . .' But as soon as Marie-Sylvia opened her mouth to speak, calling him her 'pussy love,' her 'baby tabby cat,' and her 'little devil that stays out all night,' the spell was broken: 'pussy love' sat motionless for several seconds in the hollow of his mistress's skirt, like the corpse of a cat that had died in a ridiculous position. Duplessis took advantage of the respite to wonder whether to go outside after eating or go back to sleep on the ledge of the stove. 'We'll see. For the time being, we'll eat.' He jumped nimbly to the floor and headed for his empty bowl, meowing imperiously. 'Enough of this nonsense, bring on the meat!' 'Poor little kitty's hungry? So soon? Mummy's going to make you a nice lunch.' Marie-Sylvia dragged her bedroom slippers to the fridge, reached for a dish and stopped in mid-action: 'Good grief, Mummy forgot to buy your liver! You ate it all this morning, treasure!' Duplessis gave a start. 'What? Did I hear you right? No more liver?' He looked at his mistress, eyes round, unblinking, evil. 'You want some cereal and milk?' 'Some what!' Duplessis shot off like an arrow and threw himself at the door. 'Mummy can't go out and buy it right away, she has to close the store!' Fur bristling, back arched, Duplessis clawed the bottom of the door. 'Okay, we'll go to see Monsieur Soucy and ask him for some scraps. . .' Marie-Sylvia let the cat slip out the back door, walked through the store, grumbling, and ran smack into Madame Lemieux, the little woman just arrived from Saint-Eustache, well pregnant, poor thing, who'd come to buy lighter flints for her husband who was too lazy to leave his rocking chair. 'Madame Lemieux! I didn't hear you come in!' 'And I've been standing here coughing like a lost soul for a good five minutes, like somebody with TB!'

She craned her neck towards the back of the store. 'Somebody
out there?' 'Just my cat. . .' 'You mean, you talk to your cat? As
if he was a real person? You call him "treasure"? And "my man"?
You sure that's a cat in your kitchen, Marie-Sylvia? You sure
it isn't a boyfriend, an admirer, a. . .?' Marie-Sylvia, sincerely
offended, raised her hand in protest. She had turned as red as
a beet and was trying to catch her breath. 'My Lord, what's
wrong with you, for the love of. . .? You'd think I'd just told
you the Pope was dead! Get a grip on yourself, Marie. Pius the
Twelfth is alive and well!' Madame Lemieux laughed quietly.
She'd heard that Marie-Sylvia was very sensitive on the subject
of men, and as a newcomer to the neighbourhood, she'd decided
to stick her neck out and see if it was true. Marie-Sylvia finally
got her breath back. 'Maybe Pius the Twelfth is all right, but
you've got a screw loose, that's for sure!' 'Don't fly off the handle
so. . .' 'It's easy for you to say that! You'll leave here and tell
the whole neighbourhood that I've got a kitchen full of men. . .'
'Oh, come on now, Marie. I never said your kitchen was full of
men. . . Anyway, it just takes one to ruin a woman's reputation!'
'It was my cat! My cat! Duplessis!' 'Duplessis! The former
Premier of the Province of Quebec in your kitchen! And
you call him "treasure"! I knew he was a bachelor, but I didn't
know he was a tomcat!' 'You don't understand a thing! The
name of my cat is Duplessis!' Madame Lemieux rested her
elbows on the glass counter. 'Marie-Sylvia, I'm pulling your
leg. I know all that. Now, give me some Ronson flints for my
husband.' The latch moved and the women turned around to see
who was coming in the door. Duplessis was stretched out on the
top step, his left front paw swiping furiously at the metal door
latch. 'Look, there he is. There's Duplessis.' 'Did you show
him how to do that?' 'No, he learned all by himself.' Madame
Lemieux approached the door, holding her stomach. 'I don't
know if the real Duplessis could do that!'

When the children went to spend the day in Lafontaine Park,
the problem was staying together. The park was enormous, but

as long as Thérèse, her brother and their cousins were satisfied with walking around the two lakes, visiting the tiny, dirty zoo or running through bushes and embankments, everything was fine. Thérèse led the games, with Marcel clinging to her skirt, and Richard and Philippe blindly following the leader, laughing when Thérèse laughed, yelling when she was afraid, applauding when she won a game of tag; but when Marcel, his trousers dirty, shoelaces untied, hair dishevelled, stopped smack in the middle of a dirt path and said in his flute-like voice: 'When do we play?' the situation got trickier. Richard and Philippe were sitting on the ground, pulling out blades of grass with which they hoped to make kazoos, while Thérèse tried to discourage her brother from going to the playground, which they had been circling but carefully avoiding since their arrival. For Marcel, getting dirty and playing hide-and-seek as he walked through a park, no matter how beautiful it was, wasn't playing: he could get as dirty just as well, even better perhaps, playing in the lane behind his house, with friends his own age. No, for him, playing meant swinging on the high swings, the ones that were built for the littlest children, where they imprisoned you inside four wooden slats that slid on chains, making a noise like a happy ghost; it was tearing open the sky with your feet as you shouted: 'I'm kicking the sun in the belly!'; it was being the lightweight at one end of the seesaw, scared that you'd shoot into the trees; it was climbing to the end of the moving ladder to save limpy-grandma from the fire, then, thinking better of it, and shouting to Thérèse: 'No, we'll let her toast — and then we'll spread peanut butter on her and eat her!'; it was being afraid of the attendant, who was certainly a maniac ('What does that mean, maniac?' 'Never mind, you'd be just dumb enough to go and find out!'); and most of all, ah yes! most of all, it was whirling on the whirligig until the park spun in every direction and Thérèse, in a frenzy, began screaming: 'Now you've done it, he's green again! He'll throw up all over the place and I'll get hell and he'll stink all the way home! What did I ever do to God to deserve such a simple-minded brother?' For Marcel, 'playing' meant going into the green area on Calixa-Lavallée where all the games were, the part that was also called 'the park' (when you asked someone: 'Are you going to the park?' you had to stress the word 'park,' so the other person would know if you were just inviting him for a pastoral stroll or to have fun on the parallel bars, swings and wooden slides), where, to enter, the group had to split up. In fact, only little boys under six and little girls under twelve were allowed: the officials claimed it was unhealthy for boys and girls to play games together where there might be a certain tendency for skirts to rise at the wind's slightest whim. That was the one and only reason. The City of Montreal had so decided — and all the children suffered as a result. If anyone found a ten-year-old boy having fun with his sisters or his younger brothers, pushing them on the swings or holding the ladder that they were trying to climb, he'd be chased away like some hooligan, accused of looking up his sisters' skirts (they probably took their baths together at home), while the rest of the children were left without supervision, as all the park attendants were suspect old monsters who enjoyed taking the place of the big brothers at the bottom of ladders or behind the swings. Which meant that for Marcel to have any fun, Richard and Philippe had to go off, leaving him with Thérèse, who thereby became guard and slave to his childish games. Thérèse adored her brother, but she hated spending a whole day listening to his somewhat incoherent prattling with its endless mixture of ordinary everyday acts and the poorly expressed fantasies of his imagination. Thérèse was very down-to-earth by nature and her brother's fabulous adventures in a sandbox drove her crazy. And so, after their sandwiches, when Richard and Philippe went to pee in the public toilets, Marcel looked up at his sister with pleading eyes and said: 'I pwomise I won't fwow up if we go pway on the swings!' and Thérèse raised her arms to Heaven — but not before she'd stuck a piece of gum in her mouth. 'Go and play in the dirt for a while. Dig holes.' 'Police says no.' 'We won't tell them.' Marcel, too easily persuaded, sat on his little bottom and began to dig a hole under a picnic table. 'It's too hard and I haven't got a sovel!' 'That's right, you haven't asked me for anything for a while. . .' Thérèse sat beside her brother in the grass. 'It's only noon and you're so dirty you

look like you've spent two weeks in a pigsty!' 'Do I look like
a piggy?' 'You look like a piggy and you smell like a piggy, but
we love you anyway.' Marcel burst out in a loud laugh, and
a bold squirrel that had approached the table jumped. 'But
we love you even more when you're clean. . . two minutes
before you get into bed.' Thérèse lay on her back. She could
see the sun playing through the bare branches of the trees, not
yet awakened from a harsh winter. 'Soon there'll be leaves.'
'When?' 'Soon.' 'Tomorrow?' 'Soon.' 'When, soon?' 'Marcel,
you ask the dumbest questions! Yes, tomorrow! Tomorrow,
there'll be great big leaves on the trees!' 'If I don't go to sleep
tonight, can I see them grow?' Thérèse hesitated briefly. 'No,
it'll be too dark.' Marcel got up and came and plunked himself
beside his sister, blocking the sun. 'Can I sit on your tummy?'
'No you can't, Marcel. I'll throw up my lunch.' Marcel fell onto
his sister's stomach all the same and she bent double with pain.
'Dammit, Marcel, can't you sit still for two minutes! I told
you not to sit on me and you just flung yourself on me like
a sack of potatoes. It's dangerous. You could've killed me!
Sometimes you're such a pain, I can't believe it!' Slapped
on the backside and around the ears, Marcel began to howl.
Rather than console him, Thérèse, impatient now and rubbing
her stomach, walked away from her brother onto a path. She
leaned against a tree and watched her cousins coming back
from the toilet — Philippe, running ahead; Richard, walking
behind. When Philippe came up to her, he pointed to Marcel.
'I got a feeling your brother wants to play on the swings! You
can hear him all the way to Sherbrooke Street!' 'Let him holler,
it'll do him good!' 'Did you hit him?' 'No, I chewed him out,
but he was asking for it!' Philippe ran to Marcel and picked
him up. 'How'd you like to go for a swing?' Marcel was crying
so hard that he couldn't reply. He merely nodded. 'All right,
we'll go and swing!' Thérèse was still under the tree, rubbing
her stomach. 'That's right, promise him the moon. You aren't
the ones that'll be stuck with him for the rest of the day!' At
that very moment, Richard came up to Thérèse, holding a
dandelion that he timidly offered her: 'It isn't much, but it's
all I could find. The other flowers aren't out yet.' Thérèse

turned around. 'Well, wait for them! I hate dandelions! They
stink!' Thérèse ran over to Philippe and pulled Marcel from
his arms. 'That's my little brother!' Marcel, terrified, suddenly
stopped crying. 'See! He stops crying when I take him!' A
nasty little smile appeared at the corner of Philippe's mouth.
'Maybe he stopped crying, but he's pissing now!' In fact,
upset by the quarrel with Thérèse, Marcel had forgotten to
let her know he had to pee — but he was now as she held
him, his expression blank but serious. Philippe caught his
cousin in mid-flight, just as Thérèse was throwing him to the
ground. She'd turned so white it was scary, and, as happened
every time her anger got the better of her, she stood in the
middle of the road, stiff, silent, trembling a little, as though
not really there, but withdrawn into herself, concentrating on
her rage. Richard took her in his arms and held her tight.
'Don't have a fit, Thérèse. Don't have a fit, it isn't worth
it!' Thérèse's fits were almost as famous as her mother's:
there was something terrifying about them, final, complete,
that left witnesses horrified and stunned. The fights between
mother and daughter were devastating. The women would
throw themselves at each other's faces. Thérèse answering
her mother's slaps with punches, her cries with howls, her
reproaches with curses. Beside Albertine, Thérèse was tiny,
but even so, you could sense that the former was afraid of
her daughter. No one tried to separate them any more, it was
useless; the battle had to be consummated, consumed, until
Albertine and Thérèse threw themselves into one another's
arms, crying out their love. Richard gently rocked Thérèse
and Philippe did the same with Marcel, who looked all around,
recording everything to feed his nocturnal terror. And as her
mother wasn't there to wind Thérèse up, she slowly calmed
down, relaxing in the arms of her cousin, who, moved, was
blushing. 'It doesn't matter, Thérèse, he just peed a little. It
didn't even get on your dress. Go and wash your arm and it'll
be all gone.'

Claire Lemieux took her leave of Marie-Sylvia and Duplessis on the doorstep of the restaurant. She lived with her husband, Hector, down the street, on the third ·floor of one of the most miserable houses in the neighbourhood (it was called 'the dump') in an apartment that consisted of three rooms — living room, bedroom and kitchen — that were hot in summer, cold in winter. Hector, a sort of slow, white whale, a house-painter by trade, who hadn't worked for years — not, in fact, since Claire, slender, gay and lively, had found a job selling shoes for Giroux et Deslauriers at the corner of Mont-Royal and Fabre. The job was why Hector and Claire had recently moved: the young woman had been working for Giroux et Deslauriers for a little over three years now, and she had to travel from Saint-Eustache to Montreal twice a day, half an hour by train from Saint-Eustache to Windsor Station and an hour by streetcar from the station to the store. . . . And yet, she'd done everything she could to find work in her home town not too far from her whale of a husband. But she quickly realized that working would be bad for their reputation in the village, where everybody knew one another, spied on one another and was out to get one another (a husband who stays home and a wife who works — just think of it!). Already, they'd started calling Hector, 'Lemieux the heartless'. . . . Heartless, he was, as Claire knew very well, but she preferred to laugh at it and break her back to support the two of them, instead of scratching the sore and starving to death with him. Claire Lemieux spoiled her whale; she watched him getting fatter and she took strange pleasure from the fact. Hector's sexual appetites (so tedious and limited) subsided as the layers of fat accumulated on his already soft skeleton and Claire got some peace. No longer was she subjected to his pitiful assaults, and when she wanted to make love, she made the first move — and the others. She never thought, however, of cheating on Hector. Not that she particularly loved him, but that wasn't playing the game. It wasn't done, and besides, she wasn't all that crazy about the other men she knew. Her boss thought of nothing but money (he did look up his customers' skirts when they were trying on shoes, but Claire imagined herself in their place and laughed. 'A man that looks and doesn't touch isn't any more fun than one that touches and doesn't look!'), the two salesmen who worked with her lived together (discreetly, but the phonebook never lies), and the men she saw on the street were all too old or too young. The war had kidnapped all the males who were in remotely good health, tied them up, disguised them, indoctrinated them, shipped them off to the other side of the Big Water and sent them back home in pieces or unhinged; it had left the women only their priests, who certainly took advantage of the fact, their little boys, who were too young to offer their flesh, their fathers, who told them about the atrocities of the other war to give them heart — and sometimes, their husbands, if they were disabled or prolific, for fathers of large families weren't required to go to war unless they wanted to get away from their families or if they were too poor to support them (the war smiled down from all the posters: 'Give me your husband, I'll give you eighty dollars a month!'). And so, Claire Lemieux had been very surprised a few months earlier, just before they left Saint-Eustache, when suddenly her husband came to her in the middle of the night and murmured: 'I want us to make a little ba-beee!' Claire understood immediately and burst out laughing: 'Don't worry, you dirty bugger, they won't want you for their army, you're so fat and slow, you'd lose the war for them!' But Hector insisted (for once) probably out of fear that he'd be called up and Claire thought: 'Go on, fatso, make me a baby. The time's right. . . But after he's born, you'll have to move your ass to support us!' Claire was now seven months pregnant (the little one was due at the end of June) and Hector still didn't seem aware that very soon his wife would have to quit her job to take care of their child. He ate more and more as he listened to the comedies on the radio. Sometimes, he made the effort to go for a walk along Mont-Royal. 'Getting the kinks out of my legs.' But soon he'd be back, out of breath and red, with one hand on his heart. He had trouble climbing the winding stairs and he'd reach the third landing on his knees sometimes, his respiratory tract whistling like organ pipes, his ears buzzing and his eyes bloodshot. Claire thought that he was laying it on a bit thick and found this funny.

'Hector, you're touched in the head! You get too much exercise!
It's no good for your health. Here, come and lay down.' 'Fuck
off!' But he'd lie down all the same — and the shooting pains
in his left arm would start again. Claire would leave for work
or go on eating, humming away, which had the happy effect of
driving Hector crazy. 'Here I am, just about dead, and you're
singing!' 'I hope you won't hear me after you're dead!' Claire
was really very happy to be pregnant. She'd decided to go back
to Saint-Eustache, to her mother, as soon as the child was born,
dragging her heap of soft fat behind her. She'd tell her mother:
'Papa left you a little money, so take us in — all three of us —
and I'll go back to work when I'm feeling better.' She didn't
mind Hector being the way he was; she hardly ever thought of
him as a human being, but rather as a cat or a dog. And perhaps
that's why she would have liked it if Marie-Sylvia had, not a
Duplessis with fur, but a real Hector in the back of her shop.
The baby kicked her, bringing her back to herself. She stopped
smack in the middle of the sidewalk. 'Well, you, so there you
are. . . Haven't heard from you for a while. . . I was starting
to think you'd gone for a walk "to get the kinks out," like your
Pa.' She rubbed her stomach gently, trying to find the places
where she could feel the feet move. 'Hey, that's fun! My little
Claude! Or Claudette! If I knew which you were, I wouldn't
have to say everything twice!' Hector was out on the balcony,
waving desperately at her. 'All right, all right, pinhead. You'll
get your flints!'

Victoire and Edouard were eating alone together, because
Albertine had announced that she wasn't hungry after drinking
two eggs beaten up with some milk and Gabriel had fallen
asleep in his bed after two pages of *Bug-Jargal*. Victoire had
always had a man's appetite and eaten with a man's gestures.
She cut slices of bread as thick as your hand and spread them
with a layer of butter that turned the strongest liver yellow.
Even now, at seventy-five, she ate everything: pork, the nicest
cheese, cucumber sandwiches with a glass of milk, tourtière,

cakes. If told to be careful, she would answer, mouth full:
'Leave me be, I spend my nights alone!' Only Richard and
Edouard knew about the long nights when Victoire, livid and
ghostly, painfully got out of bed and paced back and forth in
the small room, muttering: 'Come and get me, God! Come
and get me or I'll go and find you and give you a piece of
my mind that'll last till the end of time!' Sometimes Edouard
would get up and offer to help his mother, but she would
send him back to bed with a single sentence: 'If you didn't
smell so much of booze, maybe I could breathe!' or: 'Sleep
in peace, I'm paying for your sins!' When Richard timidly
asked his grandmother if she needed anything, she was less
nasty but just as firm: 'If I've managed to stay on my feet
this long, I can last a little longer!' Meekly, Richard would
go back to bed, but rarely would fall asleep again. If Victoire
heard him sigh, she said: 'Go to sleep. Pretend I'm a flock of
sheep jumping over a fence!' Richard smiled, and Victoire, in
pain beside him, would make a grimace that might just as well
have been a smile. When the great liberating belch finally came
(Victoire's theory was: 'A belch is the breath of life.'), the old
woman would sit up in bed and hurl invective at the cucumber
that wasn't going down as it should or the roast pork she'd
devoured earlier, as Albertine and the fat woman looked on
with alarm, sipping very weak milky tea. Victoire took a bite
of her ketchup-butter-brown sugar sandwich, grunting with
satisfaction, and Edouard looked away. She chewed noisily,
not realizing the tip of her nose was adorned with ketchup.
'Wipe your face, Mama, for the love of God, you look like
you've got a nosebleed!' 'You'd like that, eh?' She drew her
sleeve across the tip of her nose. 'You never tried that mixture,
eh? Never wanted to. And it's good! Real good! The ketchup
and the brown sugar go great together. . .' 'Mama, cut it out,
you're turning my stomach! You've been telling me the same
thing for thirty-five years now!' 'And it still turns your stomach,
right? You're more of a sissy than I thought. It's been a long
time since you could get to me! For thirty-five years I've been
looking at you, too, but I don't lose *my* appetite!' She burst
out laughing, without swallowing her food, choked briefly,

pounded the table, coughed, burped and wiped her eyes with the same sleeve she'd used to wipe off the ketchup. 'Blow me, I'm still good for a laugh!' Edouard could hear the fat woman laughing too, in the next room. 'That's right, both of you, gang up on me!' The fat woman blew her nose. 'We aren't laughing at you, Edouard. It's a joke!' Edouard got up from the table abruptly, knocking over his plate. His mother took another bite of her sandwich. 'It's good, you know, you ought to try it. . . Ketchup and. . .' 'Shut up, okay! We've had our share of fights, but I've never hit you with a plate. Still, it's never too late!' Edouard went into the kitchen and hurled his dishes into the sink. Victoire swallowed her bread and ketchup. 'Whew! I'm saved! The sink got it all!' Edouard passed her again on the way to his bedroom, but Victoire stopped him: 'Don't run away. I've got something to ask you.' 'If it's money, I'm fresh out.' 'I know that, I'm the one that gave you some yesterday! Now, sit down and let's talk.' 'Finished your bloody sandwich?' 'No — and you're going to watch me finish it and you're going to put up with it too. I'm your mother and you got no business telling me what to eat and when to eat it!' 'You know I'm going to end up choking you one of these days!' 'That's just what I was telling Bartine the other day. I said, "Edouard's going to end up choking me!" I can't wait! For once in his life, he'll make up his mind to do something! Now, sit down and listen.' Edouard sat down and began nervously crumbling a slice of bread. He knew very well that when his mother asked for something, there was no possible escape. She'd stop at nothing to get what she wanted. Once, she'd hidden the only three pairs of trousers that Gabriel possessed to keep him from courting a girl that she didn't want as a daughter-in-law; she'd pretended to die because Albertine refused to turn the radio to the station she wanted; she'd shouted 'Fire!' from the front balcony because it was too warm in her bedroom, and Gabriel, who was in charge of the heat, refused to stop feeding the coal furnace in the middle of January; one day (but that was something which she'd never admit, she was truly ashamed of it), she'd even stolen an ice-cream cone from Marcel, who wouldn't give her a lick of it. Edouard looked at her, amazed, almost relieved.

'It's been a while since I went down those damn stairs, and if I
don't do it today, I'm going to rip them up. So, I've made up
my mind. I'm going to go for a walk on Mont-Royal, to show
off my fat son and that ugly straw hat you gave me for Easter!
A granny's hat if I ever saw one! Now, make yourself handsome
and I'll do my best!' She crammed the last piece of bread in her
mouth and beamed a broad smile at her son.

After leaving Ti-Lou's, Betty lingered a few minutes on
the steps of the Bruchési School, although she'd promised
Mercedes that she'd come back early. Leaning on the cement
rail beside the small staircase that went up to the main door,
she looked towards the four big second floor windows, where
she'd spent the most beautiful year of her life, her second year
of school, beneath the protective wing and within the deep
folds of the robe of Sister Marie-de-Fatima, who people said
was crazy, but whom Béatrice revered, devoting to her all the
love of a little girl neglected by a mother and a father whose
dreams were too grand, who spoke of nothing but money
and escape ('Birds, give me birds and I'll build you a city
someplace else, someplace where it doesn't snow!'). They used
to say ('They' were the other girls in her class; and the bigger
ones, the ones at the Saints-Anges School, who often passed
by in groups of five or six, whispering, laughing, ignoring the
smaller girls in grade one, but warning the ones in grade two
about the crazy woman, the lunatic, creepy Sister 'Fatimette,'
who would end up behind bars in some insane asylum) that
Sister Marie-de-Fatima was crazy because, sometimes, right in
the middle of a class (often maths), she would stop, run over to
the window and fly away, murmuring: 'You've put me in jail!'
or: 'I know my body has to stay here, but at least open a door
for my soul!' She stood on tiptoe for long moments, watching
the sky, and Béatrice, though she was only seven and knew
nothing of what might trouble the soul, sensed that Sister
Marie-de-Fatima had gone flying over the surrounding roofs
to avoid exploding. The girls took advantage of the teacher's

crisis, of course, to raise hell: pulling pigtails, making faces, calling each other names or pounding their feet on the floor as they chanted: 'CRAZY, cra-cra-crazy, CRAZY!' but Béatrice remained glued to her place, watching the caged bird slowly dying beneath the jibes and laughter of the insensitive, spiteful children. When Sister Marie-de-Fatima returned to the class, breathless, her wings folded, with sky reflected in her eyes, everything in the classroom was topsy-turvy: there were bits of chalk everywhere, some of the girls were on all fours, while others were standing on their seats — but she said nothing. She went back to her blackboard and resumed the lesson exactly where she'd left off, as though nothing had happened. And her gaze always fell on Béatrice, frozen there, who seemed to be asking her: 'Was it nice, Sister?' And the nun would answer: 'If you only knew!' Béatrice got up and walked along the wrought iron fence to the third window. She pressed her face against the iron and felt the metal between her thighs. It was from this window that Sister Marie-de-Fatima had flown away for the last time. Béatrice had seen the bird take flight. That day — it was at the beginning of May, like today — Béatrice was having trouble writing the word 'angel,' which she kept spelling 'anjel,' and she had asked the nun to come and help her. 'Sister, I don't understand why you write it with a "g." It looks prettier with a "j!"' Sister Marie-de-Fatima bent over her and wrote the word in her 'beautiful' nun's handwriting, the perfectly formed letters, moulded forever by religious and community rules: rules of chastity, poverty and obedience. To thank her, Béatrice buried her head in the folds of the nun's robe. She'd started doing this at the beginning of the school year and Sister Marie-de-Fatima let her. Sometimes, she would even place her hand lightly on the little girl's unruly head, listening to her sigh and moan like a child being comforted. They never spoke to one another, but an impassioned affection had sprung up between them, an affection that united them through their expressions, by what did not have to be said, by what they understood perfectly well: Sister Marie-de-Fatima found in Béatrice's eyes the courage to continue her Calvary; while, in the nun's eyes, the little girl found the desire to learn how to fly. Suddenly, the nun began to tremble. Béatrice withdrew her head from the folds of her robe. The nun was looking down at her notebook. In an awkward gesture of affection, Béatrice had upset her inkwell. It spilled onto a sheet of paper, drowning the word 'angel' in a sea of total blackness. Sister Marie-de-Fatima cried out, pushed Béatrice away from her, and ran to the third window, which she opened so vigorously that two of the panes shattered. And Béatrice, hands and face black with the angel's blood, watched the bird spread its vast raven's wings and, with a cry of horror, awkwardly try to fly. Leaning against the fence, Béatrice heard once again the angel's fall, the dull thud of bones breaking beneath layers and layers of heavy fabric, a sound that followed her throughout her childhood. Sometimes, she heard it again when someone (Mercedes or a client) opened a window to drive out the smells of love poorly given and poorly taken. Béatrice walked away from the red brick building, unworthy witness to this first great love, stained with blood and ink, crossed Lanaudière, and walked past Saint-Stanislas church, without even glancing up.

Violette took the needles out of the bootie she'd just finished. She turned the small soft fuzzy ball in her hands for a few seconds, then, making a face, began to unravel it, pulling on the end of the green wool. Florence, her mother, stopped her by putting her hand on the bootie. 'Don't unravel it, it's fine.' Violette shrugged. 'It's smaller than the other one. Look, the one that I just finished is bigger. . . Only a cripple could wear this one!' Rose and Mauve looked at their sister, astonished at her words. Mauve frowned and spoke very quietly. 'You know very well, nobody's going to wear these booties. . .' Rose took the bootie from Violette's hands. 'I'm going to do it again. You start another one.' Florence ran her hand gently across her daughter's forehead, smoothed back her hair and tucked it behind her ears. 'Your head aching?' 'No, I just forgot. As usual.' Violette picked up her knitting needles again, selected a ball of green wool and silently continued her work. Florence waited until Rose had finished re-doing the yellow part before she spoke. 'Never undo what's been done, Violette.' 'I know, Mama, I was daydreaming.' 'If you're tired, go inside and rest a while . . .' 'I know, Mama, but I'm not that tired.' Florence spread her hands on her knees. 'Never look back. We're here so that everything will keep moving ahead. What's knitted is knitted — even if it isn't knitted right.' 'Yes, Mama.' Rose, Violette and Mauve looked at their mother, and then, at the same moment, as though by plan, they all looked down at their work. 'Is today the first time?' Florence asked in a troubled, almost trembling voice. 'Yes, Mama. Don't worry. I didn't undo anything.' Florence closed her eyes and began to rock again. The familiar creaking of their mother's chair dissipated the uneasiness the sisters had started to feel. Their needles began to click more regularly. Only Violette was still a little behind in the rhythmic movement of elbows and hands, just as a false note or a poorly executed measure remains in the mind for a long time after order has been restored in an orchestra. Then, Violette broke the silence with a forbidden question that startling her sisters rang out on the balcony like the crack of a whip, 'Mama, how long have we been here?' Florence didn't move, but her eyes filled with fear, or rather, with uncertainty, as though Violette had uttered a word so unthinkable, formulated a statement so absurd, that no reply came to mind, leaving her empty and worried. Violette pursed her lips and lowered her head. 'Mama, I want to know. I feel as if I'm forgetting everything when I knit my baby booties — and it scares me.' Florence still did not move. 'Mama, I can't remember yesterday. I mean, it's as if there was just one yesterday in my head! As if we came here yesterday and it was our first day in this part of town. . .' Violette spoke faster and faster. 'Mama, I feel as if I arrived yesterday, but, just now, all of a sudden, I remember that we saw Gabriel and Edouard and Albertine being born and . . .' Abruptly, she turned towards her mother, dropping the ball of green wool which rolled off the balcony, leaving an end dangling. 'Mama, I even remember when Victoire was born! It's the first time, but I remember! We were living in the country then, next door to her mother's place,

just like we're living next door to them now. . . Mama. . .
Mama. . . I remember when Victoire's mother was born!'
She shouted this last confession, suddenly jumping to her
feet, trembling, her hands clasped over her heart, her eyes
filled with tears. Then, Florence stood up and took her in her
arms. 'Go inside and rest. . .' 'Mama, answer me!' Florence
gently drew her daughter towards the glass door. 'All right,
we're going to talk. Then everything will be like it was before.
You'll just remember what's important. . .' She opened the
door and turned to Rose and Mauve, who had gone quite pale
as they went on knitting. 'If you feel tired, come inside too.'
When the door slammed slightly as it closed, Rose looked up
at her sister: 'Do you remember all that?' Mauve looked at
her surreptitiously, her hands never still. 'Yes. We've always
been here, Rose. And we always will be. Don't stop. That's
what we're here for.'

cat rushe.

When his second bowl of liver was finished, licked and washed,
Duplessis asked to go out without even going by his sandbox.
In vain did Marie-Sylvia plead with him, cajole him, threaten
him ('Three days! You were away for three days and now
you want to take off again! I haven't even had time to see
you! You spent the whole morning sleeping! Stay till tonight
at least. . . I'll stroke you and make you purr. . . I won't
move, you can sleep in my lap . . .'), but it was all in vain.
Duplessis clawed the bottom of the door, meowing as though
it were the middle of July, when the moon is red with desire
and passions explode at the ends of alleys. White with rage,
Marie-Sylvia opened the door, screaming: 'Okay, go out! But
don't bother coming back! Ever! I never want to see you again!
And don't come meowing at my window tonight. It won't do
you any good. You're staying out!' But Duplessis was already
far away. He jumped over the Ouimets' fence on the other
side of the lane, and now was hiding in the dandelions, his
eye on a bird perched on a low branch of the lilac tree (the
only one in the neighbourhood), excited at the prospect of

a well ordered hunt crowned by the fitting conclusion: the victim writhing in the executioner's paws, its wing broken or its neck smashed, with a heart that would suddenly stop beating as teeth searched through blood-soaked feathers for a tender spot in which to sink in triumph. But the bird (a common sparrow, if the truth be told, hard to catch and a wretched trophy) noticed Duplessis among the yellow flowers and flew off without more ado, not even fascinated by the cat's eyes that strove to be at the same time engaging, beguiling, authoritarian, dominating. Duplessis immediately lost interest in the lilac tree (why linger over failures?) and inched his way beneath the Ouimets' porch to do his business. At that very moment, a mouse slipped through the young blades of grass, and, heart pounding, reached the alley. Duplessis, occupied with a more important task, pretended not to see the mouse. He heard the Ouimets' door open above him. Then, he heard heavy footsteps that made the floor of the porch creak. He carefully buried his shit then cautiously approached the four front steps. Stretching out, he saw the feet of a woman in moccasins. The woman, long, lean, with a protruding belly, walked jerkily across the yard, then emerged into the alley without closing the wooden gate behind her. Duplessis followed her. He knew that odour very well: the woman liked cats and Duplessis was her favourite. (She called him 'the lecherous prime minister' and when she ran her hands through his fur, it had the effect of exciting Duplessis quite deliciously.) He moved ahead of her with little leaps and sat in front of her, looking her straight in the eye. The woman stopped and smiled. 'Don't bother making eyes at me, dirty old Duplessis. I haven't got anything for you today.' She walked around the cat, who ran between her feet, purring. 'I haven't got time, Duplessis. I'm on my way to work!' They came to the corner of Marie-Sylvia's restaurant. 'Your mother's probably looking for you — again!' The woman bent down, picked up the cat, opened the restaurant door and threw the animal into the middle of the room, shouting: 'Marie, here's your goddamn cat! He looks hungry!' The woman closed the door before Duplessis had time to react. He began cursing like the Devil himself. Marie-Sylvia got out of her armchair.

'You're back, my sweet! Come up on mummy's lap!' A few moments later, Marie-Sylvia, her hand bleeding, opened the restaurant door, and as far as Mont-Royal, you could hear: 'Out! Get out, you stinking rotten animal! I don't care if somebody picks you up and gasses you, so that I never hear another word about you!' Duplessis shot across Fabre Street. Immediately, a smell struck him and he remembered why he'd wanted to go out in the first place. Somewhere on the second floor of the second house, a little bit of a man with whom he'd had frequent conversations, who seemed to understand him, and whom he, Duplessis, understood very well indeed, lived with a bunch of lunatics, each one more hysterical than the other, and it was that man whom Duplessis suddenly wanted to see. It was the very special smell of that house (for Duplessis, all houses and all humans were smells, but there was something remarkable, something stubborn and tenacious given off by the occupants of that apartment, which he never entered, but one of whose inhabitants was dear to him. Very often, Duplessis came and slept on the doorstep, his nose against the crack at the bottom of the door, happily revelling in the magical, soothing, regenerative emanations given off by this little bit of a man he could talk to, who listened to him calmly, and who, O miracle!, answered in his roaming cat's language) that reminded Duplessis he hadn't seen Marcel for three or four days and that the little boy must miss him. He crossed the lane, went past Doctor Laporte's house, which gave off a disgusting smell of cleanliness that was maintained by too strong disinfectants and lingering perfumes. Duplessis intended to climb the steps, to slip his muzzle into the mail-box at the bottom of the door, and then to meow until Marcel opened the door, ecstatic, adorned with the smell of dried pee, lisping in cat-talk his human thoughts; but then something attracted his attention at the bottom of the steps, in front of the house next door, where two ageless women were knitting: a ball of green wool (a ball of wool, What bliss!) rested supreme in the middle of the pavement, promising all sorts of acrobatics, mad races and exciting games for a cat whose only toy, Marie-Sylvia, was fat, bulky and very difficult to move. Duplessis literally threw himself onto the wool and began to struggle with it, pretending it was the bird that he'd missed a while ago, or the mouse he'd turned his nose up at, or any other animal that's hard to catch but which he'd finally got the better of, and now was delighting in tearing it up, biting it, and almost suffocating himself as he imprisoned his claws in the rebellious strands. In the very heat of the battle, when most joyful, Duplessis shouted to the ball of wool: 'No use putting up a fight, you silly witch, you know the end is nigh! Give up! Give up and I won't harm you!' Florence came out of the house and sat in her rocking chair. Immediately, as though stunned, Duplessis calmed down, crumpled to the pavement, and looked at the woman, his eyes twice as big as usual. 'She fell asleep. Everything will be okay in an hour. Keep working.' Rose looked over her left shoulder and said very softly: 'Mama, why's Marie-Sylvia's cat playing with Violette's wool. . .?' Her mother cut her off in a firm but neutral voice. 'Cats can see us. Cats and sometimes crazy people.' On his backside, Duplessis began to clean his mouth with his paw, then stared at Florence again. He blinked. 'You bet I can see you!'

When Madame Ouimet arrived at Ti-Lou's (she had the key and never rang the bell, as Ti-Lou hated dragging herself and her crutches down the hallway: 'When people come to the door, they see me with my three legs and it's humiliating.'), the latter was still sitting by the window where Béatrice had left her. Her eyes were closed and her head bowed, so Madame Ouimet thought she was asleep. The young woman took much care as she cleared the little table, careful not to knock the plates together, wrapping the silver spoons in one of the two cloth napkins, centering the delicate, fragile cups in their saucers to avoid any inopportune spillage. She was about to leave the room, bearing the lunch tray, when Ti-Lou said abruptly: 'That you Rose?' She started and nearly dropped the tray: 'Hey, you scared me!' Ti-Lou hadn't moved, her head was still down, her eyes closed. 'I could've sworn you were asleep.'

'I've told you a million times, I never sleep in the daytime.' 'I know, but I thought just this once. . .' 'Never, understand? I never sleep in the daytime! It's hard enough getting to sleep at night!' Rose Ouimet headed for the kitchen, thinking: 'Never sleeps during the day! I'd like to know what she does when she spends the whole afternoon in her bed with her eyes shut, not moving a hair. Meditate?' Rose pushed open the kitchen door, grumbling. 'I hate it when people treat me like a nitwit!' She put the tray on the table and opened the icebox to pour the rest of the milk from the silver jug into the nearly empty bottle. 'You're out of ice! When does the iceman come?' The reply seemed to come from very far away, as though the living room was on the grounds of the Bruchési School. 'Around four in the afternoon. What time is it now?' Rose Ouimet picked up a card printed in large letters: 'Please leave 50 lbs.' and slipped it onto the nail that her own mother had driven into the wall many years before. Rose Ouimet had been cleaning Ti-Lou's apartment for only three years, replacing her mother, Rita Guérin, who was now too sick to 'do houses,' as she put it. 'Two o'clock. And you're out of milk!' Ti-Lou and Rose Ouimet weren't crazy about each other, but Rose was a good worker and Ti-Lou paid well, so they put up with each other, but shared no warmth or contact, which made the crippled woman very sad for she had been very fond of Rita Guérin's smiling face and the songs from the St Lawrence River that she would sing all day long, driving away the old wanton's intolerable present and replacing it with an imaginary past, a past filled with the good smells of the country and homemade bread. But Rose Ouimet, too serious for her years, didn't sing like her mother, and sometimes Ti-Lou thought she could even see the mark of unhappiness — of unhappiness too great, of suffering too intense for the lean, dry body — cross Rose's face, tracing purple shadows around her eyes when, as often happened, the young woman stopped suddenly during her work and stared into space, frowning, her mouth hard, as if she were contemplating some vision of horror, and silently, inevitably, giving in to it. Ti-Lou had pleaded with Rita Guérin to come back to work, even offering to double her salary, but Rose's mother resisted, shouting into the telephone like a woman still unaccustomed to those electric contraptions: 'Why should I kill myself for a few extra bucks a week? I want to enjoy the little bit of time I've got left!' (Rita Guérin was barely forty-five and Ti-Lou had raised her eyes to Heaven as she pounded the wall with her fist.) 'I'm sick of cleaning up after other people, I'm taking a rest! I'll send you my girl, Rose. She's a sourpuss, but she's a good worker.' Rose Ouimet was, in fact, very efficient, but her presence depressed Ti-Lou, who often wanted to take her by the shoulders and shake her, shouting: 'You're only twenty-two, for Chrissake, wipe that martyr's look off your face! Don't frown like that and don't scrunch up your eyes! You'll look like a prune before you're thirty! If your life's such a pain in the ass, then change it!' But when you walk on three legs, two of them made of wood, it's not easy to take anyone by the shoulders and shake them awake; it's a matter of balance. Ti-Lou preferred to take a stronger dose of Doctor Sanregret's drops and sink into that blessed lethargy, so dangerous but so gratifying, that she called her 'divine coma,' rather than watch the dismal Rose Ouimet's unhappiness slinking about the apartment, hugging the walls, hiding in the corners, ready to leap on its victim at any moment, paralyzing her in the middle of the hallway, broom in hand, or surprising her on hands and knees in the bathroom, her head in the washbasin. There was nothing about Ti-Lou's past that Rose Ouimet didn't know — and the former sometimes wondered if that wasn't the real reason for her coolness. Rose Ouimet knew everything about Ti-Lou because her mother had repeated everything the Ottawa wanton had told her, so she didn't want to listen to her employer talk about her past. When Ti-Lou — either for something better to do, or simply because she wanted to — had tried to tell Rose about her unbelievable life, the young woman always managed to avoid the issue by muttering: 'That's not what I'm here for' or: 'I haven't got time for that' or: 'If you want somebody to keep you company, I'll send my sister, Gabrielle. She can talk a blue streak. I'm here to scrub and that's what I'm doing!' Ti-Lou quickly understood that Rose, though so young, blamed her for her past, whereas her mother

enjoyed it and was even a little jealous of it, sometimes declaring
between two swipes of the mop: 'You were in Ottawa in 1900
and I was in Montreal in 1920. You were having fun in a place
everybody else thought was a dump and I was bored to tears in a
town everybody raved about,' then she would again take up her
song with no further explanation. Ti-Lou had several portraits
of pretentious and ugly men in carved frames, that Rose Ouimet
was loath to touch. Just once, she asked her employer: 'You
knew all these men?' and made a face at Ti-Lou's affirmative
reply. And Ti-Lou asked her: 'You don't like men?' to which
Rose responded: 'Only floozies like men. The rest of us put up
with them.' Rose Ouimet ran her hand over her rounded belly.
'Goddamn balloon!' She was expecting her first child joylessly
— cold, remote, resigned. She came out of the kitchen, held
her stomach as she crossed the house, and burst into the living
room, asking: 'Where do I start? With the house or you?'

Béatrice climbed very slowly up the first of the two staircases
that led to Mercedes' apartment. She stopped every four or five
steps, leaned against the wall or the banister and sighed. 'It's
such a beautiful day!' She stopped at the top of the first staircase
and sat on the doorstep of her own room, where she hardly
spent any time at all now, but kept 'just in case all hell breaks
loose.' It was her refuge, the only place in the world where
she could be alone. Sometimes, Béatrice, tired of the awkward
caresses of drunken and inexperienced soldiers, would go down
to her room, shut the door and cry silently in her bed or by
the window that looked out on the alley. Sometimes she even
missed her former life: the buttons, the ribbons, the tortoise
shell slides; no responsibilities and innocent nights when she
did nothing but sleep; her pay at the end of the week, little but
steady, in a brown envelope that you didn't open right away,
if you had any money left from the previous week, to see how
long you could front it out; the Passe-Temps movie house on
Saturday night: three films, four and a half hours in a stifling
hall, with many of the dirty seats broken and the strong smell of

unwashed workers and over-perfumed women; the long hollow hours of Sunday afternoon when you'd tell yourself: 'I wish tomorrow would hurry up! Anything except these goddamn Sundays!' But these little fits never lasted long. Béatrice knew Mercedes was waiting for her, counting on her, and that the work had to be done. When Béatrice came back to her friend's apartment with its red and yellow lights, the shadows under her eyes were slightly larger than usual and the soldiers liked that. Arms seized her, lips crushed her and Béatrice quickly forgot about movies and hollow Sunday afternoons. Béatrice decided to change her clothes before going up to Mercedes. As she entered her room, she immediately noticed a piece of white paper folded in four that someone had slipped under her door. She bent down and picked it up. 'Hope it isn't somebody from home come for a visit. . . That's all I need!' A somewhat sybilline phrase that Béatrice didn't understand immediately had been hastily scribbled on the paper: 'Meet me at Lafontaine Park.' No signature.

'Now, that's dumb — leaving a message without signing it! But maybe the name wouldn't mean anything to me. Maybe it's a client that wants to do it in the bushes!' Béatrice smiled. 'I wouldn't mind. Just once. Out in the open. But more than likely the ground's still wet.' She changed quickly, slipping into the dress that she kept for special occasions, for Mass or going out on a Saturday night — but she hadn't gone out on Saturday night for ages; Saturday was a busy night — the yellow cotton dress that made her look so young and emphasized her smooth brown skin, the dress that made Mercedes say: 'Usually, I look like your mother, but when you wear that, I look like your mother's mother. No matter what I do to try and look younger, I've still got a good twelve years headstart on you!' Béatrice whistled as she brushed her hair. 'I'll tell Mercedes we ought to take the afternoon off, then we'll go to the park, but I won't mention the message. We'll see what happens.' Satisfied with what she saw in the small round mirror, Béatrice smiled a broad smile at her reflection. 'I look just like a calendar girl!' She took a few dance steps as she headed for the door. 'I'd like to go out some night!' She picked up the note and slipped it in her purse.

She climbed up the second set of stairs, humming, 'Ramona, you stink of feet, tobacco too,' joyous, heart pounding. 'Hey, a message. My very first one!' At Mercedes' apartment, she stopped short and a dreadful foreboding seized her heart: the door was ajar, something weird for Mercedes, who shouted twenty times a day: 'Did you shut the door? And lock it? You can't be too careful with some of the jokers we get here!' The smell of vomit extended onto the landing. Without thinking, Béatrice pushed the door open, sure that she'd find Mercedes awash in her own blood or beaten to death, lying in her own excrement — but the big room was deserted. It was, however, in incredible disarray: everything had been smashed, knocked over, searched, broken, trampled on. The mattress, slashed open, was on the floor. The dresser drawers had been pulled out, thrown against the walls and had landed on the floor, and the bathroom door had been pulled off its hinges. Béatrice ran through the tiny apartment shouting: 'Mercedes! Mercedes!' like a madwoman, tripping over objects strewn on the floor, bumping into overturned furniture. Some vomit inside the bathtub and more right next to it. 'Bunch of pigs! Filthy pigs!' She saw again the three soldiers who had tried to stop her on the stairs that morning and felt anger rising up her spine. 'If only I could get my hands on them! I don't know what I'd do, but it'd hurt like hell!' She felt somewhat reassured when she realized that for sure Mercedes wasn't in the apartment. She went back into the bedroom, sat on the bedsprings, and let her sobs come as she pounded the foot of the bed with her fists, stamped her feet and cried: 'Goddamn bunch of filth!' twenty or thirty times, though it didn't make her feel any better. She had just started to calm down when she saw the shadow of Monsieur Soucy, the concierge, outlined in the doorway, his arms laden with packages that he hadn't even thought of putting down when he heard Béatrice shouting. 'What's going on? You can hear you hollering out on the street! What happened? Did you get beat up? And where's your friend? I knew it'd happen! I knew it! I can't set foot outside for two hours without a ceiling falling on somebody's head or some idiot forgetting to turn off the tap! I'm calling the

police!' Monsieur Soucy disappeared before Béatrice had time
to react. The words struck her like a whip and she straightened
up, as if slapped. Police! She picked up her purse, which she
had dropped near the door, and ran out of the apartment, down
the stairs, past Monsieur Soucy, who shouted: 'And where do
you think you're going, Mademoiselle Béatrice? The police'll
be wanting to talk to you!' Béatrice left the building without
slowing down, in the direction of Lafontaine Park. 'Mercedes
left that message. She fled to the Park! Mercedes is waiting for
me!' Rose, Mauve and their mother, Florence, watched her
pass without batting an eye. Florence, however, said: 'That
girl's heading for trouble!' But Florence was mistaken. Béatrice
wasn't heading for trouble. Béatrice was on her way to twenty
years of glory, splendour and power.

Philippe had discovered a subterfuge with which to enter the
playground openly and publicly, without a word from the
attendant, though it was a ploy that required Thérèse and
Marcel to play roles — and Philippe was a little worried
about the latter (the former was, in his words, 'a born actress'
and could if needs be make anyone believe that she was a
'forty-year-old mother who still looks young' or a 'four-month-
old baby advanced for its age'). As for Richard, his elder
brother. . . Philippe had a way of totally excluding him from
his games, dropping him whenever he was no longer useful.
This confused Richard, left him speechless, arms dangling and
mouth gaping, wounded, dismayed, and generally in a position
that was fraught with difficulties. At school, when they wanted
to beat him up in the yard because he'd just done something
nasty, Philippe would run to his brother, who was peaceful and
weak, bring him back into the heat of the battle and forget him
there, without even recalling, later, either the battle or, more
important, his own misdeeds. If he needed money, he came and
cried on Richard's sleeve, but once his brother gave him part or
all of his possessions, Philippe would disappear without a word
of thanks and come back a few minutes later carrying an ice

cream or a paper cone of chips, 'forgetting' to offer his brother
a lick or a piece of greasy potato. Philippe hovered around
Richard as long as his brother could be of some use to him,
but disappeared without fail as soon as Richard needed him.
And so, when Philippe's plan was adopted (Thérèse and Marcel
understood nothing, but were ready to put up with anything if
it meant they could play on the swings), Richard found himself
alone at the end of the path where the four children had taken
refuge after going to clean up Marcel and his mess. He asked
timidly: 'What about me?' but neither Thérèse nor Philippe
picked up on his question, only Marcel, who bent over his sister
to ask: 'Coco coming too?' To which Thérèse replied stoically:
'Coco's a stick-in-the-mud. He doesn't want to play on the
slides or the sandboxes with us. He's going to the municipal
library to read, eh Coco?' while Philippe looked elsewhere.
Richard immediately got up, murmuring submissively: 'I get
it,' which seemed to relieve his brother and his cousin. Not
turning around, he walked away without another word, his
shoulders slumped. He'd wait till he was all alone before
giving in to his hatred for his weakness, to his contempt for
his lack of courage, kicking out at trees and weeping with
rage. 'I know, I'm a scaredy-cat!' As soon as Richard had
disappeared behind the huge building that housed both the
art gallery and the public toilets (a building that Richard and
Philippe's father, Gabriel, called, 'The Art Urinal'), Philippe
let out a great guffaw that embarrassed Thérèse. 'Watch out,
Philippe, maybe he can hear you!' 'That's okay, it'll teach him
to stick to us like a leech!' Marcel looked up at his cousin:
'What's that?' 'What's what?' 'What you just said.' 'A leech?'
Philippe looked pleadingly at Thérèse, but she just shrugged.
'You ask too many questions, Marcel. People will think you're
ignorant.' Thérèse got to her feet and picked up her brother in
her arms. 'If you wet your pants again, Thérèse is going to leave
you all alone in the middle of the park!' Marcel flung his arms
around his sister's neck and squeezed very hard. Thérèse could
feel Marcel's heart beating against her breast. 'The dusteroos'll
eat you up. The bogeyman'll get you!' Marcel abandoned his
embrace and looked at his sister, incredulous: 'There's no

dusteroos here. There isn't any bed!' Thérèse put her brother down. 'You know, Marcel, there are house dusteroos, but there are park dusteroos too!' Dusteroos were the piles of dust that accumulated under beds when Albertine or the fat woman were too busy to mop every day. And dusteroos proved very convenient when you wanted to frighten children at night and get them to sleep: 'If you set foot out of bed, the dusteroos will bite you!' Thérèse had been afraid of dusteroos; Richard had been afraid of dusteroos; but Marcel was terrified of them. As for Philippe, at eight, he still wasn't exactly sure if they existed or not and if he boasted about them, claiming he'd never believed in them and that he'd always just pretended to believe in them to please his parents who went to so much trouble to terrify him, it was because one evening, out of bravado, he got off the sofa he shared with Thérèse to go and check and saw — he was sure of it and when he thought of it, he could feel the hair stand up on the back of his neck — he saw something move (in the dark, everything moves) and stood there, glued to the spot, pale with fear, short of breath, shit trickling between his legs. Thérèse hoped to find a clump of moss at the bottom of a tree to back up what she'd said and force her brother to be quiet for the rest of the afternoon. She'd tell him: 'Look, park dusteroos aren't grey. They're green. Even worse!' As she walked away from the bench, Thérèse put her hand on her cousin's neck. 'At least Richard would've known what a leech is!' Then the three children went towards the playground, sure of their victory. Thérèse had told Marcel: 'When we get near the games, don't say a word. Let us take care of everything. Otherwise, we'll leave you behind and go to the library with Coco!' Marcel swore that he wouldn't say a word whatever happened. As soon as they'd crossed the heavy chain-link fence that surrounded the playground to 'protect' the children, as it was claimed, Philippe, out of the blue, without even saying: 'Watch out, here I go,' went into contortions, crossing his eyes, sticking out his tongue, limping so grotesquely that he looked like a puppet with tangled strings, which made Thérèse say: 'Don't go too far, Philippe. You'll scare them and that'll be worse!' Marcel asked fearfully: 'Is

Fwip sick? Do we have to take him home?' Thérèse crouched beside him. 'No, Marcel. Flip isn't sick. It's just a game. . . You'll see, they'll let him come in with us and we'll have lots and lots of fun. . . Now, you be quiet.' She stood up and turned to her cousin. 'Limp a little, Philippe, but just a bit. . . And make one arm crooked, just one. . . Good, that's right. . . Don't hold your head so crooked. This isn't a horror show!' Philippe moderated his efforts in an attempt to look a bit spastic (he had in mind a classmate with muscular dystrophy whom he always made fun of and whom he exasperated with his sarcasm and his imitations) and the trio bravely approached the first set of swings: Philippe hobbling beside Thérèse, who was holding back her laughter, and Marcel, watching him, dumbfounded. Thérèse took a handkerchief from the pocket of her dress and concealed her giggles behind it. When she'd finished pretending to blow her nose, she realized that Marcel, carried away by Philippe's game, had begun to contort himself as well, mimicking his cousin's every gesture and expression with obvious delight. Just then, she noticed the park attendant approaching them, looking concerned, and she chose that moment to shout at her little brother: 'Marcel, will you stop making fun of your big brother? It isn't nice! I've told you a hundred times!' She took Marcel by the arm and began to shake him, hoping to make him cry so that he wouldn't say anything silly. But Marcel shouted in his shrill voice: 'I was just playing!' When the attendant came abreast of them, he let out a 'What's going on here?' in a voice that said a great deal about his limited intelligence and his general lack of subtlety. When Thérèse looked up at him, she was struck by his good looks and stood there, somewhat taken aback. The playground attendant wasn't the doddering, grimy old man she'd been expecting, but a young man in his early twenties with fine features and brilliant eyes. Instead of answering him saucily, she began to stammer, looking down, blushing, getting her words mixed up, all of which had the effect of making more credible the unlikely story she and Philippe had concocted: their mother, tired of looking after her disabled son, asking her daughter, so reasonable and responsible, despite her youth, to take the child and their younger brother to the park so she could get a few hours' rest. . . As Thérèse told her story, Philippe, who was watching the attendant from the corner of his eye, saw the man's hesitation melt, to be replaced by a heavy-handed pity that he thought funny and couldn't wait to imitate. Marcel, though he'd sworn to keep quiet, nearly spoiled everything. When Thérèse had finished her explanations and finally looked up at the guard, who she thought was definitely very handsome, the little boy said quite candidly and very loud, probably to make himself more interesting: 'He isn't my brother. He's my cousin!' For a moment, everything seemed in the balance. Philippe would gladly have stepped on his cousin right then and there, but he was imprisoned in his role, and as for Thérèse, she was too exhausted by her idiotic story and too excited by the attendant's beautiful eyes to come up with a believable answer in a hurry. Eventually, it was the attendant himself, in his great naïveté, who got them out of the hole by saying reproachfully to Marcel: 'It's not nice to be ashamed of your big brother! Jeez! If I had a brother like that, I'd take care of him!' Marcel hid in his sister's skirts, for he thought the gentleman was a jerk. The attendant gave Thérèse a smile that nearly made her faint. 'You have a good time with your brothers, girl. . . And if you need me, just shout. My name's Monsieur Bleau. . . Gérard Bleau.' He rumpled Philippe's hair in a gesture of friendly protectiveness, then walked away. As soon as his back was turned, Philippe stopped his act. 'I'm worn out!' In his great candour, then, Marcel once again uttered a remark that his sister, and particularly his cousin, found profoundly depressing, raising a problem neither of them had thought about: 'Will Fwip have to act like a dumdum all day long? How can he play if he's all cwooked?'

'How do I look?' Victoire, dressed to kill, painted, ridiculous, stood before the fat woman, a mauve straw hat on the side of her head, her skinny body draped in a brown crêpe dress that hung unevenly around her twisted legs, her face invisible beneath a garish layer of Albertine's makeup. The fat woman had always been frank with her mother-in-law and the older woman appreciated it, often saying of her daughter-in-law: 'Maybe she's silly, but she's okay. Not like my daughter, Albertine. She's so scared of me, she'd sooner die than tell me she dropped a plate.' In fact, Albertine regularly broke pieces of crockery that belonged to her mother just to get her goat, and every time, she howled: 'One less cup! Your estate's going to hell, Mama!' or: 'I hope you aren't too stuck on that goddamn Chinese plate because if you are you better get ready to bawl your eyes out!' The fat woman was a little taken aback. She had never seen her mother-in-law so badly dolled up and she wondered how she could tell her. The total frankness that came naturally to her would require her to say something like: 'Go and hide, you'll scare people!' or: 'I think you ought to start all over — from scratch. . .' toning down her words with a smile of complicity or a burst of laughter. But the fat woman knew that Victoire had decided to go out, come what may, and it would have been cruel and useless to delay her pleasure, so she merely spoke of the hat which, in any case, her mother-in-law detested. 'You're right. It's an ugly hat. When Edouard gave it to you at Easter, I couldn't figure out why you hated it so much, but now. . .' Victoire came a little closer to her daughter-in-law's armchair, bent over her and said with obvious insincerity: 'Listen, I know just what you mean. But I'm going out with Edouard, so I haven't got any choice — I've got to wear it!' She'd lowered her voice, but she was whispering so loud (when she went to confession, everyone could hear her and the priests would tell her: 'Talk in your normal voice, you won't make so much noise!') that she awakened Gabriel, who was sleeping in the bed beside his wife's chair. As he opened his eyes, the sight of his mother made him sit up. 'Calvary, Mama, what're you doing all decked out like that? It isn't Hallowe'en!' Victoire didn't flinch. She simply stared even more insistently at her daughter-in-law. 'Do I really look that bad?' The fat woman shrugged. 'Answer me!' 'Well, you see. . . Maybe it's a bit too much. Mauve and brown isn't the best combination in the world. . .' Victoire straightened up and cut off her daughter-in-law, clicking her tongue in satisfaction. 'Even better! I've decided to put Edouard's nose out of joint and I think I'm off to a good start!' Finally, she turned to her son and said gently: 'Go back to sleep, Gabriel. You're tired. Your mother and your brother are going out to pass the time amusing the other walkers on Mont-Royal. Go to sleep. You'll hear about it soon enough!' She turned and, with dignity, walked out of the bedroom. The fat woman smiled, shaking her head. Her husband looked at her. 'Know what?' She took his hand and patted it. 'Either your mother really wants to get even or she's decided to shift her battle with Edouard onto new territory.' Gabriel noticed the book on his wife's lap. 'Now you're talking like *Bug-Jargal*! Pretty soon, nobody will understand a word you say!' He sat up in bed, leaned on the arm of his wife's chair and kissed her on the mouth. 'Did he move today?' 'And how! I've got the feeling he can't wait to come out!' 'You pick a name yet?' 'Yes. If it's a boy, Pierre; if it's a girl. . . Denise.' 'You sure — about Denise, I mean?' 'Yes.' Gabriel and his wife had lost a daughter, Denise, their eldest, two years before, and the night they'd decided to make another child, the fat woman said: 'If it's a girl to take the place of the one we lost, we'll call her Denise.' They'd never talked about it again, but Gabriel hoped his wife would change her mind. The fat woman ran her hand through Gabriel's hair and over his damp forehead. 'If you really don't want to, we'll try to find another name. But, well. . . I'd like it.' Gabriel laid his head on his wife's vast bosom. They stayed like that for a long time: Gabriel, on his knees in the bed, head against his wife's breasts, as if he were asleep; the fat woman, stroking his hair, his neck, his face. 'I love you, you know.' It was hard for him to say those words, the fat woman knew that. Her husband, skilled tavern orator and life of the party, was astonishingly reticent and bereft when it came to speak sweet nothings. An almost pathological sense of propriety kept him from talking about 'those things,' as he called them, and when the time came to prove his love for his wife, a slap on the bottom or a wink of complicity had to be interpreted as passionate declarations, replacements for the letters he'd never written, the flowers he could never afford and the words that almost always stuck in his throat. 'You smell good.' After a long caress, the fat woman murmured: 'Go on, shut the door.'

The kettle had been whistling for several minutes before Ti-Lou heard it. Rose Ouimet was on her hands and knees in Ti-Lou's cupboard, a bucket of water beside her. You could hear her scrubbing and swearing. 'This floor looks like it hasn't been washed since Adam screwed Eve!' Rose had helped Ti-Lou into her bed, where now she reigned, surrounded by chocolates and pillows. 'Rose, the water's ready for my bath. . .' Rose didn't hear — or pretended not to hear. The kettle continued to whistle. Ti-Lou took a chocolate-covered cherry, her favourite, placed it on her tongue and burst it open against her palate. The juice flowed into her throat. Ti-Lou closed her eyes. She chewed slowly, swallowing just a bit at a time, keeping the pulp of the chocolate and the juice of the cherry imprisoned for as long as she could between her tongue and palate. When there was nothing left in her mouth, she savoured the after-taste that tickled her taste buds. 'Rose, if the water boils away, you'll have to put some more on because I have to have that bath!' Rose Ouimet sat up, and ran her arms across her sweaty forehead. 'What'd you do in this cupboard, for the love of. . . It's all sticky!' 'If I told you, you'd be shocked. . .' 'Okay. Enough of your jokes. I'll get your bath ready.' She threw her scrubbing-brush into the pail of water and walked out of the bedroom, muttering. Ti-Lou selected another chocolate, one with maple filling, and concentrated on the taste of maple that blended so well with the chocolate. In order to clean the cupboard floor, Rose had to take out Ti-Lou's improbable collection of left shoes that had been lying around for years. Once her pride and joy, they had become, since the removal of her right leg, the object of curses and loathing. When Ti-Lou was still powerful and wanton, she'd boast to anyone who cared to listen that she owned one hundred and eight pairs of shoes (actually only fifty-four pairs, but the she-wolf of Ottawa always multiplied everything by two), and as many pairs of gloves (she was always seen, however, wearing the same gloves, long black silk ones, but perhaps different pairs), and when a client, a little more skeptical than most, ever dared question her power and influence over Ottawa, Ti-Lou would spring from her bed, as if he were a holy man and she a demon, dash over to the wooden wardrobe, fling open the doors and say: 'Look! A hundred and eight pairs! Can a woman have a hundred and eight pairs of shoes and not be powerful?' As the recalcitrant client, in any event, did not know anyone who was even interested in owning more than four or five pairs of shoes, he would apologize politely, amused by Ti-Lou's naïveté. . . . Some even went so far as to offer her a hundred-and-ninth pair, to which Ti-Lou inevitably replied: 'You think I'm crazy? A hundred and eight's enough. More than that would be an indulgence!' She had learned the meaning of the word 'indulgence' one night while entertaining personalities from France: an ambassador, two cultural attachés, and the inevitable tame bishop, Monsignor Brunet, who spent his time haunting the corridors of Parliament in search of 'persons interested in meeting an Ottawa society lady, the most beautiful and the shapeliest. . .' (Ti-Lou suspected several cabinet ministers of hiring Bishop Brunet to advertise her house and the ministers suspected her of the same thing, but truth was that the bishop was crazy about Ti-Lou and would balk at nothing to find a reason for coming to see her). That night she'd gone to her room to change three times (parading before her distinguished visitors first, in a fuchsia-coloured frock 'to remind my guests that summer exists, even in the middle of February,' then, in an emerald green dress of repulsive ugliness, a dress of which she was particularly fond; then, in white, for 'the purity of my soul' and in black, for 'the purity of your intentions' — all in appallingly bad taste — painted like a clown, but much funnier, winking an eye and swaying a thigh to excess, and Bishop Brunet had come up to her in the night and whispered in her ear: 'The way you show off your wardrobe comes perilously close to indulgence!' Ti-Lou took his remark

as a compliment with only a zest of criticism; she liked the way
it sounded, and the word 'indulgence' had taken its place in her
vocabulary.) Opening her eyes when the taste of chocolate and
maple had ebbed away, she saw the heap of left shoes (after
her operation, she had thrown out all the right shoes, insisting
on putting them in the rubbish herself, even though the new
crutches made her comings and goings difficult) that towered
beside her bed and she began laughing bitterly. 'Sometimes you
think you've forgotten your problems, but that bitch of a life
can always bring them back by multiplying them by a hundred
and eight!' 'You talking to yourself now?' Rose was standing in
the doorway, holding the kettle. 'I've always talked to myself
because I've never met anybody interesting enough to have
a real conversation with!' Astounded at the pretentiousness
of her remark and, in particular, at its inaccuracy, she who
had spent her life talking about herself in great detail, always
overdoing it, omitting only the boring details — and even then,
not always — Ti-Lou glanced down and nervously coughed.
'Is it ready?' 'Yes. Want me to carry you?' 'I can get there
on my own!' Rose Ouimet turned her back, hoping she would
have the hardest possible time extricating herself from her bed.
Ti-Lou seized her crutches, placed her left foot on the floor
and, with a push, managed to stand up without too much
effort. 'While I'm in the tub, after you scrub my back, you
can hide all those goddamn shoes! Nobody ever teach you
any tact, you silly cow?' No reply. 'Do you hear me?' She
was now walking down the hallway. 'If the bathroom wasn't
so far away either! You hear what I said, Rose? Yes or no?'
Rose Ouimet came out of the bathroom and for the first time,
Ti-Lou noticed how badly her pregnancy suited her. 'That kid
must know its mother doesn't feel so good.' 'Sure, I heard you.
You yell loud enough! If you didn't have a hundred and eight
pairs of shoes, the pile wouldn't be so big!' 'I haven't got a
hundred and eight. I've just got fifty-four!' 'Then how come
you always say you got a hundred and eight?' 'I count them
by pairs. Fifty-four pairs makes a hundred and eight!' 'But
you never say fifty-four pairs. You always say a hundred and
eight!' 'Yes, but I've just got one of every pair! You never

noticed I just got one leg, you cow?' 'Well, that's just it. You threw out half your shoes, but instead of dividing in half, you multiply everything by two! A hundred and eight pairs makes two hundred and sixteen shoes, not fifty-four!' 'Say, who's the boss around here, anyway?' Rose Ouimet opened her eyes very wide. 'Just because you're the boss, don't mean you're right!' 'Yes, it does — and quit pestering me!' A shooting pain at the tip of her stump startled her. She lost her balance, dropped one of the crutches and leaned against the wall. 'What's wrong?' Ti-Lou had turned dreadfully pale. She was shaking like a leaf. 'It hurts. Good God, it hurts!' 'Where?' 'I don't want that pain to start all over again!' Ti-Lou looked at Rose with pleading eyes. 'If it starts again, it's the end!' 'No, it isn't. It'll go away. . . . Here, lean on me and get in the tub.' Ti-Lou slipped off her bathrobe. Rose Ouimet helped her get in the water. 'Not too hot?' 'It's fine. It feels good. . .' Rose Ouimet, her hand in a bath glove, began to scrub Ti-Lou's shoulders and neck with the soapy water, but then something attracted her attention: the end of Ti-Lou's right leg was floating on the surface and a black spot had blossomed behind the scar at the tip of the stump. 'Funny, the end of your right leg's all black!' Ti-Lou howled as though her heart had been ripped out.

Usually the smell was so strong that the few visitors who ventured that far cut short their visit, plugging their noses and snickering, the parents sometimes embarrassed, the children always laughing themselves silly. As for Richard, he found safe refuge in those musty smells — and every time his frail body was assailed by some pain too hard to bear, he would run here, without stopping, and lean against the circular fence that kept in the turtles — already half-dead from heat and malnutrition, dried out, wrinkled, sick, their shells soft and grey. He never stopped to look at the two bears since the day he realized that the poor creatures had a skin disease that was getting worse from week to week; he ignored the monkeys, whose obscene gestures made him blush, as they masturbated all day long to the great delight of the pimply-faced adolescents who came there solely to see them find release; sometimes he'd glance, very quickly, at the solitary fox that howled in frustration as it ran back and forth in its cage during the mating season; but the turtles. . . . He could spend hours watching these hideous things trying to cool off in the tepid, stagnant water, their heads raised towards the sky in a gesture of prayer, their mouths open, toothless, motionless, actors in a tragedy. It was their immobility that fascinated Richard the most, the picture the creatures presented of unchanging misfortune, subdued yet permanent, frozen forever in time and space, denying the past, already masters of the future, moulded by defeat and wallowing in it. Richard would have liked to be one of these turtles. He was one of them when the anguish of his soul prevented his body from reacting: he had chosen the turtles' immobility rather than try to resist his morbid desires and get on with living. He was a born victim and the turtles reflected his image of the world in which he was evolving — or rather, not evolving. But this superb day in early May, beautiful and mild as it was, was too early in the season for the animals and the little zoo was closed. Richard walked among the deserted cages, seeking the stench of sick animals clinging to the branches of trees or the bars of their prisons, but winter had long since driven out all traces of misery, and the pleasant smell of spring was everywhere. The strong, insistent whiff of animals rotting on their feet would not come again to pacify his soul until the summer holidays began. Richard always wondered where they hid the animals in winter. He enjoyed imagining them closed up in a deep, damp cellar underneath the park, with no air or water or food, so their summer prison would seem like a reward. He crouched on the ground still saturated with water, beside the turtles' cage, and let his loathing surge out of him like a torrent swollen by spring waters, smashing everything in its way, carrying clumps of earth, logs that broke like matches on sharply pointed rocks, invading everywhere, submerging everything before anyone had time to react. Some day, he'd jump on his brother, Philippe, and tie him to a tree as the Indians used to tie up the white missionaries; he'd sit on

the ground in front of Philippe and shower insults on him,
bellowing and gesticulating, calling down the wrath of God, the
only punishment worthy of him; then, he'd hit him on the face,
the body, enjoying the sight of his body turning blue, hearing
his voice become, at last, pleading, pleading; then he'd skin
him alive, one small piece at a time, putting out his prying eyes,
tearing out his viper's tongue, stripping him bare, plucking off
his obscene monkey's limbs, and finally strangle him with his
own hands, as he screamed in his ear: 'Die, dirty dog! Go to
hell with the rest of your kind! And leave me alone once and
for all!' A gentle warmth took hold of him as he dreamed, the
happy vengeful destroyer of Evil, agent of Good, worthy of the
most Deserving Saints and Bravest Soldiers, but he realized to
his great shame that an erection had caught him by surprise and
a warm sticky liquid was wetting his pants. His first ejaculation.
And at last he understood that the turtles' immobility could be
gratifying.

Victoire hadn't set foot out of the house for more than two
years. The last time, she remembered all too well, was at
the very beginning of the war: December, 1939, the famous
night when Albertine's husband, Paul, announced that he'd
enlisted and might have to leave for Europe any day. The
news had somewhat dampened Christmas Eve at the house
of Victoire's sister, Ozéa, who'd been living near Marie-Anne
for forty years, and who thought it was still a fashionable
neighbourhood, even though she saw more and more families
from Hochelaga moving into the neighbouring houses. Ozéa
often said to Victoire: 'I can't figure out why you stay where you
are? There's a million children on that street. Not a minute's
peace!' To which Victoire replied: 'Lord, Ozéa. You're as deaf
as a stone! Just open your window and listen! There's now
as many kids on your street as where we are!' Ozéa merely
smiled. 'You're jealous. You've always been jealous because
you married a man without a pot to piss in and my Gaspar's
got enough money for a whole collection!' Nevertheless, Ozéa's

Christmas Eve ended in a total hullabaloo, as Paul, who had decided to get royally pissed with the family one last time, started telling everybody exactly what he thought of them: he insulted his brother-in-law, Gabriel, calling him soft, heartless and afraid of his own shadow; he heaped insults on Edouard, whom he always called his closet sister-in-law, even going so far as to slap his face and call him 'mummy's fairy,' which made Edouard laugh, but not Victoire; finally, in the small hours of the morning, he took his wife and mother-in-law aside to blame them for his ruined life, his domestic unhappiness, the beginning of his alcoholism, his early baldness, rotten teeth, weak muscles and even the holes in his socks and the sweat stains under his arms. All in a loud voice in front of the whole family and Ozéa, in particular, who pursed her lips and placed her hand over her heart. Ever since that night, Victoire had refused to go out, even to Mass. She never spoke to Paul again; in fact, he disappeared from circulation quite quickly, the nails in his soldier's boots ringing on the sidewalk and his beret planted firm; pleased, proud, imagining that he was finally going to make a success of his life. Nor had Victoire seen her sister, Ozéa, who, in fact, hadn't tried to get in touch either. That Christmas night had been the ridiculous event, the grotesque break that can separate members of a family forever. Victoire was ashamed of her son-in-law and her daughter, who had taken advantage of the situation to throw an ugly hysterical fit that went on far too long — and nothing could ever make up for this humiliation. She shut herself inside the house then and never went out again. Only Josaphat-the-Violin, Victoire's older brother, still paid regular visits, but for a long time the old woman was even ill at ease with him. 'Maybe Josaphat doesn't remember, but I do!' However on this glorious spring day without really knowing why, Victoire suddenly felt the need to go out to fill her lungs and eyes with new life, new sap that would regenerate her and give her the courage to face the dreaded heatwaves that were fast approaching. Victoire was a winter woman and she found summer depressing. But when she saw herself all dressed up and ready, she felt a moment's hesitation. She held Edouard's arm and was about to put her foot on the top step, when she suddenly stopped, stiffened and leaned on the banister. Did she really feel like parading along Mont-Royal on the arm of this big baby she adored, but whom she knew was ridiculous, even laughable? 'Are you sick?' Edouard fastened on the word 'sick,' one of the words that his mother used so often, which seemed to hold her entire life together, hoping she'd decide at the last minute not to carry out her plan. Edouard made the great mistake of letting his hope show and his mother smiled. 'Me, sick? Since when? No, I just felt a bit dizzy. Get a good grip on me now, then we'll be in business.' She took her son's arm. 'Let's go!' Rose, Mauve and Florence, their mother, had heard the brief conversation and Mauve, surprised, murmured: 'Mama, Victoire's going out. . .' Rose got up, walked down the steps, terrifying Duplessis who was still playing with the ball of green wool. Leaning against the fence she looked up at Victoire and Edouard who were slowly coming down the stairs. Mauve walked over and stood beside her. 'My, she's aged. . .' Florence stood there motionless, hands placed sedately on her knees. 'Mama, come and look. She's having a hard time getting down the stairs!' 'I know she is, I don't have to look.' At each step, Victoire sighed. At the eighth step, she said: 'Whew, halfway there!' She stopped to get her breath. 'What'll it be like on the way back?' She noticed Duplessis who, ignoring Rose and Mauve, had thrown himself on the ball of wool. 'Look, there's Marie-Sylvia's goddamn cat playing with thin air! I'm telling you, that cat's out of its mind!' She began to go 'Ssst! Ssst!' to frighten the cat, but Duplessis decided not to hear her. 'Mama, you're going to fall!' 'I am not! I've walked downstairs before, for heaven's sake!' 'But not when you were trying to scare a cat! Do one thing at a time! You can scare the cat when you get to the bottom!' Victoire and Edouard began walking down the stairs again, slowly, one step at a time. 'Rose, Mauve, come and sit down.' Florence hadn't looked up. Rose and Mauve obeyed reluctantly. They sat on their straight-back chairs without taking their eyes off Victoire. At the bottom of the stairs, Victoire straightened her dreadful hat. 'We're over the worst. I always thought those stairs were

too steep!' Still clinging to Edouard's arm, she stopped at
Florence's front steps, feeling as if she were being watched.
Florence had just looked up at her. Rose and Mauve saw that
their mother's expression had become infinitely tender. There
was even the beginning of a smile on her lips. Victoire turned
her head abruptly towards the house where the women were
knitting. 'What's going on now, Mama?' Victoire dropped
Edouard's arm and, taking short steps, approached the fence.
'Leave the cat alone. He'll go away by himself. . .' Without
knowing, though perhaps deep down feeling it, Victoire was
looking straight into Florence's eyes. Rose and Mauve held
their breath. Victoire placed her handbag on the fence. 'Funny,
eh, Edouard? That house has always been empty. It was empty
when we moved here forty years ago and it's still empty today.'
She was looking now at the door, the windows, the front steps.
'And it's always clean.' She removed a glove and ran her hand
over a section of the fence. 'Fresh paint, just like every year.'
She looked up at Florence again. 'Funny, wherever I've been,
wherever I've lived, there's always been an empty house next
door. When I was little, in Duhamel, the house next door
was abandoned and my father wouldn't let us go in. It was
abandoned, but it was always as clean as a polished doorknob.
As if somebody was taking care of it. In the winter, they closed
the double windows and in the summer the screens. In the fall,
it smelled of ketchup and in the spring of fresh paint. But we
never saw a soul. Ever. Just like here.' At that very moment,
the door opened behind Florence, and Violette came out. From
the window in the living room where she was lying, she had seen
Victoire stop in front of their house. 'Mama, she's looking at
you! She sees you!' 'No, Violette. She isn't crazy enough —
not yet.' When Victoire saw the door open, she gave a sudden
start. She stepped back a few paces. 'That door opened all
by itself! Isn't it locked?' Edouard took her arm. 'These old
houses. . . Everything opens by itself. . . Must've been kids
playing inside. . .' 'Go and shut the door, Edouard!' 'Mama,
it's after three and we still haven't gone anywhere!' 'Go and
shut that door!' Edouard opened the gate and walked onto the
little cement path that went across the lawn. He climbed up

the three front steps, past Florence, who hadn't moved, past Violette, who'd moved over a few paces, and slammed the door. 'Okay, fine. Now, let's go.' When Victoire and Edouard had gone, Florence burst out laughing as her three daughters looked on in horror. 'I hope the door isn't locked!'

Albertine paced back and forth past the closed door of Gabriel and the fat woman's bedroom. 'At their age — I ask you! And her nearly eight months gone! Sometimes I think I'm living with a bunch of perverts. . .' Now that she was alone, she could give in to her usual bad mood, as her promise to Thérèse to be less silly only concerned others. . . 'I promised I'd try and be nice with the rest of them, so I wouldn't scare Marcel, but I didn't promise anything about myself!' When Thérèse and Marcel left for Lafontaine Park shortly before noon, Albertine, feeling somewhat relieved of her promise, was tempted to curse and scream. She felt angry words rise in her throat, ready to come out splattering everyone, gluing her mother to the wall, lashing her brother Edouard with contempt; but she held back, telling herself it might be better to try and end the day the way she'd started it, that, since morning, it hadn't been all that hard, really, to be kind and gentle on the outside, though her insides knotted and unknotted with her anger; that she was serving an apprenticeship, and, who knows, by working on her new personality she might even make herself believe that life wasn't so bad, that a smile always wipes out the irritations, rages and storms that wear everybody out. 'Take a deep breath, count to ten and smile. . .' She'd nearly blown up a little earlier when she was washing her sister-in-law's hair and she had to control herself to keep from abandoning the other woman, head full of soapsuds and neck dripping wet, as she shouted: 'Before you were like this, goddammit, you used to be able to wash yourself! After the kid's born, you can wash yourself again! If you want a baby at the age when most women are grandmothers, it's your tough luck!' She'd managed to control herself — but at what a price! When she

left her sister-in-law's room, her work done, the soapy basin
slipping through her arms, she felt the first warning: the iron
ring that squeezed her forehead, her temples, the nape of her
neck, at the onset of one of the horrible migraines that would
come after a battle with her daughter or some dumb trick by her
son. She went to empty the basin in the kitchen sink. 'I mustn't
get a headache. If I get a headache, I'll smash everything in the
house!' And when she saw her mother on Edouard's arm — all
dolled up like a scarecrow on its way to Mass — stop on the
doorstep, turn around and say: 'I know you're bending over
backwards to act decent today, Albertine, but let me tell you,
it doesn't suit you! You look like a cow that's chewing a cud
full of bile!' A wave of pain struck at her brain and she raised
her arm towards the old woman, to plead with or strangle her,
she didn't know which. The pain stayed there, hooked behind
her left eye, pounding to the same rhythm as her blood. Now,
the ever present contrast between her solitude — badly married
as she was, badly fucked, quickly disgusted by a selfish,
awkward husband — and her brother's happiness which she
couldn't help finding grotesque, that contrast, full of childish
laughter and knowing sighs, needled her, like stinging abuse.
She walked back and forth past the room, coughing, blowing
her nose, noisily knocking over dining room chairs, unable to
admit that she envied Gabriel and the fat woman. Her head hurt
dreadfully, and from time to time, she stopped in the middle of
the hall or in the kitchen doorway, as if struck dumb, eyes filled
with tears, shoulders shaken by sobs until, unable to hold out
any longer, she threw herself against the closed door and began
pounding as hard as she could, screaming in a voice filled with
despair: 'You don't have the right to enjoy it! You don't have
the right! Not under my eyes! Not as long as I'm here! Do
your dirty business all night long if you want, but let me
have my days in peace!' The door opened and Albertine fell
into her brother's arms. The fat woman was looking out the
window. Her arms hung down on either side of the armchair.
Bug-Jargal had fallen to the floor.

This was how Ti-Lou put it: 'I've always been very hard on my body. Work and suffering never scared me, and the good Lord's my witness, I've worked like an ox and suffered like a saint! In my house in Ottawa, I didn't take any days off, no sir. It was seven days a week, fifty-two weeks a year — and that was that! It was some lease I signed at that house! . . . But praise be to Heaven, I was healthy as hell, with a constitution like a horse, so whenever I had some little ache or pain, I'd knock it out with a double rye or gin, and then, I felt no pain! I sprained my back three times, broke an arm, had disgusting headaches and more shameful diseases than I can keep track of — but it never kept me from my work! If you want to reign, you've got to forget yourself, because if you think about yourself too much, other people take advantage, and then they take your place! When you're at the top, you can't afford aches and pains! So even when it was all I could do to stand on my feet, and even when I couldn't stand on my feet at all, I acted as if everything was okay. I'd smile and strut my stuff and I'd go on giving the full treatment to men who didn't deserve a basement bargain! Once, I remember, my back was sprained, I was bent double, I could hardly move, but even so, I entertained the Prime Minister himself, sitting up in bed with pillows all around me — and I stayed like that all the time that he was there — and he never knew I wasn't well! What do you think about that? Ti-Lou didn't come cheap, but you sure as hell got your money's worth! My house was all painted white and I paid for the paint myself. . . When I retired in 1930 and moved here, because Ottawa's no city to retire in (it's too dull), because people there knew me too well and there was a danger my old age might be ruined by jealous women or a new generation of cabinet ministers that knew too much. . . when I moved to Montreal, I said to myself, "Ah! Saint-Joseph Avenue, doctors, dentists, retired folks like me. I'm gonna be just fine. Nice and peaceful. . . not too far from Mont-Royal and the stores, but not too close either. . . The church across the street (I still had a few dresses to show off that weren't full of worm holes), the little school too, the kids yelling during recess, Heaven on earth!" So, I moved in here twelve years ago, after partying for thirty years, with my head full of memories, my bank account full of postdated cheques, and the table in the living room full of ads from travel agents and shipping lines: Ah, Cunard! That word made me dream all my life! Ships, islands, the ocean, Bueños Aires, Montevideo, Vera Cruz, Miami, Rio de Janeiro! Around the world in a floating palace, with Ti-Lou finally getting her turn! I'd earned it and I was going to pay for it myself! But then, three weeks before I left, I started limping like a cripple: shooting pains down my right leg that hurt like a son of a bitch and I had a hell of a time getting to sleep. . . . I sent for Doctor Sanregret (he only had to cross the corridor) because I wasn't in any mood to hang around for hours with his coughing and spitting down-and-outs. . . . And damn me, if I didn't have diabetes! No more sugar! Forbidden! Me, off sugar? No more chocolates? No more fudge? I told that doctor he didn't know me well enough and then I booted him out. And stayed here with my pain. For the first time in my life, illness got the better of me: I didn't take that trip because my leg hurt too much. But I was pigheaded and I didn't cut out sugar. Even today. . . When it hurt too much, I asked Doctor Sanregret to prescribe some of those drops, of which I needed more and more, the pain got worse — but so what? I put up with it and didn't breathe a word. I'd noticed the little toe on my right foot was turning black, but I thought I'd hit my foot against something or other. . . Then, one fine day, I was taking my bath — I remember like it was yesterday — and my toe was as black as coal. The rest of my foot was starting to go black too. . . I told myself, I'd better get the doctor over here. I got back in the tub and started washing my right foot. . . and there I was, holding my little toe! I had the washcloth and I could see my little toe right in the middle of it; it looked just like an old dried-up raisin. . . and it didn't even hurt!' When Ti-Lou came to this part of her story, she always stopped for a few seconds to give her listener time to take in the full horror of what she was saying; then, when she was quite certain of the effect, she'd add candidly: 'Want to see it? I've still got it. . .'

Of course, no one had ever wanted to see her blackened right
toe and no one ever knew if the temptress of Ottawa really
possessed that little lump of coal. . . Ti-Lou went on: 'Three
days later, I woke up with my right leg cut off. Me, Ti-Lou,
terror of ministers' wives, queen of Parliament, there I was like
a World War I veteran who had stepped on a mine just before
being sent back to Canada! I screamed for one whole year. . .
I felt as if I was just half of myself. You know what I mean?
Those legs had put in some good years! Those legs had damned
a hell of a lot of people; they'd enjoyed thirty years of dancing
and screwing! It's no joke, learning to walk again when you're
fifty! Crutches. . . I could go on about those goddamn crutches
for weeks and I'd still have things to say about them! You stand
at the mirror in a brand-new dress and you've got three legs,
two of them made out of wood, that keep you from moving
—it's the worst thing that could ever happen to a hooker! And
now. . . when my eyes get glassy, you know that I've forgotten
everything, that the drops are working. . . . But when my eyes
are dry, watch it: if I'm in a good mood, don't believe me; and
if I'm in a bad mood, don't talk to me; and if I'm really pissed
off, stay away!' When Rose Ouimet had dried Ti-Lou and put
her to bed, the old woman was still crying. She kept repeating:
'It's over. It's over, Rose. Everything's finished!' Rose had a
lump in her throat that kept her from speaking. She wished she
could console Ti-Lou but something told her it wouldn't do any
good. The black line at the bottom of Ti-Lou's leg was the final
sentence, the ultimate death sentence — and nothing, neither
words nor caresses, would make the slightest difference. Ti-
Lou asked for her drops. Rose brought them from the living
room. 'You can go now. Never mind the cleaning. I'm in no
mood to watch you lumbering around the house with your
belly sticking out. Go and lie down. You're tired.' When Rose
Ouimet left, distraught, the grandfather clock at the end of the
hallway was sounding three o'clock. 'That's a hell of a price to
pay — even for a scarlet woman!'

The memory of Marcel, and his smell of dried pee, caught
Duplessis by surprise in the very midst of his destruction of the
ball of green wool. He disappeared from Florence's lawn so fast
that the four knitting women (who saw everything) didn't even
notice. Only Mauve, from the corner of her eye, thought she
spotted a shadow dart between the wooden slats (she'd pulled
her chair over to the left so that she could rest her head against
the column that held up the balcony), but she'd just dropped a
stitch and wasn't paying attention to the cat. Rather than follow
the sidewalk, Duplessis decided to cross flower beds, lawns
and fences to get to Mont-Royal. It was a longer route, but
more pleasant. Even more marvellous at the height of summer
because of Madame Rivest's flowers, which attracted bees and
butterflies, treasured victims of Duplessis ('Butterflies are hard
to catch, but they're so good! And bees, my dear! It's worth
the risk of getting stung for the divine luxury of biting into
those fat juicy bodies. . .'), or the Beausoleils' grass offering
the neighbourhood cats an ideal hunting ground and refuge,
with natural hiding places and green tunnels, especially when
the sun was at its highest. Duplessis told himself there was
something touching about the new grass, the crocus blossoms
and the omnipresent dandelions: the grass would grow fast
and furious; the crocuses would disappear to make way for
lily-of-the-valley; the dandelions would turn to balls of white
silk that he'd have fun demolishing with one swipe of his expert
paw, spreading to the four winds flimsy ballerinas that would
land on the earth, drifting wherever the breeze might carry
them, frozen figures — complicated, but so graceful. As soon
as he realized that Marcel wasn't around (at this time of day
the little boy would normally have been up to no good under
the stairs or in the street, but no joyous cry, no uncontrolled
laughter could be heard), Duplessis decided to go and look
for him in the only other place he could be: Lafontaine Park.
The previous summer, when the friendship between Duplessis
and the little boy was transformed into true passion, which left
Duplessis throbbing at night, intoxicated with love and anxious
to go to sleep, so that the next day, the moment when he'd
see his friend, would come more quickly, Marie-Sylvia's cat

understood one crucial point: when Marcel disappeared for a whole day, making him anxious and concerned, it meant he'd been literally carried away to the park to be in some weird fashion propelled and on a piece of wood between two lengths of rope. Marcel would squeal in a way that Duplessis was pleased to think was inspired by horror and the tiger cat, superbly brave and glowing with passion, would throw himself beneath the swing to save his friend. As soon as he saw the cat, Marcel would begin to laugh, shouting: 'Plessis! Plessis!' and ask the others to stop pushing him. Duplessis would jump onto Marcel's lap, purring hard as caresses and kisses came his way. Then, convinced he'd, at the very least, saved Marcel from mortal peril Duplessis would escort his friend home, meowing with joy. And so, Marie-Sylvia's cat walked unhindered across the L'Heureux' lawn, then the Amyots', and the depressing asphalt square of the Guillemettes', who thought that they'd done good in asphalting the front of their house, but were quickly disenchanted when in the middle of August the tar started to melt and stick to the soles of their shoes, and then, at last, the huge square of freshly turned-over earth, the Rivests, known as 'the gardeners,' because, every year, they managed to grow things no one else even thought of planting (the fat woman often said: 'The year that I saw pumpkins puffing up like balloons in their front yard, I thought, this time, they're going too far. . . but when they gave us each a big pumpkin at Hallowe'en, I thought, well, maybe they're crackpots, but it works!'). He stopped against the Jodoin's fence to listen to a conversation between Gabrielle Jodoin, so beautiful and gay that the other women baptized her 'the lark of Fabre Street,' and Victoire, who'd stopped in front of her house to the great dismay of her son, Edouard. 'When are you due?' Gabrielle Jodoin rubbed her stomach, smiling. 'End of June. Same as my sister, Rose.' 'My daughter-in-law, too.' 'That's right, she's got one on the way too. . .' 'Hardly "on the way". She looks like she's going to have twelve!' 'I hear she isn't too well?' 'She's all right, but she has to stay in bed all the time. . .' 'She's got a lot of time on her hands.' 'Well, she's got lots to complain about as far as that's concerned, but she wanted that baby so badly!'

'Me too! It's my first, but it won't be the last! Mastaï thinks
we ought to stop after three, but I want as many as I can.'
'You won't be saying that a few years from now, Gaby.' 'Don't
worry about me. I'm crazy about kids!' 'Not like your sister,
Rose. . .' 'Oh, her. . .' Gabrielle Jodoin gestured hopelessly,
then decided to laugh. 'Know what she said yesterday? We were
up to our elbows in dishwater — they'd come here for supper,
her and that nut case she's married to — and all of a sudden, she
says to me: "You're so crazy about being pregnant, I wish you
could carry mine." Now, I ask you, is she crazy in the head? I
had a good laugh, but all of a sudden I realized, she was dead
serious. . .' 'That sister of yours never should of got married.'
'Don't say that. We had a double wedding and when I see how
bad things are going for them, I'm scared it'll happen to us
too. . .' 'Don't get yourself worked up about that, Gaby. Even
if your Mastaï didn't invent the wheel, he's got a lot more going
for him than her Roland.' Edouard sighed, exasperated. 'Come
on, you two. I got more to do than listen to you gabbing like a
couple of women who talk for talk's sake!' His mother didn't
even look his way. 'Tell me. What've you got to do that's so
important?' Gabrielle burst out laughing. Duplessis chose that
moment to walk across the lawn. He went between the legs of
Gabrielle, whom he rather liked, greeting her with a friendly
meow. Victoire started. 'That goddamn cat again! He's going
to follow us all the way to Larivière et Leblanc, for Chrissakes!'
Duplessis ran all the way to Mont-Royal without stopping. He
was afraid that Victoire and Edouard were also on their way to
the park and he didn't want Marcel to disappear into the arms
of the fat man, who reeked of some perfume that always left
his little friend smelling disgusting, like a slightly off corpse
or rotten flowers. 'I have to get there first or they'll spoil my
whole day!' He crossed Mont-Royal without slowing down and
almost caused an accident between a chip-wagon being pulled
by a horse and a bashed-up 1935 Ford: the horse bolted in
fright at the sight of a lump of tiger-striped fur darting past
him, but the chippy knew the horse well and the accident
was neatly avoided. Scarcely had he reached the far side of
Mont-Royal, when Duplessis stopped short and felt his heart

freeze: just at the corner of the lane, fifty feet away from him, stood his great enemy, the dreaded Godbout, a solitary, usually peaceful dog, who turned obstinate and vicious whenever a cat, especially Duplessis, whom he particularly abhorred, tried to cross his territory, which extended from Mont-Royal to Rachel. Godbout had seen Duplessis and he was ready for him, cursing and grumbling, front paws well apart, mouth open to reveal terrifying teeth. To not lose face, Duplessis began to clean his muzzle with his front paws, as if he hadn't seen the dog. He could feel his heart pounding, but he never let it show. Godbout, however, was nobody's fool. He came up to the cat, barking like all of Hell's demons. Duplessis let his paw dangle in mid-air, looked Godbout in the eye and said: 'Go bark up another tree, dear heart, you're interrupting my ablutions!' Two and a half seconds later, the battle was on and blood started to flow.

'I'm so tired, I think I'll die here!' Philippe had taken refuge behind a tree, the only place in the playground where the attendant couldn't see him — or so he thought. He was sitting at the foot of the tree, exhausted by two hours of grimaces and contortions. He had managed to get in the playground, but the two hours there had been rather difficult: how do you have fun when you must keep inventing a character who isn't you, who is also trying to enjoy himself in his own crippled and deformed way? At first, Philippe found it amusing to try and imagine how a cripple would behave in the middle of the playground, but he quickly realized that it was no place for them to have fun: the slides and ladders were too risky; the whirligig out of the question unless he sat on it and let someone else push him (but the great joy of the whirligig was precisely to make it spin by yourself); the sandbox was full of dirty, squalling children — that left the swings, and even there, he had to pretend! Marcel joined his cousin at the foot of the tree, surprised to see him suddenly stop crossing his eyes and his arms and legs. 'Flip stopped pwaying?' 'Flip's worn out,

goddamn it! Go and play in your sandbox — and if the guard
comes back, you tell me. . .' Marcel sat between his cousin's
legs. 'Marcel's tired too!' He leaned against Philippe's chest.
'Sleepy-bye. . .' 'That's right, go to sleep and they'll get us!'
Marcel contemplated the branches above them, covered with
buds. 'Leaves on the twees tomorrow. That's what Thérèse
said.' He shut his eyes and immediately fell asleep. How many
times had Marcel come and fallen asleep against his cousin,
abandoning himself in his arms, after supper, or later, while
Philippe, Thérèse and Richard were doing their homework
on the dining room table, when Marcel would climb up on
his cousin's chair with the excuse of giving him a peck on
the cheek, then linger in his arms, and finally, fall asleep,
trusting and content? Thérèse was a little jealous of Philippe
and told him: 'You're really a pain when you put him to sleep
like that!' To which Philippe replied: 'Good thing that there's
somebody in this house to put him to sleep; there's no shortage
to yell at him!' Marcel wriggled, wrapped his thin little arms
around Philippe, sighed and smiled. 'Looks like I'm stuck here
for a while.' Philippe decided to try and sleep as well. He leaned
his head against the tree trunk and closed his eyes. He usually
took a nap with Marcel on Saturday and Sunday afternoons,
and sometimes even after school. It was his way of reassuring
himself, of forgetting the grammar he couldn't make head nor
tail of, the arithmetic he always managed to understand after
everybody else, the religion he couldn't care less about, the
geography in which he inevitably got lost. Philippe was a
mediocre student and knew it. He'd even come to terms with
it in a way: 'I'm a dumbbell, but I don't care. When I'm old
enough to leave school, I'll go and work with Papa. . .' Unlike
Richard, who did his homework religiously every night, armed
with pens of every colour, rulers to underline his headings, and
impeccable notebooks, Philippe was so untidy that he rarely
finished his homework and, then, only after a lot of fruitless
slogging and sweating. When Richard came home from school,
he was rested, with the calm of those who are sure of themselves
and convinced of their superiority; but Philippe was nervous,
anxious, and Marcel's regular breathing, as he snuggled against

his heart, provided him with the self-confidence that he lacked
and which he made up for with boasting, tricks, jokes and
even blows. Unable to fall asleep in such an uncomfortable
position, Philippe opened his eyes and looked at his cousin's
small face. 'If I didn't have you. . .' Thérèse's laughter crossed
the playground, tearing the afternoon in two. Thérèse laughed
this way only when something very important was happening
and her laughter was always the line of demarcation between
two periods of time — before and after her laughter. Philippe
thought: something has just happened to prevent the day from
ending the way it started, but he made no attempt to discover
what the girl was doing. He knew he'd find out everything
eventually. For the moment, he was interested in nothing but
Marcel's breathing and his smile.

Mastaï Jodoin, carrying his empty lunch-box, was walking
towards his house. He was humming 'Les Goélans,' a song
he hated, which his wife had put into his head that morning
and he couldn't get rid of. He'd driven his streetcar all day long
humming that song, which he interrupted with a loud curse
whenever a car cut him from the right or a passenger took too
long getting off. Mastaï Jodoin had a reputation as a peerless
streetcar driver, so he was allowed to rant and curse in peace,
even if the rules of the transport company strictly forbade it.
If a passenger complained about the lack of breeding of driver
number 423, the reply was always: 'Maybe he swears like the
devil, but he hasn't had a single accident in five years! Would
you rather risk your life with a driver as meek as a lamb?' In
fact, they'd tried hard to persuade Mastaï Jodoin not to swear
in public; in the beginning, he'd even been punished in various
ways: he'd been put on the Rachel line, the most boring line
in town, he'd been made to work Sundays and holidays, he'd
even been suspended for several days following some escapade,
but nothing changed. As soon as he was at the controls, Mastaï
would let fly some well-chosen oath, with a nice wink at his
ill-at-ease inspector, and sometimes, he'd even say: 'You won't

get me, my friends! I'm the one that's gonna get you!' He was asked to try to contain himself when a priest or a nun got on his streetcar. 'I don't like priests and old crows are a joke. Why should I hold back for them?' Nonetheless, whenever a couple of nuns showed up at his ticket box or some priest or brother greeted him with a 'Bonjour, my good man,' as they got on, Mastaï Jodoin's language was changed a bit and variations on known curses would ring out and turn the nuns pale and the priests red. Sometimes, to amuse himself in the middle of an afternoon, when only old ladies and housewives were on board, he'd call out the stops in a somewhat unorthodox manner: 'De Montigny, up yours!' 'Laurier, for shit's sake!' 'Rachel, brothel!' Then, he'd burst out laughing as he saw the horror-stricken faces of his passengers. 'Got you, eh, Madame? Falling asleep were you, my dear?' Often he'd be helping an old man or woman get on or off — out of kindness, for the rules of his job didn't require it — but as soon as his noble gesture was done, he'd close the door and shout: 'By Calvary! Next time I'll kick you out on your ass, my sweet!' to the great displeasure of the other passengers, who had, in fact, just been admiring the young conductor's kind and thoughtful behaviour. Mastaï spied his wife, Gabrielle, waiting for him in the distance, leaning against the fence and waving to him cheerfully. Gabrielle was outside waiting for her husband as she did every summer's day. It was the first time this year and Gabrielle was excited. 'It means that the nice weather's here to stay!' She'd come out a good half hour before her husband's arrival, to have time to stroll around the yard and hum a tune to the baby sleeping in her belly. Her conversation with Victoire had been a pleasant diversion. And she'd watched Victoire walking away on Edouard's arm, nodding her head. From far away, Mastaï shouted: 'How's my baby today?' As soon as he was near her, she replied: 'Before, when you used to talk about your baby, I knew it was me. But now, I don't know. . .' Mastaï put both hands on his wife's belly. 'Okay, I get it. From now on, I'll ask, "How's my two babies?"' 'And everybody'll think I'm expecting twins!' 'That'd be too much!' They exchanged a long kiss right in the middle of the street, an amazing thing in this neighbourhood, where all feelings were hidden as much as possible. From her balcony, where she was sitting to get a little sun, Claire Lemieux watched Mastaï and Gabrielle Jodoin, a glimmer of envy in her eyes. Her big white whale of a husband was asleep on the living room sofa again. 'It's bad enough that it's been ages since we've kissed like that, but I'm the one that comes home from a goddamn shitty job everyday!' She swallowed some more warm Coke. 'I'm going to break out in pimples again. . .' She placed the bottle on the balcony floor. 'But who cares? Nobody'll notice!' Mastaï wrapped his left arm around his wife's shoulders and with his right hand took two theatre tickets from his pocket. 'My beautiful Gaby, tonight I'm taking you to see Poune!' Gabrielle Jodoin squealed with delight and grabbed the tickets. 'Poune! I've been dying to see her for ages! Let's eat early so we can get there in time for the double bill!' She hopped up and down, clapping her hands. 'Oh, I'm so glad! What's the comedy show this week?' '*The Bar on the Corner* — they say it's a laugh a minute! I nearly took you to see *The Woman from Maxim's* with Antoinette Giroux but I was scared it'd be too serious. . . I wanted a laugh!' 'Me too! I want to have some fun!' Suddenly, she placed her hands on her rounded belly. 'He's excited too, the little bugger. He's kicking me!'

Mercedes had spent the whole day wandering, first on Mont-Royal where to pass the time she visited stores on both sides of the street, then in Lafontaine Park, where she hung around smoking cigarette after cigarette, a little disappointed because they hadn't yet taken out the green wooden benches, but happy to smell once again the fragrance of spring rising from the grass and the sun drinking up all the earth's dampness. Mercedes knew Béatrice wouldn't come to meet her before half-past two or even three o'clock, so she decided to go all the way around the park lingering in front of the Notre-Dame hospital, where she was born, and the municipal library, where she'd never set foot and which she thought was open only during summer

holidays, since children didn't have time to read in the winter.
As for adults. . . she hadn't known anyone who had time to
read since their teens. . . It had taken her exactly an hour and
a half to walk around the park, and at precisely half-past two
she was back where she'd started. She wondered if the three
soldiers were awake, and if so, what they'd done. 'I hope they
don't remember a thing and think that they lost their money
somewhere else! But I'd better not count on it. . .' It was the
first time she'd robbed clients. Not that she hadn't wanted to
before, but fear of reprisals had always stopped her. She'd
known so many girls who came back on a Sunday morning
with a black eye or a bloody face from trying to fleece a client.
'Goddamn men! You can do anything to them — spit in their
face, humiliate them, kick them around like dirt — they like
it, it excites them! But don't try and take a cent from them!
They'll get their dignity back in one hell of a hurry and have
you waiting on them hand and foot!' At Larivière et Leblanc,
she'd had a hotdog and a Coke, taken out the fifty-two dollars
that she'd found in the soldiers' pockets and spread the money
on the counter. The sight of this money (so much all at once and
so easy to pick up!) had warmed her heart. 'Béatrice and I could
use some new shoes — new sheets too. . . . And we'll get it all
free!' But her thoughts always returned to the three soldiers.
'I got a feeling the apartment's too hot tonight. We'll have to
sleep in a hotel. Tomorrow, there won't be any danger.' She
was used to thinking no further than tomorrow. In the houses
where she'd worked, Chez Suzy on Sanguinet, or at Fat Petit's,
everything was always settled within twenty-four hours: fights,
money problems, even diseases. It would never have entered
her mind that the soldiers' hatred could be so tenacious that
they'd come back the next day to seek vengeance. For her,
soldiers paraded once and never came back. Since Béatrice
still wasn't there, she crossed Rachel and went into the corner
store to buy some more cigarettes. 'The place smells of horse
manure! When'll they get a truck like everybody else?' Armed
with a brand-new pack, she went back to the park and lit up.
On the little path that began at Fabre and then veered off
to the right, a little boy was walking slowly, visibly upset.

Mercedes recognized the eldest of her neighbour's children, a serious boy, who always looked away when she approached. She walked towards him, glad of the diversion. When the boy saw her, he stood there, frozen, and Mercedes noticed a dark spot drying on his left leg. She guessed that it was sperm and she smiled. Richard blushed and turned to get away as fast as possible. 'Hey, little boy, are you lost?' Richard stood still and answered without turning back. 'I'm old enough to know where I'm going!' 'You going home?' 'Yes.' 'You all alone?' Mercedes had come up to him. Richard answered, still without looking at her. 'My brother and my two cousins are playing in the girl's park. I think it's dumb, so I'm going home.' She held out her cigarettes. 'You smoke?' 'No!' 'Not even on the sly?' 'I'm not interested in things like that!' 'You do other things in secret though, eh?' Richard crossed his hands in front of his penis and blushed even more. 'You don't have to go all red like that. It's normal. You're old enough. . .' Richard moved away from her, but in the wrong direction: he was walking deeper into the park. 'Why won't you talk to me? I won't eat you!' For the first time, Richard faced her. When she noticed his big red ears, almost transparent, Mercedes nearly burst out laughing, but she restrained herself. 'A woman that smokes cigarettes on the street could do just about anything!' 'Ah, so that's it. . .' Mercedes was always forgetting that a woman who smoked on the street got a bad reputation. Accustomed as she was to being banished wherever she was or whatever she was doing, she cared little about such details; sometimes, she deliberately lit a cigarette in public, out of bravado, sending out clouds of smoke she'd more willingly blow in the faces of women than men. She threw her cigarette to the ground and stepped on it with her right foot. 'Now I'm more respectable, eh?' Richard looked away again, but this time he didn't move. Mercedes put her hand on his shoulder. 'Something's bugging you, right?' Richard lowered his head and began to sob. Mercedes sat down, right in the middle of the little path, and drew Richard to her side. And for nearly two hours, she listened to the story of his life: what bothered him, how he hated his brother, his frustrated passion for his mother and the new

sensual pleasure that he didn't understand but which felt so
good. So, while Béatrice, crazy with worry was looking for
her, Mercedes, hidden by bushes on an out-of-the-way path,
was hearing the confession of an over-sensitive little boy. With
this child, she experienced again — but for the first time with
joy — the role of confidante that hundreds of men had imposed
on her, the still and silent person who was part of the five-dollar
trick, a role often more difficult to play than the one of the
fulfilled mistress which, in the end, required nothing more
than technique, whereas the other, this substitute for the
confessional, required a patience that was inhuman, so similar
were the problems of her various clients in their mildness, their
pettiness and their meanness. Richard's problems were serious
and beautiful compared to those of the men who had forgotten
long ago and too quickly that they'd once been children, who
had replaced their doubts about existence and the meaning
of life — if they'd ever had any — with beer that made
them heavy, and ill-digested lust, performed and paid for in
five minutes. Richard told his story with gasps and hurts of
violence, never taking his eyes off Mercedes, submitting to her
gaze and demanding absolution. Mercedes listened to him and
dispensed that absolution, relieving the boy's frail shoulders of
their burden of guilt, encouraging his confidences, provoking
them when they came reluctantly, and washing away with her
smile the horror of his confession.

Gabriel was sitting at a table, looking lovingly at four cold
beers. The fat woman had told him: 'You can come home
plastered, but not so plastered that you can't stand up. I
don't care if it's Saturday, but the rest of the world doesn't
have to know it too!' Gabriel had already disposed of four
bottles, anxious as he was to feel the warmth that begins at the
solar plexus and gradually radiates through your whole body,
making your limbs heavy, relieving your head and chest of all
their cares and tracing on your lips a blissful smile. 'Waiter!
Four more!' Now that there were four fresh cold beers in front

of him, he didn't touch them. He was waiting for the right moment. He often said: 'Four beers get the motor running, but the next four make me take off!' He'd wait till his motor was running before he filled up again. He watched the drops of liquefied condensation slide down the glasses, tracing a path, clear transparent furrows that revealed the golden beer in all its splendour through the moisture that clung to the glasses. As he followed the course of the drops of water to the table, he thought of his sister, Albertine, and saw her blow her nose and wipe her eyes after her outburst that afternoon, daring to look at him and his wife only surreptitiously, apologizing in a hoarse voice that contained a hint of shame. For once, he hadn't been weak with her. He'd closed his bedroom door after telling her gently: 'Now you go and let us finish what we started. Go in your room or out on the balcony and think about something else.' When he came back to his wife, she murmured: 'When can we be by ourselves? We'll soon have three kids, Gabriel, and we can't bring them up right in a circus like this!' Gabriel knelt before her, resting his head between her thighs. 'If we were all by ourselves, we'd be so poor! We're better off here!' He heard a sob catch in the fat woman's throat. 'But who says that we wouldn't be happier, Gabriel? At least it'd be our own poverty! Here, I feel as if nothing belongs to us! Not even that! They took away my responsibilities, they took away my children, and now, I can't even spend ten minutes alone with my husband! At night, you're at the printshop; and in the daytime, we have to be careful because our room opens onto the dining room. . . And when the baby's born, we'll have to keep it in here, in our room, and it'll grow up in the dark!' He promised his wife everything then: a new apartment, a new life, a new job for him where he'd work days; everything she'd been asking for since they'd come in this house that was too small, to be looked after by his mother, who was fond of him but only had eyes for Edouard, and Albertine, who'd never forgiven him for marrying for love, who constantly told anyone who would listen: 'They didn't get married for love, it was just so they could do *that*,' knowing very well it was precisely the absence of 'that' from her own marriage that had nipped it

in the bud. But Gabriel knew he didn't have the courage to
condemn his family to the hovel his starvation wages would
limit them to, nor the thin soup and constantly needed clothes
— a whole way of life so boringly melodramatic that he'd try at
all costs to avoid it, a humiliating poverty that would drain all
his courage and lead to weakness and self-destruction. Here,
at least, with the money he contributed, Edouard's board,
the money that Paul sent Albertine, and their mother's life
savings, they all managed to live decently enough, eating well
and often, sleeping in clean, comfortable beds, keeping warm in
the winter, and sometimes even having some fun at mealtimes.
Gabriel feared that he wouldn't be able to give up all that for
some hypothetical future. He promised, knowing very well he
was doing so only to gain time. He started: someone had just
tapped his shoulder and the bitter smell of ill-digested beer
and the stink of unwashed clothes tickled his nostrils. Willy
Ouellette, a mouth-organ player, as famous for his spot-on
retorts as for his approximate music, was leaning over him,
saying with a smile: 'Maybe you aren't my very best friend,
but that's no reason to act like you don't see me!' Without
waiting for Gabriel's invitation, Willy sat down at his table,
placing before him his harmonica and the beggar's bag that
he carried with him everywhere, which contained everything
he possessed: an unlikely series of handkerchiefs for the cold
that he'd been trying to cure for a good twelve years now and a
collection of threadbare underwear which he washed regularly
in the wash basin in the tavern bathroom and then put to dry
on the radiators in winter, or spread on the grass in the parks
in summer. He was rather repulsively dirty, his disgusting
smell discouraging any conversation longer than ten seconds,
responding automatically to any reproach that he might receive
because of his smell: 'I ain't that dirty, you stinking fart. I got
a whole set of clean pants!' Then, he'd take out several pairs of
underwear and wave them under the nose of his interlocutor.
'You know any French Canadian with this many? Don't you
worry now. You might think doctors look clean, but go and
check their pants. It isn't so pretty! Maybe my hands don't
shine like a mirror, but my ass is as white as snow!' Willy

Ouellette seized a glass of beer and drained it in seconds. He wiped his mouth on his shirt sleeve, belched and smiled. 'Say, you got a grin like the cat that stole the cream. You just screw your wife?' Gabriel burst out laughing and pushed the three remaining beers at Willy. 'Play me a tune, Willy, and make it a long one. I've got a lot to forget!' Willy pounced on the three beers, drained them in record time, then got up, shouting to the world at large: 'Listen, everybody, Gabriel's just gone from being an acquaintance of mine to being a real good pal — and I'm gonna celebrate by playing something I haven't played for years, because it used to make my mother bawl. She died asking me to play it for her, but she didn't get to hear it, because before I could get my mouth-organ, she passed away like a little chicken, with her head dropping on her chest and her hands clutched over her goddamn heart that'd just given up the ghost: that song's called "Clair de Lune," by Debussy, or maybe Ravel, who knows — anyway, by some Frenchman.' Gabriel shut his eyes and let the music lull him. He'd have needed his four other beers to take off, but he decided that the music would do the job just as well, so he began religiously following the wrong notes that Willy produced, mixing 'Clair de Lune' and 'Summertime' with disconcerting sincerity. A completely unexpected notion occurred to Gabriel, who opened his eyes at the shock: 'Deep down, Gabriel, you're nothing but a goddamn crybaby. A goddamn crybaby — and lazy on top of it!' Without waiting for the end of the piece that Willy Ouellette was murdering so effectively, he shouted: 'Waiter! Four more!' And Willy Ouellette interrupted his concert just long enough to yell even louder, a resounding: 'Make that eight!' which made the seven or eight drunks who'd come to sit near the new-found friends burst out laughing.

Everyone on Mont-Royal — storekeepers, workers, delivery-men, salesmen, waitresses, even the usher at the Passe-Temps — knew Victoire, or at least they'd heard of her, the older ones often saying to the younger ones who'd been recently

hired: 'We can complain all we want about what a pain in
the neck our customers are, but not one comes anywhere
near that one! Now, there's a pain in the neck! She'd come
in here and buy nothing more than a peanut, but she'd drive
everybody crazy, knocking things over, saying we hid the best
things for the rich ladies from Saint-Joseph, and most of the
time, she'd walk out without buying a thing, leaving us to
clean up her mess! We were so scared of her sometimes, we'd
call the other stores and tell them to pretend they were closed!
That's the truth! We were doing them a favour! She would
walk Mont-Royal all the way from Roche to Papineau, both
sides of the street, and turn it upside down in one afternoon,
then afterwards, she'd go back up Fabre with one pair of
stockings in her brown paper bag or a one-cent sucker stuck
in her mouth like a trophy!' Françoise, the head waitress at
Larivière et Leblanc's lunch counter, would tell at the drop
of a hat about 'the time that crazy bitch ate three butterscotch
sundaes and after every one, she told me I'd forgot to serve
her, and then she left without paying, shouting at the top of
her lungs how she'd never set foot again in a place where you
wait hours for your sundae and never even get a whiff of it!'
That time, in fact, Victoire had realized she'd forgotten her
purse and, too proud to admit it, she decided to gain some
time by eating sundaes until a way out came to her. After
the third sundae, when she was about to retch and a migraine
was sawing through her skull, she suddenly straightened up
and started giving hell to Françoise, almost without realizing
it, as if she were having a nightmare, scarcely knowing what
she was saying, but saying it with conviction. Luckily for
her, it worked: she left the store unscathed, her reputation
still intact, or so she thought — and feeling not a shred of
guilt. 'Don't tell me three butterscotch sundaes are going to
break Larivière et Leblanc!' And when she disappeared from
circulation, stories started going around about her, each more
harebrained than the next — all over Plateau Mont-Royal.
They started by saying that she'd simply moved and so much
the better, but this too-easy conclusion didn't satisfy anyone;
they needed something they could get their teeth into, a tragic

end or at least some great misfortune, to fill the gap caused by
her absence. Monsieur Applebaum, the manager of Grover's
on the northeast corner of Fabre and Mont-Royal, claimed
that he'd seen her get hit by a garbage truck, but nobody
ever believed anything said by Monsieur Applebaum, who had
a reputation for exaggerating, and anyway, there was something
a little too pat about this explanation. They preferred stories
in which the words 'mysterious disappearance' replaced the
word 'dead,' because that way it was easier to imagine Victoire
unhappy, in pain, repentant. Dying but not dead. No matter
how much you believe in the fires of hell, the final and
irrevocable punishment for a dissolute life, a good thrashing
in some backyard, a devastating fire or an incurable disease
are a lot more frightening to contemplate and a lot more
exciting to wish on your enemies than the Devil's forked
tail and ridiculous sniggers. The news got around then, that
Victoire's house had been razed by a tremendous fire, that it
had driven her completely mad, poor old woman, and now,
she was in an insane asylum, 'at Longue-Pointe, with the
hopeless cases,' victim of a disease resembling leprosy; but a
lot more painful and, in particular, horribly ugly to look at. A
visible cancer. Purulent sores. Scabs. Buboes. Françoise, for
her part, refused to listen to such nonsense. She preferred to
imagine Victoire lying on the operating table, tied down and
wide awake, stuffed with ice cream and butterscotch sauce,
showered with insults and bodily blows. And so, when Victoire
and Edouard, an odd couple if ever there was one, emerged on
Mont-Royal, turning left towards Marquette, Victoire suddenly
straightened up and then hunched her back like a beaten dog, as
a strange silence fell over the neighbourhood. It was Saturday
afternoon: the street was teeming with housewives doing their
shopping, whimpering children drooling onto their mothers'
skirts, drunks sitting or, rather, laid out in the tavern doorways.
No adolescents. The few young men walking on Mont-Royal
that afternoon did so on the arms of pregnant women, whose
presence served as alibi to their country in time of war, as
guarantees of their honesty, and most of all, their innocence.
Abandon a pregnant woman for the Old Country! Never!

Victoire and her son hadn't taken thirty steps when, already, heads began to turn and salesmen with measuring tapes around their necks or tailor's chalk in their hands came out of stores. When Victoire and Edouard walked past his store, Monsieur Applebaum from Grover's was waiting on a skinny woman determined to find some cloth to match the colour of her hornrimmed glasses. Monsieur Applebaum dropped the roll of red-and-brown spotted fabric he'd just unearthed in the back of the store and ran to the door as if someone had kicked him in the butt. 'She isn't dead!' A sardonic little smile appeared on Victoire's lips. She glanced furtively to the left and right to see the effect that their presence was having — and her eyes wrinkled with delight. 'Two years now, and they haven't seen hide nor hair of me. And I bet my nightie they all thought I was dead!' As for Edouard, he wished he were, indeed, dead. He knew his mother's reputation all too well, his own career having started as a sales assistant in a shoe store on Mont Royal. He'd heard people talk about her in terms so appalling that he'd never admitted she was his mother. And amazingly for years Victoire played along: whenever she came to the store where her son had managed to land the manager's job through flattery, compliments and scheming, she also pretended not to know him. She treated him just like the others, yelling at him, threatening him, making abundant use of the words 'cheat' and 'thief,' trying on fifteen pairs of shoes and buying nothing; sometimes, even going so far as to tell him in front of everybody: 'I pity the woman that brought you into the world!' or: 'If I had a numbskull like you for a son, I'd kill myself!' or again: 'You should be wearing a shoe on your head, not a hat!' And when Edouard came home at night, she would literally throw herself at him, cover him with kisses, laugh so hard that she had to wipe her eyes with her handkerchief. 'By God, I had a good laugh! You should've seen the look on your face! Like a potato about to sprout!' Edouard never really understood why his mother behaved like this. Enraptured of him as she was, she should have been delighted that her son was manager of a shoe store, that he had a position of trust, with heavy responsibilities on his shoulders; but instead, she humiliated him in front of everyone, even going so far as to express pity for his mother! How could he understand the affront this manager's job represented to Victoire, compared to the ambitions and dreams that she'd entertained, maintained and nourished for him since his birth? How could he guess that she desired power for him, poor child; he, who had always let himself be shunted about, bereft of any idea of grandeur, knowing nothing of the thirst for power until the day when, suddenly, everything became clear to him — desires, thirsts, dreams, ambitions — the cursed day when he realized that he was different, in a society that condemned any disposition, tendency, talent, taste that didn't fit its criteria of normality and where he had hidden his 'abnormality,' stuck it away beneath a mask of indifference, in the persona of a store manager? How could he imagine that his mother knew he wasn't like the others and that the shame she felt because of it, concealed even from her, could turn to pride only if he could face talking to her about it? Victoire knew that Edouard became someone else when he walked out the door and she never forgave him for that. The shoe store manager was a stranger to her because he was too different from everything she'd always dreamed of for her darling son, her heart's delight, her baby. Hadn't she given birth only to a handful of gutless wonders? Gabriel, who'd taken refuge in the bosom of his fat wife, Albertine-the-victim, and Edouard — *a manager of a shoe store?* Clinging to one another on the sidewalk, Victoire and Edouard had never looked so much like strangers. She was sure of the effect she was having and relished every moment of it, while he, even though he'd left the neighbourhood long ago to go and sell shoes in the west end of town, at Ogilvy's, where rich people shopped and he was the only French-Canadian salesman on the floor, so bilingual now, that even his boss called him Eddy and customers always addressed him in English, still he felt the burning humiliation of this 'innocent walk' on the arm of the most hated old woman on the street — his mother. At the corner of Marquette, Victoire stopped in front of a jewellery store window. She dropped Edouard's arm and leaned against the glass. Edouard stepped back a few paces. It was as though the street had stopped living. Everyone, customers as well as salesmen, came out of the stores to look at Victoire staring at the jewellery. Edouard folded his arms over his big belly, looked down, and finally, leaned against a telephone pole. Die. Right there on the spot. Never feel again those mocking looks. Or else survive and confront them. Whirl around and laugh in their faces. 'Good joke we've been playing on you all these years, eh, you jerks? We had you fooled all this time and you let us play our game and never suspected a thing. . .' No. No courage for that. Withdraw. As usual. Shame. The usher at the Passe-Temps came out too, and was shouting: 'Edouard! Edouard! At last, you got yourself a girlfriend!' Victoire turned around and walked over to her son. All this hypocrisy on top of everything else! 'I'm hungry!' They crossed the street as Mont-Royal looked on in amazement. Victoire kept nodding at all the people they met, sometimes murmuring a scarcely audible 'Bonjour' or: 'How are you?' Françoise, the head waitress, was watching them through the window of Larivière et Leblanc. Victoire gave her a big smile, as if she were a friend she hadn't seen for years, and hurried into the store. Combative and happy, she faced Françoise, and said in a very loud voice: 'Three butterscotch sundaes please!'

'Thérèse, that's a nice name. You don't hear it very often.' 'My mother used to read a lot of French novels before she got married and she decided if she ever had a daughter, she'd call her Thérèse. I'm the only Thérèse in grade six and there's three classes of thirty-one pupils!' Thérèse was comfortably settled on the big green wooden bench, her feet barely touching the ground. Gérard Bleau, the playground attendant, rolled cigarette after cigarette, frowning when it was time to strike a match, as if this were a difficult task requiring concentration almost beyond his capacity. 'There's three Jeannines, just in my class. And two Claires. Claire Côté and Claire Thivierge. There used to be four Denises, but one of them left because her mother needed her to take care of her new baby brother.' 'What about your little brother? How come he's like that?'

Captivated by the beauty of the young man's face and by the
hunt from which she had emerged victorious, a victory that had
delivered her victim to her bound hand and foot, Thérèse had
forgotten Philippe and Marcel for a good half-hour, so she was
a little startled by the attendant's question. She looked towards
the ladders where she had left her brother and cousin. 'Don't
go looking for them. They're under a tree. For a kid with St
Vitus' Dance, I'd say your brother calms down pretty fast when
he sits down! The minute he was under that tree, he stopped
twisting and turning — just like that! And he stopped shaking
all of a sudden too. Is he always that way?' Thérèse wondered if
the attendant was laughing at her, if he'd already seen through
their little game, but there was no irony in Gérard Bleau's grey
eyes: they were innocent, pure, wide open — and astonishingly
empty. 'I guess he isn't too bright.' Before she spoke, Thérèse
coughed nervously to conceal her emotion. Really, he looked
more and more beautiful. 'No, he isn't like that all the time.
Depends on the day. He's tired today. Sometimes, he's a
real pain in the neck and nobody can stand him, but today
he isn't bad at all.' Thérèse laughed. A chilly little laugh.
'I say whatever comes into my mind.' She had circled the
attendant long enough before the attack. First, she pretended
to be playing hide-and-seek with her brother and cousin, then
hopscotch, but when she realized that Gérard wasn't paying
attention to her, she started walking around the bench in ever
smaller circles, never taking her eyes off the head of the young
man who went on smoking, unaware of her presence, glancing
absentmindedly every now and then at the few little girls on the
playground. 'I'm a big spider. A big black spider with hairy legs
and scissors for a mouth! And a great big fly just got caught in
my web! Mmmmm. . . Now, let's go up to that fly nice and
slow. We don't want to scare him right away. . . And when he
finally sees me, it'll be too late. . . I'll throw myself on top of
him and eat him in one bite. . . No, no, maybe I'll take my
time instead.' When she walked behind the attendant, she
felt a pang in her heart and her breathing became faster. 'My
Lord, he's gorgeous!' He had unfastened the two top buttons
of his shirt, revealing a scrawny chest with little hair. 'Just

like a movie star!' Once, he looked at her. Smiled. Thérèse
immediately looked down and turned her head away. She'd
often been told never to stare at men, that it might put ideas
in their heads. 'Ideas?' For the moment, she was the one who
had the ideas. . . 'I'm a mother cat that's just had babies and
he's a mouse that wants to eat them up. . . Here, mousie. Just
try and touch them, you mean rotten mouse. . .' It was she who
approached him, spider-cat, with confused desires, foolhardy
little girl, for whom men were beautiful objects whom you
parade around and show off, then put away when you don't
want them any more. 'When I'm finished with you, your own
mother won't recognize you!' She thought of her own mother
for a few seconds: her mother bending over her, scrubbing her
mouth with a soapy washcloth. 'I'll tell you when you're ready
to wear lipstick! Eleven years old! Next thing we know, you'll
be asking for high-heeled shoes and nylons! Do you want the
men to run after you? Like a hooker?' But she refused to explain
what a hooker was. 'If I tell you that, I'll have to tell you other
things and I'm not in the mood.' But the memory of her mother
vanished when Gérard Bleau slipped his hand inside his shirt to
scratch his chest. 'I wish he'd take his shirt off!' Amazed at this
thought, Thérèse paused. 'I wonder why?' No reply occurred
to her. She just wanted him to take off his shirt. But her desire
troubled her deeply and she was unable to resume the hunt. 'It
isn't just that. There must be something else.' Suddenly, she
saw herself in Gérard Bleau's arms, her mouth almost glued to
his, like in the Ipana toothpaste ad that she'd cut out of one of
her uncle Edouard's English magazines, the ad that showed a
man and woman with their arms around each other, just
about to kiss. . . 'So that's it!' In two seconds, she'd crossed
the ground separating her from the handsome attendant, sat
on the bench facing the one where Gérard Bleau sat calmly
smoking, and asked point blank: 'What kind of toothpaste do
you use?' The hunt was over. She knew what she wanted. She
saw in Gérard Bleau's astonished expression a hint of fear that
flattered her. He replied: 'Pepsodent,' without laughing, and
she said, 'Mine's Ipana.' That was when he asked her name.
And she was proud to tell him. And then, they were off. 'He

wasn't born like that, you know. . . He fell from the second
floor when he was little. . . He didn't get hurt, but it did that to
him. . .' Anything at all. Just as long as the conversation went
on. But how could she bring him into it, guide him along that
mysterious road of which she knew absolutely nothing? What
made a man want to kiss a woman? A woman? Thérèse saw
her mother again. 'You haven't got any problems. You're just
a little girl. Enjoy it! And stay that way as long as you can. You
don't know how lucky you are!' Lucky! She cursed the 'luck'
that made her powerless, ignorant and bereft in the face of a
desire that she didn't understand, a new desire that, against
her will, made her heart pound, a hunger that she didn't know
how to appease, an unfamiliar thirst that frightened her, but
fascinated her too. 'Why don't you want to play with the
others?' Suddenly, an insult. A kick. As usual: go and play.
Don't bug the grown-ups. Play with your dollies. Look after
the baby. You're too young to be here. 'They're asleep. . .'
Gérard Bleau threw his cigarette butt to the ground and stepped
on it. 'They'll have to wake up some time!' Something about
this clinging little girl was starting to get on his nerves, but he
didn't know what. Her insistent gaze, perhaps, her piercing
eyes. Yes, that was it. Her eyes. He was surprised to find
himself buttoning his shirt again. The way she stared at him.
As though he were a mannequin in a store window. A toy. He
felt like a toy. Unconsciously, he picked up his tobacco pouch.
He was trembling a little. 'I told you to go and play!' He had
raised his voice without realizing it. She frightened him. He
was afraid of this little girl of — what? — ten, eleven? He
shrugged. Just then, Thérèse leaped up, grinning. 'Today's
my birthday! I'm twelve years old!' 'Oh yes? Happy Birthday.'
'Usually when it's somebody's birthday, you give them a kiss!'
Without waiting for him to reply, Thérèse took two steps and
stood between the attendant's knees. He moved his head back
a little. 'Let's have a little kiss.' She bent over, serious now, and
kissed him on the mouth. It was very brief, but Gérard felt the
beginning of profound anguish; more than that, he felt fear, the
real thing, mixed with guilt and remorse, total panic, as if he'd
just committed some irrevocable act that cut his life into two

distinct parts: the part before the little girl and the part after.
But *he* wasn't the one who had committed the act! It was the
girl! *She* had kissed him! It was not him! He was innocent! His
erection surprised him in the midst of his terror and he bent
double as Thérèse ran away. 'I'm such a dope! My birthday!
A birthday kiss doesn't count! It isn't a real kiss!' She'd have
to start all over again.

He'd taken refuge under a balcony, the closest one, he'd slipped
into the first dark hole he saw, he'd lain on his side, shaken
by spasms, his gouged eye dripping. He didn't even have the
strength to lick his wounds. He took short breaths because
of his broken ribs. He didn't understand. He couldn't accept
it. All this pain. This useless suffering. Gratuitous. Godbout
had taken him in his jaws and shaken him like some ugly
old rag, then thrown him up in the air and jumped on him.
First, Duplessis tried to explain that he only wanted to walk
past, that was all, that he had business in the park, that he
didn't feel like walking around the whole neighbourhood. . .
but Godbout kept a jealous eye on his territory and never, never
would he let Duplessis past. 'I took over your area because you
were too gutless to hold onto it, so tough titty, Kitty! You've
got no business here! Scat! Shoo! The south side of Mont-Royal
doesn't belong to you any more, so you can take de la Roche
or de Lorimier if you want to get to the park. I don't want to
smell your piss on one of my posts or on my hydrants! Because
I wouldn't put it past you to start marking out your territory
behind my back. I know you, I've been keeping an eye on you
for months, whenever you put on one of your scenes in the
neighbourhood! I can see you sniffing around your old tracks
and hanging around your favourite spots. . . And don't think
you're going to come up on me from behind and chase me out
of here like some vulgar beggar. Oh no! This is my territory
now and I'm staying!' The confrontation that followed was
inevitable. Duplessis hadn't been up to it. At first, he was
surprised by Godbout's aggressiveness: the dog had no reason

in the world to be annoyed with him; on the contrary, he'd beaten him to a pulp only a few months before, so now he was master of a neighbourhood rich in restaurants and well supplied with garbage cans. . . But then, Duplessis told himself that it was normal for Godbout to still be afraid of him. 'He knows very well that I'd never give up for good. That I'm getting ready for a comeback. He's no fool. In his place, I'd do the same.' And Duplessis moved clumsily. Godbout went through the motions of biting him (a warning), but Duplessis clawed him in earnest. And that was what started everything. A mistake. As soon as he felt the blood on his muzzle, Godbout went wild with rage and the carnage began. Duplessis was a strong cat, and aggressive when he had to be, alert, lively and agile, but Godbout's obstinate anger went beyond the bounds of caution and common sense and the cat could see in the dog's eyes that for one of them this battle would be the last. Duplessis wasn't in the mood. Not today. He defended himself, of course, but his heart wasn't in it. Right in the middle of the mêlée, when he was clinging to one of Godbout's ears while the dog shook his head in every direction, trying to dislodge him, the cat mentally shrank back. For a moment, he saw the scene from the outside, completely detached, and the absurdity of the situation hit him in the face: a flea-bitten cat and a mangy dog fighting over a right-of-way — how silly! While a little boy who was madly in love with him was waiting in the park, he was demeaning himself in this squabble with a narrow-minded brute who'd sell his mother (or kill her) for a chicken bone, which would then get stuck in his throat. He let go, landed on his paws, hesitated briefly (what he really wanted to do was run away and too bad about his reputation. Love is more important) — which was fatal. Godbout leapt at his throat, clipping his eye on the way so that it burst like a grape, and Duplessis felt the shadow of fear pass over his soul. He jumped with pain and meowed to signal that death was near. 'Die! Die rather than suffer like this!' Godbout lay down on the other side of the garden fence where Duplessis had taken refuge, watching the cat as he licked his blood-reddened claws. 'At least you could let me die in peace.' 'No, I want to be good and sure that you're dead. I want to be the first one to announce it.' 'If the gate wasn't closed, would you come and finish me off?' 'No. Anyhow, I could jump over it. I'd rather watch you die nice and slow, nice and easy. And enjoy every minute of it.' 'You hate me that much?' 'Yes.' And Duplessis knew that Godbout would start howling the moment he was dead. That he'd howl the news of his final victory, his irrevocable domination. That people would come out on their balconies and say: 'Somebody just died. I hope it's nobody we know!' and eventually, a child would shout: 'Doesn't matter. It's just a cat. I can see it. He's under the balcony. . .' Just a cat. A foolhardy cat. A cat in love who, without involvement, had just spent two whole nights fulfilling a crazy lady cat. Detached. A cat who had detached himself from that hygienic act just as he'd detached himself from this mortal battle. He stretched his head a little so that it jutted out from under the balcony. 'If the little boy that smells of dried pee comes by, my life, my love, my heart's delights, at least I'll see him before I die.'

'You really think I'm too hard on Marcel?' In the middle of her Saturday afternoon dusting, Albertine had stopped in front of the open door to the fat woman's bedroom; the latter had invited her in. Albertine sat on the foot of the bed, as did all the visitors who came to see Gabriel's wife. Legs squeezed together, duster on her lap, she didn't dare look her sister-in-law in the eye. The sounds of Gabriel and his wife making love were still too present in her memory, too fresh, so if she looked the fat woman in the eye, the latter might be able to read there envy, disgust, contempt, respect — too many feelings all jumbled together, hesitant, shaky, all different. The fat woman waited for Albertine to speak first. She felt one of her sister-in-law's rare confidences coming on, a confession as brief as it was sudden, that Albertine would let drop in the most incongruous places and at the most unexpected times: over the stove on Christmas Eve as they were making doughnuts; coming out of Mass one July morning when everyone else was in raptures over the beautiful summer day; or once, when she was bringing the post to her room on a pleasant morning. . . Brief, choppy sentences; voice low, a murmur. Everything expressed in fifteen seconds — with no warning at the beginning or at the end. This time, though, only one question came out. The fat woman waited two long minutes before she replied. Just in case. Then, realizing nothing else was coming, she leaned a little to the right so that she could take her sister-in-law's hand. Albertine had anticipated her gesture and avoided it by placing her hands on either side of her on the bed. And the fat woman found herself holding a dirty rag. She picked it up, squared her shoulders and began dusting the arm of her chair, the place where she always rested her elbow, where there was never any dust. 'Why are you asking me that out of the blue?' Albertine then told the fat woman of her conversation with Thérèse the night before. And her promise to try in the future to be nicer to her youngest child. The fat woman smiled. Albertine sighed. 'I don't think I'm all that mean.' The fat woman answered with another question. 'Bartine. . . do you really think I'm too old and fat to have another baby?' Albertine jumped as if someone had pricked her. Then she looked her sister-in-law in the eye and everything came tumbling out so fast and with such force that when she'd finished her voice still rang in the fat woman's ears. 'Yes! Yes, I think you are! Yes, you're too fat! And too old! You know what people out on the street say about you? Eh? They say you're filthy! They say only somebody really filthy would want a baby after forty! They say when a woman gets to forty, it's time for her to rest! That it's too late to start washing nappies and bringing up children! And I think so too! When the kid starts school, you'll be fifty! When other women are fifty, they're grandmothers, dammit! And do you want to know what you'll look like when you start to take him out? Like his grandmother, that's what! His grandmother! People will tell you: "You look young for a grandmother!" And you'll have to tell them: "I'm not a young grandmother. I'm an old mother!" You can't wait, eh, you just can't wait! People will point at you and it'll be your own fault! And if you keep on. . . if you don't stop. . . Anyway, if you go on doing what you did this afternoon, on top of everything else, you'll be having even

more! Lord Almighty, do you really want to rip your belly apart
like that till you're fifty? With another baby the house will be
too crowded. It'll drive us all crazy. And if it takes you a long
time to get over having it, who'll be stuck with it, eh? Me,
that's who! I'm the one that'll wipe his behind and wash his
nappies! But did you ever ask me what I thought when you
decided to have that baby, you and your handsome Gabriel?
Eh? Oh, it's fine to have babies, but you have to be able to take
care of them. And let me tell you, I'm nobody's servant. Ever
since you've been stuck in here, I've done everything in this
house. But don't think for one minute that I enjoy it. Besides
wiping up after the whole house, I have to clean you up too,
just like a baby!' Albertine got to her feet as she spoke. She
bent over her sister-in-law, who had looked away from her.
She stopped speaking as abruptly as she'd begun. The good
smell of homemade soup was beginning to drift through the
house. The clock in the dining room chimed five o'clock. The
fat woman shut her eyes. Albertine picked up her duster. 'If
you feel ashamed of yourself, just try and imagine how the rest
of us feel when we go out on the street!' The fat woman opened
her eyes again. 'You just answered your own question, Bartine.
About Marcel. And everything else.'

Germaine Lauzon burst into the house of her sister, Gabrielle
Jodoin, just as the radio said that it was five o'clock and that
the news would follow. 'Five, already? Well, I won't stay
long. I've got the supper to get ready and Ernest doesn't
like to wait.' Germaine Lauzon gave her brother-in-law a big
smile. 'Bonjour, handsome! Off work today?' Mastaï Jodoin
was whistling as he peeled his third potato. 'I was done at
4:07 today and I don't go back till 5:18 Monday morning.'
'You drive me nuts with your hours and your streetcars! Why
can't you start at eight and finish at six like everybody else?'
'If we started and finished at the same time as everybody else,
how do you think they'd get to work, dingbat?' Gabrielle Jodoin
took the potatoes, ran them under the tap and tossed them into

a pot. 'Now, don't start tearing each other to shreds, you two, or there'll be no end to it!' Germaine sat at the end of the table, puffing. She was much fatter than her sisters, Gabrielle Jodoin and Rose Ouimet, and her pregnancy (eight months gone like them) was giving her some trouble. 'I'm going to have a little sit, otherwise, I'll bust!' She patted her belly, trying to put to sleep the child who had just kicked her so hard that she could feel it. 'I can't do a thing any more. I get out of breath right away. I'll tell you, I just went over to Souci's for a quart of milk and I feel as if I'd been running for two hours! And I wasted my breath because they were out of milk. . .' Gabrielle opened a cupboard. 'Anyhow, I hope you didn't come here looking for sugar! I'm right out! It's hard to put your hands on any these days.' She took down two soup bowls, two spoons and the salt and pepper. Germaine shrugged and ran her hand over her brow. 'You think I just come here to borrow things?' 'Want some soup? The rest won't be ready for an hour, but Mastaï's hungry.' 'Oh, why not? A little soup before supper never did any harm!' Gabrielle took down a third soup bowl and placed it in front of her sister. 'What kind is it?' 'The soup? Barley.' Mastaï was rolling himself a cigarette now. He spoke gently, evenly, as though nothing were happening. 'I'm taking your sister to the theatre tonight.' A small bomb. He was sure of its effect and watched his sister-in-law react, a mocking smile coming to the corner of his mouth. Germaine stiffened and turned first red, then white. The theatre was her great passion (throughout her childhood, she told anyone who would listen that, some day, she'd be going to Hollywood or Paris, that she'd be a great actress. . . the drama of a child with no imagination, whom everyone finally tired of, and whom the family nicknamed 'The Actress,' a nickname that stuck, that she detested now like some shameful sin or a birthmark), but her husband Ernest Lauzon, a mechanic at Canadair, a young man completely bereft of fantasy, whose sense of humour consisted of looking at the comics in the Sundays with an imperturbably serious expression, sometimes murmuring: 'I don't get it!' or: 'That's dumb!' that drove Germaine absolutely mad with rage (she liked the comics too). Ernest Lauzon, then, forbade his wife to go to the theatre saying that it would get her too worked up and put ideas in her head. What ideas, he would have found it hard to say as, to him, the very word 'idea' represented mysterious needs that he didn't know, wasn't interested in and never thought about. The only thing he knew was that when Germaine came back from the theatre, she looked right through him, glassy-eyed with joy, as though he didn't exist. He'd once confided to his brother-in-law, Mastaï Jodoin: 'When she comes home, she talks about Jacques Auger as if he was the good Lord in person and she talks about Albert Duquesne as if they'd made a date to meet in the backyard at midnight the next day! I can't get over it! We've only been married two years and I'm sure as hell not going to let her spend her nights dreaming about Albert Duquesne! She says he's got a beautiful voice! Why shouldn't he? He hasn't got anything better to do!' Germaine plunged the spoon into the soup without a word. Mastaï put down his cigarette, which he would finish between the soup and the rest of the meal. 'I'm taking her to the National.' Germaine blew on her soup, making as much noise as she could when she swallowed so that she wouldn't hear her brother-in-law, then added a little salt. 'Good soup. Barley's good. But Christ, it's hot!' And Mastaï slurped too as he ate his first spoonful. 'There's two shows. Six hours altogether.' Gabrielle Jodoin looked at each of them in turn, her husband whom she loved so much, her reason for living, and her fat sister whom she'd got to know better since they'd both become pregnant (Germaine and Gabrielle had grown much closer in the past seven months, while their sister Rose, who was pregnant as well, had withdrawn into herself, hiding away in her house and using every means to conceal her pregnancy) and she felt that twinge of jealousy that she experienced when they got on each other's nerves, like children, something that happened often; it wormed its ways into her, making a hole, a void, in place of her heart. 'They fight and pick on each other just like an old married couple! I'm the one that seems like the sister-in-law when they get together!' Germaine still acted as though Mastaï had said

nothing and went on eating her soup. Only a slight trembling
in her hand, which she tried in vain to repress, bore witness
to the turmoil inside her. In fact, she wanted to claw her
brother-in-law, cut him into bits and stamp on the pieces.
'He knows that pisses me off! So why doesn't he cut it out?'
But Mastaï kept his trump card till the end, as always. He had
a way of setting up tricks and a sense of timing that made him
a peerless storyteller and a player who was highly skilled, to
say the least: when you least expected it, when you thought
everything was over, when you thought that you could finally
laugh at his joke or submit to other people's mockery, he was
always there with something unexpected that was even more
hilarious or infuriating. 'I bought tickets for you and Ernest
too, but then I remembered your lord and master doesn't like
the theatre, so I gave them to a bum that was walking past the
National. He was real glad. He even promised to give himself a
wash before he went to the theatre, so we wouldn't feel sick. It
would've been dumb to waste good tickets like that, know what
I mean? Best seats in the house!' Germaine Lauzon slowly put
her spoon in her soup bowl. 'I was coming to ask you over to
play cards tonight. Rose and her husband will be there. And
Mama's coming too — with Pierrette. If you feel like it. . . You
just have to walk across the street. Thanks a lot for the soup.'
She got up and walked down the hallway, as her brother-in-law
roared with laughter. Gabrielle followed her sister to the front
door. 'Maybe we'll come, Germaine, but I don't know for sure.
If we aren't there by eight, it means we won't be coming.' The
door closed softly. Neither Mastaï nor Gabrielle saw the tears on
Germaine's fat cheeks, but Gabrielle knew they were there.

'Why do you think we all voted "No" last week? Because we all
got a yellow streak? Well, we haven't! But we don't want to go
and get killed in a war that's got nothing to do with us!' A dozen
men were sitting around Gabriel as they did every Saturday
afternoon — labourers, retired men and even a few winos who
came to finish off the day in the tavern, knowing very well

they'd have to listen to what they called, among themselves, 'Gabriel's sermon,' the inevitable political harangue that the fat woman's husband launched into after his eighth or ninth beer, which could last until very late at night if the speaker was on form and his audience attentive. Gabriel had earned the affection and respect of all the establishment's clients because of these speeches, which were always naïve, but expressed perfectly well the preoccupations that got people worked up in these days of insecurity, hesitations and questioning. His influence was even beginning to take on a certain importance without his realizing it, the men often waiting to know what he thought about some social or political question before they expressed their own opinions. He had even, to a large measure, been responsible for the 'No' vote of all the men in the neighbourhood. 'If Canada wants to give England a hand, it's their funeral! But I don't want to murder people and lose my limbs for a country that never did nothing for me!' The men applauded. But Willy Ouellette, still sitting across from his friend, didn't know what to think. 'Isn't that right, Willy?' Willy Ouellette seemed to be dozing in his chair, holding his mouth-organ. His thinking wasn't clear, far from it, but something was nagging at him. 'I just think. . .' He ran his sleeve across his mouth where there was still a little foam from his beer. 'I just think it's too bad about France. If you ask me, we gotta save France. . . our mother country. . . our roots. . .' Gabriel got to his feet and came and stood before Willy Ouellette, who moved back in shock. 'France! France abandoned us! France sold us down the river! Save France so it can go on shitting in our faces afterwards and laugh at the way we talk and think they're better than us!' Without really knowing why, Willy Ouellette decided to stand up to Gabriel, perhaps so as not to lose face; perhaps too, because, in his heart of hearts, a small fleur-de-lys flag was still feebly waving. 'I think you're laying it on a little thick there, Gabriel! Just because France dropped us a few hundred years ago, doesn't mean we should let her die at the hands of the Nazis!' 'It's no reason to go and die for her either! I don't want to die for France and I don't want to die for Canada either! And I sure as

hell don't want to die for England! So why should I go? Can you
tell me? Can you see yourself fighting in the middle of a bunch
of Englishmen and Frenchmen from France that always turned
up their noses at you, against a bunch of Germans that never
did nothing to you?' 'If we leave the Germans alone, they'll
invade the whole place, even over here, and turn us into atheists
and pagans!' 'That isn't true! The Pope in Rome, what side
do you think he's on, eh? He's on Mussolini's side — and
Hitler's!' 'Now Gabriel, don't tell me you're on Hitler's side,
and Mussolini's too!' 'Of course not, I didn't say that. . . I'm
no Fascist. . .' Gabriel would soon be out of his depth, he was
well aware of it, but he couldn't find a way back. This was the
first time anyone had dared stand up to him. He pounded the
table with his fist, a gesture that was usually effective and final,
but this time, amazingly, it left no echo. 'I'm not going to go
and die for nothing, for some country that's always made fun of
me!' 'Maybe it's better to die for nothing, like a man, Gabriel,
than have everybody think you're yellow-bellied for the rest of
your life. . .' Gabriel paused, the first pause since the argument
had started. Willy Ouellette took advantage of the pause. 'One
thing for sure, we're all going to look like a bunch of goddamn
cowards! You think Canada's going to believe the only reason
we don't want to go to war is because we think it's none of our
business? Don't kid yourselves! The Province of Quebec's the
only part of Canada that voted "No"! All the others said "Yes".
So now they've got another good chance to laugh in our faces.
They're already saying we make babies just so we won't have
to fight, because men with families don't have to go — and
now, we come right out and refuse to pass a law to make all
able-bodied men go and fight for England!' 'They promised
us we'd never have to fight for England!' 'Sure they did, but
then they changed their minds. What do you expect? It's them.
It's the government that's in charge! And we're the only ones
that voted "No," so now we'll have to go and fight anyway.'
Gabriel suddenly sat down again. The roles had been reversed
without anyone wishing it. Willy Ouellette hadn't wanted to
take the wind out of Gabriel's sails. He didn't know where his
arguments had come from; he hadn't even looked for them or

thought them out. There he was, suddenly, almost the winner of the argument, facing a Gabriel he didn't recognize, who seemed to want to run away, step back, give in. A painful silence fell over the tavern. Gabriel picked up the last beer on the table and drained it in one gulp. Then, the decisive question, the final blow, came from Ti-Paul Boudreau, the waiter: 'I hear your wife's expecting, eh Gabriel?' Gabriel leaped to his feet and the words poured from his mouth, distorted by emotion, disfigured, hoarse, broken. Pleading. 'I didn't get my wife pregnant so I wouldn't have to join up! Please, don't think I did that! I got her pregnant. . . because I love her. . . and she wanted another baby!' Gabriel retreated before his obviously incredulous audience and ran away like a beaten dog. The saddest, most confused man was Willy Ouellette who, without wanting to, had just humiliated the greatest tavern orator in the neighbourhood, his new friend, and sown doubt — that sore, that incurable wound — in the hearts of his brothers.

Violette had been back at work for several minutes: purl one, knit one, green wool, blue wool — or yellow, or pink — glance down at the street between two booties or sip some cold tea, but something about her behaviour had changed. Her hands weren't so agile. She wielded the needles with uncertainty and the booties that she was knitting were really too small now. They were ridiculous balls of wool with no precise shape that wouldn't fit the foot of any baby, no matter how puny. Florence saw all this, but said nothing. She would have to wait until night, until bedtime, when it was completely dark, with only the blind eye of the moon as witness, before she spoke. . . Only then could she sit by her daughter's bed and tell her. Everything. Explain? No. Tell. Victoire's family. The generations, the individuals, clans, relatives, the prolific love-matches between blood relatives, the barren marriages of convenience, the new branches, the dead ones that needn't be cut off because they fell off the tree by themselves, Victoire's great-great-grandfather, Thomas-le-Fun, who had fought against the Americans, thereby gaining a wooden leg on which he had carved the words: 'Sacrificed at Saint-Denis,' his son, Gaby-Gaby, who never stopped growing and who finally died from it, his bones bursting, disjointed, his daughter, Nénette, who had twenty-seven children in twenty-seven years and died giving birth to her last daughter, Victoire's grandmother, cursing her husband, her fate, her priest, her body, and the role of caring servant that was reserved for women, a saint who was refused the last rites and who hadn't been buried in consecrated ground, a witch who dared speak out, a cursed woman who had covered the village with her imprecations until the priest threw himself at the feet of his bishop, exclaiming: 'Come and wash the sky of my village, Monseigneur. The sun's gone away and it's black everywhere!' And Victoire herself, yes, she'd tell her about Victoire, about her youth, about her loves (especially Josaphat-the-Violin, her brother, the one great passion in her life), about how she'd been torn apart, heartsick, when she had to move to Montreal to follow the man she didn't love, who adored her, Télésphore, so gentle but so soft, and her life as a recluse on the second floor of the house on Fabre Street — and finally, about themselves: Florence, Rose, Violette, Mauve, straddling the generations, perpetually tending and knitting, hidden watchers, surveying and looking on, united, protecting cradles from afar, counting the births, but not the deaths — and happy? Happy. They, who patiently knit up time. They, who watched over Victoire's family from the very beginning and would watch over it until it was extinguished. Why? What did it matter? She might even, perhaps, tell Violette the future: the fat woman's multiple child, all the simultaneous births: Rose Ouimet, Gabrielle Jodoin, Germaine Lauzon, Claire Lemieux, and that other birth, to Marie-Louise Brassard, who hovered behind the lace curtain in her living room, wild with fear, who thought her first child would come out her navel. But Florence thought, she'd keep that all for herself. To put Violette to sleep, she would tell of the past. She would keep the future for herself. What was the good of telling everything? Knitting as she went along, keeping

her eyes open, offering no interpretations, rejoicing or suffering
with Victoire, with Gabriel, with Albertine, with Edouard —
and later, much later, recreating it all with the boy-girl child
who would be born to the fat woman, suffering with him,
taking refuge in sounds and images, reliving his family's past,
to prevent it being extinguished by indifference — this was
their lot, the lot of Florence, Rose, Violette and Mauve. But
predictions? No. And yet, Florence knew everything that would
happen — or almost — but she refused to gather her knowledge.
Wait. Watch. Knit. Baby booties to perpetuate the line. Violette
burst out laughing, a harsh and nervous laugh, bringing her
hands to her mouth, she dropped her knitting. 'Mama, I closed
up my last bootie! I was daydreaming and I knitted it shut. . .
I knitted a perfect circle!' Florence took the circle in her right
hand and dropped it into her apron pocket. 'Go and get supper
ready, Violette. I'll take your place.' 'It isn't my turn.' 'Go and
make supper.'

Marie-Louise Brassard had gone into hiding behind the lace
curtain in her living room. Throughout her pregnancy, for
seven months, as long as a tunnel where nothing moves, where
everything is frozen, hollowed out in the midst of the void,
leading to nothing but fear, Marie-Louise had taken refuge
at her window, as though seeking help there. Sometimes she
stood, but most of the time, she sat on a straight-back chair
that she brought from the kitchen and placed sideways, the
seat and the chairback grazing the lace, while she sat, always
bored, except when she was afraid. She took her place at the
window every morning with a cup of tea in her hand. Her body
faced the wall where a huge crucifix reigned between two lights,
but her head was always turned towards the outside, towards
life. She rarely moved and she let her tea get cold on her
lap, occasionally bringing the cup to her lips, an automatic
movement performed almost in spite of herself. Sometimes
she turned her head towards the living room, but then she
would quickly look back at the street again. She had hung

a curtain between herself and life and she watched life from between the cotton flowers. Unlike Marie-Sylvia, who spied and interpreted every movement on the street, Marie-Louise Brassard was content just to take note of everything — the gestures of the passers-by, the way the light changed when a cloud passed over, even the sound of an occasional car. All was forgotten as soon as it passed. At noon, she got up, went to the kitchen and ate a devilled ham sandwich or a fried egg, then came back to sit behind her curtain for the rest of the afternoon. When the baby kicked, as it did more and more often now, Marie-Louise would stare in fright, wondering if her time had come. Every time. Because Marie-Louise Brassard, product of the ignorance and intolerance of a rural society that imposed silence where explanations were necessary, a society that fostered envy, hypocrisy and guilt as three essential virtues, and that, most of all, considered sexuality an evil (not simply a sin, but *the* sin, the sole and ultimate one, to which women must submit in order to assure progeny for the race), was lost in fear of her child. No one had ever told her anything about sexuality, she, who, on her wedding day, still thought babies were delivered by the Indians from Caughnawaga, had been not surprised, but horrified when Doctor Sanregret, whom she'd gone to see about her nausea and stomach aches early in her pregnancy, told her she was 'carrying' a child, a child that would be born early in the summer. She hadn't dared ask any questions, as her mother had told her that one doesn't ask questions, ever, about anything between the belly-button and the knees, but, by sitting on her chair and thinking things over, by frightening herself and questioning her ignorant body, by muttering bits of conversation that she'd overheard at home when she was little and too young to understand, she finally reached the conclusion that her baby would come out through her navel. All her terror, then, was concentrated there, in the middle of her body, and when her child struck out with its little feet to remind its mother that it was there, alive and happily preparing for its arrival in the world, she thought, every time, that the doctor had lied to her, that the little devil would rip her belly apart before summer. There were drops of sweat on

her forehead, her breathing became jerky, choppy. She was
overcome by fear. Often, she would put both hands over her
navel, as if to plug it, and she would croon, bent over: 'Go
away, go away, you bloody nuisance. Your mother doesn't
want you and your father's out of his mind.' Léopold Brassard,
like Gabriel, worked nights and slept during the day. In fact,
they both worked in the same place (Gabriel on the presses,
Léopold a linotypist), but they never spoke, merely greeted
one another with a timid 'Bonjour!' when they punched in
together or at the beginning of their half-hour break at ten
o'clock at night. If they left for work at the same time, each
would keep to his own side of the street, parallel roads that
refused to cross. They avoided looking at one another at the
corner of Fabre and Mont-Royal and never sat together in the
streetcar. . . And when Léopold came home from work around
two in the morning, he never went to bed. He would wander
through the house, reading the comics, making something to
eat, big meals (excellent, as a matter of fact; he was a better
cook than his wife and it was he who prepared their food at
night), which he ate as he watched the day break. Then, he
would wait for his wife to get up before going to bed. They
had never been able to get used to each other. Léopold was as
ignorant as Marie-Louise and when this large snivelling person
that he didn't know what to do with arrived in his bed it had
been the greatest humiliation of his life. They took turns in the
conjugal bed. His wife's enormous belly was as great a source of
amazement and terror for Léopold as it was for Marie-Louise.
The child was the fruit of their wedding night, the only night
that they'd spent together, horrible, Léopold scarcely knowing
what to do and doing it badly; Marie-Louise scared to death
when that thing she'd always seen flaccid on her little brothers
penetrated her without her knowing why. She even went so far
as to think Léopold wanted to piss inside her, given that he
was drunk and didn't know what he was doing. Léopold and
Marie-Louise Brassard moved to Montreal immediately after
their honeymoon (a weekend in Quebec City, during which he
hadn't once been sober and she hadn't once stopped crying),
because Léopold got a job at a printshop on Sainte-Catherine.

Marie-Louise was cut off from her village and transplanted onto this foreign street where she knew she'd never put down roots. Like a poorly tended plant, Marie-Louise was dying at her window — from boredom and from fear. In the midst of a maelstrom of passion, joy, cries, jokes, weeping and laughter from the street, she was totally motionless. The street was stifling her like an asphalt cloak.

At the hour when the sun was beginning its slow descent over the wealthy neighbourhoods, Lafontaine Park looked like a forest at dusk. The shadows grew longer, creeping onto the lawns where now, in early May, there grew only frightful little signs that read: 'Keep off the grass,' while the squirrels, less timid, came out of their hiding places and frisked about, chattering wildly; and hydrangeas, like bouquets, formed dark spots in the shadows of the trees. The air was cooler, rather damp, and everything was covered by a weighty calm. It was as though nature was waiting, as though something important was about to happen. In the slanting rays of the setting sun, everything seemed to be in profile. Béatrice too. She was leaning over the railing, standing in the middle of the bridge that joined the two artificial lakes which hadn't yet been filled with water and looked like garbage dumps, full of greasy papers and beer bottles. It was the first time she had seen the lakes empty and it made her sad. 'People are pigs! When will they learn not to dump things wherever they happen to be standing?' She would have preferred not to know that the lakes were artificial, holes that had been dug and filled with cement, basins that had to be drained of their water in the fall and their garbage in the spring, and that the fountain in the middle of the smaller lake was filled with cracks, split open, soon to crumble. In summertime, on splendid silky nights, the lake, crowned with its fountain that changed colours minute by minute, was magical. Everything in the park was beautiful, easy, perfect. But, on this late afternoon, in the golden light of a sun whose journey was coming to an end, its ugliness was hard to bear. 'When you look on the other side of the lake, it's as pretty as a picture and you'd think you were in the middle of the woods, all by yourself and happy, free, but then, you look down and that dump hits you in the eye and you know there's no hope.' Béatrice had given up any hope of finding Mercedes. She didn't know where to go. Above all; she didn't want to return to her apartment. 'I'm flat broke. I haven't got a place to sleep. I mean, I've got one, but I'm scared to go there. All I've got is what's between my legs. It's all I've ever had.' Combing the park, she'd gone right past Mercedes and Richard four or five times without seeing them, perhaps hearing bits of Richard's confession, but unable to imagine that those sobs, that breaking voice, the moans and whispers that she heard, were addressed to her friend whom she could more readily picture in the arms of a client on the verge of apoplexy than bending in sympathy over the suffering of a little boy. She had gone up and down all the paths in the park, all the alleys. She'd seen timid lovers looking down as their hands brushed — and bolder lovers coming out of the bushes, scratched and pink with guilty pleasure. She'd seen pale old men smile at the sun and even greet it, and children playing noisily in the playground. She'd seen a young girl kiss a man on the mouth (her father? the park attendant?) and two little boys fast asleep, neighbours from Fabre Street, under a tree, arms wound lovingly around one another, breaths mingled, calm, serene, abandoned. But not a sign of Mercedes. Nor of any clients either. She lay in the shadow of a maple tree for an hour or so, just thinking. Had the three soldiers kidnapped Mercedes, killed her? Or had the police finally come and raided them (they'd been expecting it for so long)? Who sent the note that she'd found under her door? And what would become of her? Where could she go? Back to her aunt, Ti-Lou, to tell her everything? In the end, all these questions put her to sleep. She dreamed that she was putting on a show in the big hall and that she was on the stage, stark naked, pretending not to notice it and going on with her performance in the midst of the mocking laughter and jeers of a jubilant audience. She awakened soaking wet, lying in the sunlight, exhausted, as if she had just spent one of those agitated nights that are more tiring than restful, and she decided to come and watch the sun die behind the trees in the park. 'There's a time for everything. Like grandma used to say: "Nothing's as important as the only free show the good Lord puts on for us. If you've got any problems when the sun goes down, just forget about them and let yourself be taken over by the orgy of colours your Creator gives you every night. It cheers you up and cleans you out and purifies your soul!" The old witch was right too. Sunset is like a knife that slices the day right in two! When you look at it, you aren't either happy or unhappy. You're just small.' She waited anxiously for the moment (in one hour? two?) when, for a short time, she'd no longer feel anything, neither fear nor sorrow, nor concern, nor that sense of destitution in the face of a problem that wasn't really all that complicated, but which troubled her because she didn't understand it. Leaning against one of the cement tree trunks that served as armrests for people crossing the bridge, made of imitation field stones (cement again), Béatrice began to hum.

Victoire finished her butterscotch sundae and wiped her mouth on the corner of her paper serviette. 'Get a move on! We're going to the Park!' Edouard's ice cream almost went down the wrong way. 'It's five o'clock, Mama!' Victoire had taken a dollar bill from her purse and carefully placed it on the counter. 'We never eat before six-thirty, seven, on Saturday in the summer, so we've got all the time in the world for a little walk.' 'It isn't summer yet.' Victoire looked at Edouard for the first time since they'd sat down at the counter. 'If we miss supper, we miss supper. I haven't set foot outside the house for two years and I feel like taking a little walk in the park! Can't you get that through your thick skull?' She drummed on the counter with her fingertips to attract the attention of Françoise, who was chatting with a customer, leaning forward, her hands spread on the cold marble. Then Victoire turned back to her son, a glimmer of pity in her eye.

'Don't worry, I'll walk faster and you'll be back in time for your soup. Now, don't tell me you'll be ready to eat again in half an hour!' Edouard looked at her, amazed at the change in her tone of voice. 'Don't answer, Edouard. I can tell that you'd say yes and that's depressing.' Françoise added up the bill and took the dollar from the counter, then she muttered, very low, just loud enough for Victoire to hear. 'Look at that! She's paying her bill!' Victoire looked her straight in the eye without replying. The bill came to fifty cents. Françoise brought back the change in dimes, in the hope that Victoire would leave at least one of them as a tip. When she saw the five ten-cent pieces, Victoire smiled. 'Could you change these for a fifty-cent piece please?' Françoise went back to the cash register muttering about customers who preferred their change in large denominations. 'They think it looks better to take out a fifty-cent piece than a bunch of nickels and dimes. Cheapskates!' She brought the fifty-cent coin to Victoire, who immediately put it safely away in her purse. The old woman hissed in Françoise's direction: 'If she thinks she's getting one red cent from me, that one, she's sadly mistaken. If there's one thing I can't stand, it's waitresses that talk behind your back!' Edouard had noticed none of these goings-on, as he was busy scraping the last of the butterscotch from his glass dish. Victoire tapped his arm and got up. 'No use scraping the bottom, my boy. It's all gone!' Françoise stood, frozen by what Victoire had said. She would have liked to leap over the counter and snatch the ridiculous straw hat off the old witch's head, but lately her aggressiveness had been causing problems (she'd slapped one client who tried to untie her apron and told a Madame from boulevard Saint-Joseph to fuck off when she claimed the rice pudding tasted burnt) and she swore she'd keep her head, no matter what — at least until the end of May. Edouard followed his mother, docile as a great flabby dog. Françoise followed the curious couple all the way down the counter, as far as the front window. 'If it wasn't for this counter, she'd've been dead a long time ago, the old bitch! That's right, drag your dimwit son around after you! I should've thought of it before that you two knew each other. You've got the same

nose! Like a grotto! With no Blessed Virgin in it! No wonder
their noses are turned up like that, they're always looking for
shit!' Without knowing he was Victoire's son, Françoise had
never been very fond of Edouard. After all, he was the only
man on Mont-Royal who never flirted with her! All the men
in the neighbourhood found the buxom waitress from Larivière
et Leblanc a tempting dish and not a day went by without one
of them asking her for a date, or something more specific.
Françoise fulminated and distributed slaps and insults, but
deep down, she was very happy. When Edouard came in for
lunch, he never spoke to Françoise, except to order his meal.
He didn't even look up at her. She had developed an aversion to
this obese individual who seemed to prefer fat food to women.
But as he always left a generous tip, she never said anything
nasty to him. Françoise watched Victoire and Edouard turn
the corner, arm in arm, the old woman hobbling after the
fat man, ridiculous in a get-up that, instead of making her
look younger, made her appear even more worn-out, like
someone from another age, a creaky, elderly phantom that
gropes and gesticulates more than it shocks or scares; and the
obese man, her son, standing beside her, stiff with shame, or
with embarrassment at least, turning his head away a little when
she spoke to him, as though nothing she had to say concerned
him or, even worse, as though he were nothing but a scout
helping his first little old lady cross the street. Françoise folded
her arms over her opulent bosom. 'Wonder what her husband
was like to make an elephant like that?' After this profound
reflection, she turned away from the window, attempting to
chase with a wave of her hand the two customers from her
mind. Françoise tended to settle everything in her life this
way: her difficulties in love, as well as an aching shoulder,
even her emotions when they became too strong, on the verge
of uncontrollable. When she was very young, she'd developed
the habit of erasing things that irked her by running the
back of her hand across her forehead, the only gesture that
betrayed the great weariness she tried to hide beneath a layer
of feigned good humour and a tone of voice that was just a
bit too imperious to be really dangerous. This time, though,

her gesture was no help at all. Victoire and Edouard kept
scurrying through her mind. She leaned against the counter for
a moment. 'It wears you out, hating people like that. Life's too
short. But it's hard to forget them, that's the trouble!' Victoire
and Edouard were heading south now, down Papineau, alive
with the cries of countless children abandoned to their fate in
this dangerous road and with the noise of metal rubbing against
metal, of streetcars rattling past, sparking at regular intervals.
At the corner of Marie-Anne, Victoire paused briefly. 'Want to
go home, Mama?' 'No, I'm not tired. Just my leg dragging a
little.' She looked east. She thought of her sister, Ozéa, whom
she hadn't seen for two years, who was probably out rocking
on her balcony, a Saturday paper open on her lap. 'Your aunt
Ozéa's a heartless bitch.' She said nothing more and crossed
Marie-Anne Street with no help from her son. Edouard had said
practically nothing since they left the house. He was too afraid
of giving in to his rage, which would have made Victoire very
happy. He was afraid of saying things to his mother that he'd
regret later, things which would have delighted the old lady.
As he watched her limping, clinging to his arm, he shuddered
and wanted to scream. This exhausting relationship with his
mother had undermined his life and only now that he was over
thirty-five was he beginning to realize that he was no more
than a silvery-coloured fish, an object wriggling in Victoire's
aquarium, as she feasted on this spectacle of captivity, giving
him only leftover scraps of love to nibble on and changing his
water only when he was near to suffocate. Contact with his
mother electrified him, obsessed him, drained all his energy
— and yet, he needed it. His evening flights, the nights that
he spent outside, in other places, other arms, were basically
only unimportant episodes, intense interludes, of course, that
left him deeply marked by experience (furtive sulphur-scented
touches, small closed infernos that were consumed in a few
hours, then quickly transformed into memories that one would
like to think of as blasphemous), but they remained interludes,
for the most important part of his life was lived within the walls
of his mother's house — the squabbling, the fights, the duels,
the reunions that he thought he hated so much, were really

his own skeleton, his nervous system, his heart and blood. As long as his mother was alive, he could only move around on the fringes of her will, circling her like a dependent satellite, submissive to laws that were not of his making, stripped of any self-determination and, most of all, of choice; and the day she ceased to live he would, perhaps, die with her, disarmed, disconnected, at a loose end, a dismembered puppet forgotten in a corner, gathering dust and indifference — unless he were suddenly to blossom, experiencing all his springtimes at once, exuberant, overflowing, high on delight, drunk on freedom, in control of himself at last, holding the reins with a firm but mad hand, and riding hell for leather to make up for lost time. He knew only too well that he'd be offered this choice one day — he dreamed of it — but no matter how often he told himself that his mother's death would be a deliverance, the very notion of being deprived of her — her voice, her expression, her odours — terrified him. Victoire had taken her son's arm again, though he didn't realize it, lost as he was in his unfathomable dilemma. As they passed the church of the Immaculate Conception, Victoire suddenly emerged from her thoughts as if she'd just found the solution to a very important problem. 'No wonder Ozéa's crazy, the whole parish is full of lunatics! Priests that plant corn out the back of their church aren't for real! Even the priest back home in the country wouldn't do a thing like that, for Chrissake! They ought to be looking after my sister's soul instead of their tomatoes!' She had spoken loud enough so that the two priests, who had just spent the afternoon trying to dig even furrows in the rich earth of their garden to be could hear. They looked up at the old woman and smiled. One of the priests took out a big checked handkerchief and wiped his forehead. 'Give us your sister's address, Madame, and we'll drop our tomatoes right away!' Victoire shrugged. 'Oh, never mind. You don't seem bright enough to know the difference between a tomato and a cucumber anyway! I wouldn't be doing my sister any favour!' The two priests burst out laughing. 'I wonder where they dig up these new priests nowadays? In the loony bin? Come on, my boy. They're too depressing.' On the other side of the street, the park beckoned. For a long time,

Victoire looked at the trees. At last, she looked at Edouard. Her eyes were misty. 'Here's where I made you, my boy. Come on, I'll show you the place.'

Gabriel came and stood beside Béatrice on the bridge. He had recognized her in the distance, in the pale green polka-dot dress that she usually wore on Sundays in the summer, when she and her friend walked back and forth past his house, laughing, singing and shocking just about everybody with their insolent manner and their makeup, garish in these austere times. Albertine would say of them: 'They ought to be shot like criminals! As far as I'm concerned, I have to hold myself back to keep from smashing their windows!' Victoire merely smiled, occasionally muttering something like: 'Must be times when they'd like to smash *our* windows too! We don't make life any easier for them. If they weren't such floozies and you were a little more like one, the house'd be more fun — and the rest of the neighbourhood too!' Béatrice had seen Gabriel coming, staggering a little. She recognized her neighbour, whom she thought a nice man because he was so discreet and because he always seemed embarrassed. She wondered if he might be not quite so shy when he'd been drinking. Gabriel didn't approach Béatrice and Béatrice didn't move, on purpose; she went on humming some old hit of Damia's or some new one by Charles Trenet, she wasn't too sure which. She wondered if he'd dare speak to her. But Gabriel kept his head down. Without saying a word. The light was more and more golden and now there was some green mixed in with the blue of the sky, a fleeting green that disappeared if you looked at it directly, but reappeared as soon as you looked to the side, bright, vibrant and soft, all at once. Gabriel was thinking of how he himself had just fled, run straight here, defeated on his own ground by some bum who didn't even know what he was talking about and whom he himself had just filled with beer and a show of friendship. Ten times, he thought of returning to the tavern to smash the jaw of that stinking bundle of rags, but each time, the shame of being seen by his friends held him back. Another day, perhaps, next week or the week after that, but not now. He was suffering too much. Finally, Béatrice spoke first, not looking at him, however, but staring off towards the tops of the trees that circled the lake. 'You don't look so hot.' 'When a man gets called yellow, it messes up his day.' 'Who called you yellow?' 'Somebody that might have been right.' He seemed to hesitate for a moment, then suddenly, he approached her. 'What do you think? You know a lot about men, even though you're still pretty young? Do you really think we got our wives pregnant so we wouldn't have to fight in the war?' Béatrice looked at him for the first time. 'Yes. And I think you did the right thing.' She went back to the treetops, just as Gabriel, in turn, looked at her. She kept speaking, but very softly, as if she were speaking to herself. 'I don't know why men go and get themselves killed over on the other side. I don't understand a thing about the war.' 'If you really want to know, neither do I. Only thing the war does is move the pile of shit from one place to another! Doesn't matter which side wins. How's it going to change things for you and me? We aren't important enough, neither one of us, and we're too far away from it all for our lives to be any different if either the Germans or the Allies win! Everybody tries to scare us by saying the Germans and the Wops will come over here if they win the war. . . . Come on! It'll take them forever to put Europe back together again. They won't have any spare time to be thinking about us!' With the help of the beer, he became impassioned. (He was standing in the middle of the tavern surrounded by his friends who asked nothing more than to let themselves be convinced by what he said — and he was getting ready to spawn one of those endless speeches that had made him a local hero. He'd let himself go for hours, winning them over one by one, reading on their faces now surprise, now anger; he'd make them laugh, weep, applaud; he'd descend to the darkest melodrama to draw gasps of pain from them, then, suddenly, he'd ascend to summits of promises and good faith, hand on his heart and head held high; for a long time, he'd soar, following the winds of his inspiration, repeating the same thing a hundred times

— but in a hundred different ways; and, once again, he'd be
Gabriel, king of the tavern orators, the most listened-to and
most respected man in Plateau Mont-Royal!) 'I didn't get my
wife pregnant so I wouldn't have to go and fight, but I'm glad
she's pregnant anyway! And I got a feeling that's why she did
it! Maybe she's even risking her life for me!' He didn't believe
a word he was saying, but what difference did it make. He was
talking! And talking well! 'Let them do whatever they want,
this side or over there. I know I'm scared. I shouldn't've got
her pregnant because I know very well she's too fat and too
old. . . But I did it. And now, she's been stuck in the corner
of that room for months. She can't walk, can't even get up. . .
When Doctor Sanregret comes over, he looks at me like I'm the
world champion jerk. . . . But I'm not! I love my wife! And
I want that child! Can you understand that?' Béatrice cut him
off with an abrupt gesture. 'He's just like all the others! When
he's sober, he's too ashamed — and when he's had a few, there
isn't an ounce of shame left!' Gabriel, surprised, pulled himself
together and apologized. 'I'm a bit drunk. Had a lot of beer.
Too much. Thought I was back in the tavern with my buddies.'
Béatrice ran her right hand over her skirt as if she were brushing
off imaginary crumbs. 'That's the problem. Whenever a man
talks to me, he thinks he's talking to somebody else — his wife,
his friends. He gives me his confession as if I was a priest, but
no man ever just takes me for myself!' Suddenly, she didn't
want to see him any more. She wished he'd disappear like
the others after they'd taken their pleasure and paid for it.
She wanted to be alone in the sunset and forget everything.
She straightened up, took a few steps and came back to him.
'There's men that pay me to listen to what you've just told
me, so I don't see why you should do it for free!' 'You're the
one that asked me what was wrong. . .' She turned around
and walked to the other end of the bridge. He followed her.
'I'm sorry. If you're going back home, at least I can walk with
you. And you can tell me your problems too. . .' 'You'll lose
your reputation as a good family man if anybody sees you with
me.' 'After this afternoon, I haven't got much of a reputation
left to lose. Anyway, let people think whatever they want.'

Béatrice realized that she was getting ready to tell this man everything. Maybe he wasn't as mean as the others, after all. Though they'd talked for a good ten minutes, he hadn't made the slightest dirty remark. So Béatrice prepared to unburden her heart. But as they were crossing Calixa-Lavallée, Gabriel noticed Thérèse, Marcel and Philippe leaving the playground. Philippe was walking very strangely, as though he were sick, and Gabriel began running towards him. 'Flip, what's wrong? Are you sick?' Béatrice watched him move away. 'So soon. . .'

Albertine slammed the two empty bottles on the counter. 'You there, Marie?' Marie-Sylvia's voice came to her from the very back of the shop. 'Yes, yes. . . coming.' Albertine heard the toilet flush, then saw Marie-Sylvia emerge from the storeroom, carrying two molasses cookies and a big glass of milk. 'You eat in the toilet?' 'If I pour myself a glass of milk when Duplessis's here, he bugs me till he gets one too, so I started having my five o'clock snack in the bathroom. It's no dirtier than anywhere else, you know. . . If the bowl's clean. . .' 'Cut it out, I'm going to throw up!' Marie-Sylvia put her cookies and milk beside Albertine's empties. 'I'm going to let you down, I'm afraid, my poor Madame. . . I'm right out of Larose spruce beer. . . Sold the last bottle to Monsieur Brassard this morning. You know what it's like. There's a war on. . . I don't know if they're running out of spruce trees or not, but we're having a hell of a time getting spruce beer.' 'You blame everything on the war! For three years now, all the lazy slobs in the world have been trying to make us believe that if we can't get anything any more, it's because of the war!' Albertine picked up her bottles. 'My weekend's shot to hell now. That's my Sunday treat — to sit out on the balcony with two bottles of Larose. You know that! So how come you didn't keep me one, at least? I've been a customer here longer than those two rats that hide inside their hole because they're so scared of the big city!' Marie-Sylvia was standing with her elbows on the counter. She looked at her milk and cookies.

'You don't even listen when we complain, Marie. We'll end up taking our business somewhere else!' Albertine turned and headed for the door. Marie-Sylvia looked up suddenly. 'Have you seen my cat?' 'He clawed me and then he took off, the little beggar!' Albertine turned to her as she opened the door. 'Generally, you're the one that knows where everybody is. . .' 'I've been keeping an eye out for him all afternoon. . . I saw the two floozies go by, one after the other; I saw your kids going on their picnic; I saw Madame Ouimet going to Saint-Joseph and coming back; I saw. . .' 'But you didn't see your cat.' 'No. He's just been gone for three days. You know what it's like, nature. . . But usually, he comes home to stay for a week, all tuckered out. . .' 'I didn't see him. I was in the house the whole blessed day. . . But I've got better things to do than look for cats!' She slammed the door behind her. Marie-Sylvia shrugged. 'Charming as ever. . .' She was preparing to go back to the bathroom when the door opened again, making the little bell ring. Albertine stuck her head inside. 'How many bottles did Monsieur Brassard buy?' 'Four. That's all that I had left.' Albertine disappeared without thanking Marie-Sylvia, who settled comfortably into her armchair. 'For once. . . After all, Duplessis isn't here. . .' Even as she ate, her head was turned towards the window. Albertine was walking purposefully across the lane towards the house where Marie-Louise and Léopold Brassard lived, the second house from the corner. From their balcony, Florence, Violette, Mauve and Rose saw her open the gate in the wrought-iron fence. Mauve looked at her sisters, then at her mother. 'Will you tell me what she's doing there?' As Albertine walked past the living room window, she saw Marie-Louise's shadow behind the lace curtain. 'She's nailed down in there, if you ask me!' Marie-Louise had become a sort of legend. She was a familiar ghost people had grown accustomed to, knowing she was always there, but not bothered about her. When people passed her house, they knew she was there at her window, but they no longer even bothered to check. If they said hello, she didn't answer. Richard called her 'the eyes in the curtain,' a name that had the good fortune to terrify Marcel, who imagined there were, in fact, eyes sewn into the curtains at that window. When Marcel got on Richard's nerves too much playing on the sidewalk, the older boy would say to him: 'The eyes in the curtain will pick you up and eat you!' Marcel would stand there, paralyzed, and look anxiously on the other side of the street. 'Whose eyes?' 'Nobody's. The eyes in the curtain.' Albertine rang three times before the door opened. 'They're dead. He polished off his four bottles and blew up!' After two long minutes, a small silhouette could be seen behind the door. Marie-Louise. 'I wanted to talk to him in person, but oh well.' Marie-Louise opened the door a crack and looked out timorously. She said nothing, simply watched Albertine, who stood there for a moment not knowing what attitude to assume. 'Maybe she's dumb. Or deaf. Or crazy. Or maybe all three!' She cleared her throat and raised an empty bottle to the level of Marie-Louise's eyes. 'Bonjour, Madame Brassard. Sorry to bother you right at suppertime, but, you see, I just went over to Marie's to buy my spruce beer and she tells me she just sold the last to your husband. Four bottles. So I was wondering if you could sell me one. . . I wouldn't think that the two of you would drink all that by Monday. . . Marie said she'd be getting a truckload — no, a boatload — on Monday morning, but that's too late because I only drink it Sunday afternoon, out on the balcony and. . .' Marie-Louise had already disappeared, leaving the door ajar. Albertine stuck her nose against the glass and looked inside. 'What am I doing here? Is she going to play ball? Now I don't know what to do!' A few moments later, Marie-Louise was back with a cold bottle of spruce beer, which she handed to Albertine through the half-open door, then took one of the two empties Albertine was holding, and gently closed the door. Albertine was flabbergasted. 'Maybe I wanted to play!' She bent down and slipped a quarter into the mailbox, a slot at the bottom of the door. 'Keep the change and buy yourself some manners!'

The fat woman had tried to go back to *Bug-Jargal*, but the lines
of print danced before her eyes and she knew, in any case, that
she'd never be able to concentrate enough to follow the story.
'Too much is going on today. Escape's out of the question!'
Even the name Acapulco, printed in her head in iridescent
letters, couldn't make her dream. 'It's silly to dream about
Acapulco when I can't even get up to pee!' Her conversation
with Albertine, or rather, the long list of insults that her sister-
in-law showered on her, convinced the fat woman of the validity
of the suspicion that had been gnawing at her conscience for
some time, but which she'd dismissed or repressed. She knew
that members of her family and Gabriel's family, the women in
particular, denounced her pregnancy as obscene, a scandalous
state of affairs, a blot on the family's honesty and integrity, an
attempt to provoke fate, which, in turn, would punish her,
when she least expected it, giving her perhaps a deformed or
an abnormal child, at any rate taking revenge on her. As for
the men. . . she knew so few of them, if the truth be told.
And it was so hard to know what they were really thinking.
Her brother, Léo, had come to see her a few weeks earlier
and had looked at her strangely, concentrating on her face and
avoiding her belly, his lips stretched out in a smile. He even
looked her in the eye and told her how thrilled he was, but
everything in his expression contradicted him. She would have
preferred it if he'd shouted insults at her too, then at least she
would have known how he felt and been able to try to explain
everything. . . But no. His feigned good temper made contact
impossible and Léo left the same false smile. Edouard, at first,
seemed embarrassed when he found out that another squalling
voice would be added to the ones already polluting the house,
but gradually, perhaps out of pity for the fat woman as he saw
her body changing shape from day to day, uncomplaining,
except sometimes late at night when the tension became too
great and a fit of rage, brief but devastating, would shake her
for several minutes, unleashing floods of tears and cries; or
perhaps because he sensed that she really wanted this child,
that she needed it to go on living, and he began to talk to her
in the morning before he left for work, and in the evening when

he came home, even going so far as to serve her breakfast or supper, telling jokes and making faces to amuse her (she who was so fond of such things), running his hand over her stomach, saying: 'He's going to weigh two tons and we'll have to buy a whole herd of cows!' Her husband, Gabriel, the big child she'd been protecting for twenty years, keeping her most serious concerns to herself so that he never suspected their existence, always singing when he got up in the afternoon or late in the morning, though tears would often have been fitting, even necessary; her husband, so understanding that it sometimes bowled her over, had given her this gift without asking any questions, gladly complying as soon as she told him that she wanted another child and rejoicing when she told him that the baby was 'on the way' and that she was happy. At times the fat woman wondered if Gabriel was hiding as much from her as she did from him, if he wasn't far sharper than she thought. 'Maybe we hide the same things from each other without knowing it and we settle our problems twice, each in his own way, thinking that the other's completely in the dark.' She smiled at the thought. In fact, she really enjoyed this complicity in camouflage. But was Gabriel happy at the prospect of another child? She couldn't say. 'Yes, maybe. For sure.' The only one in the family who seemed truly pleased at the news was Victoire's brother, Josaphat-the-Violin, who had hugged the fat woman with his knotted, powerful arms, not saying a word but showing her that he understood, encouraging her, letting her know that he would back her in her struggle, support her against the others, defend her and help her as much as he could. All this she already knew. She lived it every day. She'd finally become almost immune to it. But what Albertine told her confused her, even though she was expecting it — what the street, their neighbours, friends, acquaintances were saying about her. This sentence, with no right of appeal, this refusal to accept such a vital need, this crass ignorance that put restraints and limits on her freedom and spat upon her choice — yes, her choice — to procreate, to gestate, to give birth despite the fact that she was over forty, insulted her to the very depths of her being. What right did a neighbourhood have to decide

when and where a woman was entitled to have children? What
right did they have to decree that a forty-year-old woman who
wanted a child was a degenerate? Who dared to say that being
pregnant was ugly? She wanted this child. She needed it and
she was beautiful! Her stomach contracted suddenly and the
baby kicked her. The fat woman uttered a small cry of delight
as she brought her hands down to her thighs, running them
gently over her belly, touching, trying to guess where the head
was, where the limbs were — laughing, happy, thrilled. 'You're
going to put me through the wringer, you little devil, but I'll be
glad to see you anyway!'

'It was a wonderful day! People everywhere. The paths, the
streets, even the grass. Just that once the park was full of
beautiful women wearing long dresses and men got up like
waiters in a fancy restaurant. . . You see, the people that
arranged the party had asked all the women to wear white.
The rest of us — my sister and me, for instance — we didn't
have white, so we wore the palest-coloured dresses that we
had.' Victoire was taking small steps; she was transformed,
rejuvenated. 'Back then, you see, Lafontaine Park wasn't like
it is today. It was a lot prettier. In 1906, the streets had hardly
been paved and there were hardly any cars in Montreal! Every
Sunday afternoon, your aunt Ozéa and I, we'd come and sit
by the refreshment stand and watch Montreal's high society
parading past us in their carriages. . . People took their time in
those days — they didn't shoot across the park the way they do
now, like an accident looking for a place to happen!' Edouard
listened to his mother, his hands clasped behind his back. He
knew that she could walk without his help now. She was two
or three paces ahead of him and, from time to time, she would
turn around, talk to him, wait, then dart off again. A different
woman. 'You'd've thought you were in the middle of the
country! You can't imagine what it was like! At the edge of the
lake there, if you shut your eyes. . .' Victoire stopped, closed
her eyes, took a deep breath, as if she were seeking some odour

that had vanished, dissolved long ago. 'Nowadays, you can always hear some car shrieking or the chip stall whistling!' They crossed Emily Duployé and entered that section of the park that was calm, reserved for pedestrians. Everything seemed ablaze in the setting sun. Victoire laid her hand on her son's arm. Her voice became confidential. 'When I see more than ten trees together, my heart explodes, as if I was going to die. . . I've been a prisoner in the big city for forty-five years now and I still haven't got used to it!' Edouard, overwhelmed, wanted to make some gesture towards his mother, but she turned away. 'The city of Montreal put on a big party to inaugurate the first gondola on the big lake. Believe me, that was a sight! A gondola in Montreal! We got a look at it before anybody else because it arrived the week before the party and we came and watched the workers set it up on logs, so that it could slip into the water nice and easy during the ceremony. . . We couldn't get over it! A gondola ride in the middle of Montreal! I was so excited about it I couldn't get to sleep at night. . . All the papers were talking about the big party and there were so many people that all the streets around the park were blocked. Your father and I, and Albertine and Gabriel, who were still babies, met there at nine in the morning so we'd have good places, even though the party started at two! I brought a big blanket and we all laid down on it, right out there in the open. . . Ozéa and her husband came over and joined us. . . Oh, it was a wonderful day! Some people even hid in the bushes the night before and slept out under the stars. That gave me ideas. . . When the rich people's carriages started arriving, the rest of us, the poor, got up so that we could watch them.' She pointed to Calixa-Lavallée in the distance. 'They came that way, along Rachel, then they turned right at the path that goes to the bridge, went across (they had special permission) and got out right in front of the refreshment stand. There were hundreds and hundreds of guests with invitations. . . The rest of us didn't have any invitations. We weren't even supposed to be on the same side of the lake as them. We were on the other side of the lake, across there but we could see as clear as day. Everything went on right in front of us, like a show. . . The gondola — it wasn't the same one

as today — it was prettier and a lot bigger too. Like I told you
a while ago, they'd put it up on logs so it could slide into the
water. . . It was up on the grass, on the hill. . . Your father
said it was dipping its nose a little too much for his liking,
but he was so critical, remember. . . So, the ceremony started
around two-thirty, three o'clock. . . There was a fanfare that
played John Philip Sousa and all the rest. . . Speeches. We
couldn't hear a thing, but we clapped all the same! Anyhow,
the stage faced the invited guests, so the rest of us could only
see the backs of the people that were talking. Then, afterwards,
the mayor's wife walked over to the gondola with a bottle of
champagne and she hit it so hard that the goddamn bottle
broke! She got quite a surprise, let me tell you, with hot
champagne spilling all over her hands! But it didn't seem to
bother anybody else; the guests all clapped as if nothing had
happened. It takes a lot to upset those people, you know. I
wanted to offer her a cloth to wipe her hands off, but your
father said she could use her dress. I think that's what she did.
Anyway, she took off her gloves — I saw that with my own eyes
— and they were all wet. And just then, a worker comes up with
an axe and gives the first log a good whack. I don't really know
how it worked, but the logs started rolling down the hill with
the gondola rolling after them. . . We were all standing up,
clapping like crazy. . . The gondola took a dive when it hit
the water — and then, it sank straight to the bottom! It just sat
there with its nose at the bottom of the water and its rear-end
in the air, the motor dangling over the grass. Maybe you can't
imagine it, but that spoiled a lot of people's fun. . . Not your
father though. He got down on all fours on the blanket and
started laughing like a soul in hell. I was so ashamed — it was
no joke! But then, everybody else around us started laughing
too, and pretty soon, the only people that weren't laughing
were the fancy pants on the other side of the lake. They were
all holding on to their tickets that gave them a free boatride
and let me tell you, their jaws dropped down to their knees.
The mayor disappeared; the councillors all took off; even the
wardens from the Immaculate Conception parish, who'd been
standing there during the ceremony as stiff as sticks, thawed

out and went and hid in the refreshment stand. Then, all of a sudden, the gondola started cracking, like rotten old wood, and the rear-end landed on the grass. The motor blew up and then it caught fire. Your father couldn't take any more, he nearly bust a gut laughing. Then, the people around us started clapping again and the men were shouting all kinds of things: "Put out the fire, it isn't St John the Baptist's Day yet!" "Next week, put the mayor on logs!" "Say, Mr Mayor, reminds you of the city budget, doesn't it? Waterlogged to the neck, with its motor buzzing around." In less than fifteen minutes all the carriages had disappeared and the rich people's side was empty; the rest of us were walking around the lake to see the damage. It really bothered me, but everybody else seemed to think it was funny, so I started laughing too. The men made jokes about it all afternoon. There was a fellow from Saint-Henri who'd brought his accordion, so it wasn't long before we had another party going. I still couldn't tell you where the beer came from, but it came and we celebrated St John the Baptist's Day a month early!' Victoire had stopped walking as she spoke. She was leaning against a tree. 'You wonder how come I'm telling you all this today, out of the blue, eh?' Edouard smiled. 'I guess that's the day you made me. . . You told me a while ago that you were going to show me where. . .' 'Come here. . .' She took his hand, drawing him towards a bush with buds that had started to open. 'On our way home for supper, right around now, your father said: "Victoire, the kids are dead on their feet, we ought to put them down on the grass and lie down for a while ourselves." I knew what he was getting at, so. . .' She looked at Edouard for a long time. 'I wasn't all that crazy about. . . but I wanted another baby and I knew it was the right time. . .' Edouard was looking down. It was the first time he'd heard his mother make any reference to sex and he was embarrassed. But Victoire went on with her story, looking back towards the bush. 'Then he asked me: "Is it risky now?" and I told him no. He didn't want any more children. I never knew why. . . And he said: "That's good!" And then, we made you.' She walked into the grove, ignoring the branches that caught at her dress. She bent down slightly. 'Right here.'

She turned abruptly towards her son. 'I'm so bored with my life, you can't imagine! I haven't got a single blessed thing to do! I feel so useless!' Edouard ran towards her and took her in his arms. 'Stay with me, son. You're all I've got now!'

Gérard Bleau was so badly shaken by the incident with Thérèse that he hadn't noticed it was past the closing time of the playground. Very few children were left at such a late hour: five-year-old twins, who hadn't stopped squabbling all day now, continued their games beneath the vacant stare of their mother who had hardly moved since morning but merely said, from time to time, in a tired, plaintive voice: 'Gisèle, my head's splitting!' or: 'Micheline, cut it out, or Mama's going to fling you out of the swing!'; a little boy who had spent the whole afternoon on the whirligig without getting sick was screaming now because he was alone and couldn't make it spin; a few little girls in the sandbox giggled as they dug up turds deposited by some feline in search of love; and the trio from Fabre Street: Thérèse, Philippe and Marcel, whom Gérard Bleau dared not look at for fear of meeting the little girl's eyes, were playing on the big slide, uttering cries of delight that most likely could be heard all the way down to Sherbrooke. The day that Gérard Bleau had spent keeping an eye on the children had been fascinating for him because it wasn't his usual job. He'd agreed to replace a sick friend who had sung the praises of hours spent in the sun amidst children's cries and the singing of birds — but he had not enjoyed most of the day. Gérard Bleau was a mechanic at Provincial Transport and he usually spent Saturday getting shamelessly drunk, starting at ten in the morning and drinking beer after beer, until he was legless — no matter where, no matter how. It was the same every week. But Sunday, he'd get up, fresh as a daisy, with a song on his lips, and go hunting. The women in the neighbourhood knew him well and some would come out on their balconies to watch him pass by or they'd even approach him — the darling of Dorion, the Don Juan of Sherbrooke. That morning, though,

Monsieur Gariépy, whose house he roomed at, got up with a
raging toothache, maintaining that he'd kill all the children in
the park if he went to work. Monsieur Gariépy, the playground
attendant at Lafontaine Park for nearly twelve years now, was
old and ugly, but the children adored him. They called him
'Grampa' and rubbed against him like selfish little cats. From
May to September (weekends in May and June and every day
in July and August), you could see Grampa Gariépy, a dead
pipe in his mouth, frowning, keeping an eye on the children,
handing out punishments and rewards, as if he were the good
Lord in person. Sometimes, he eyed the little girls a bit too
closely, especially the plump ones, whom he called his 'chubby
little angels,' but he never made any improper advances; he was
content to walk behind them when they climbed the ladders
or the slides. But, Grampa Gariépy was getting on and the
prospect of spending another summer in the park didn't fill
him with delight. Which was why he wanted to say no when
they called him the week before to say that the playground
would open on the second of May and that he should be
there at ten o'clock on Saturday morning. He'd even talked
about it to his wife, who greeted the news with a scream.
Grandma Gariépy had no desire to spend the summer with
her old man hanging around the house and she insisted that
he agree to work for another season. In the end, he gave in
— as usual. But this raging toothache — for real since the
stumps of Grampa Gariépy's teeth were dying in tartar and
pipe juice — was the old man's salvation — for that weekend,
at any rate. So, Gérard Bleau set off for the park with no
particular enthusiasm, with even some apprehension, as he'd
never been fond of children, considering them to be interfering
little showoffs. Not one child had come all morning and Gérard
felt like running away to the nearest tavern, thinking it was too
early in the season for parents to bring their children to the park
to play. Bored to death, he hung around the two park benches,
cursing Grampa Gariépy's toothache. At noon, a few mothers
turned their children over to him, asking him to feed them
around three and wash their faces and take them to the public
toilets. Amazed, Gérard said nothing and let the women go. He

fed a few children in the middle of the afternoon, but he neither
washed them nor took them to the toilets. The children who
knew where the toilets were went by themselves and the others
calmly went in their pants — without stopping their play. By
four o'clock, Gérard had around thirty children to look after,
but using his charm (he knew he was handsome and had no
qualms about using his angelic good looks), he went to see
the few mothers who were there, and asked them to take over
for him. He fluttered his eyelashes and used his tenor voice
and it worked — as usual. (Hadn't his own mother told him
before she died: 'I gave you good looks. Now, use them! If you
know how to do that, you'll never have to work! Use women,
let them support you, save your money — and most of all —
never get married!') He was at a loose end and the afternoon
was beginning to seem twice as long. The arrival of Thérèse,
Philippe and Marcel was a pleasant diversion that allowed
him to focus his attention on the unfortunate little cripple,
towards whom he thought his behaviour was highly charitable.
He even spent a good half-hour trying to imagine a day in
the life of the young invalid, but imagination wasn't Gérard
Bleau's strong point and all he managed to do was contemplate
Philippe having a pee. Gérard Bleau had never been afraid
of women; on the contrary, he had followed his mother's
advice and quickly learned to use women, soon becoming an
out-and-out charmer, sometimes spending hours at his mirror
trying out new pouts and winks. It was so easy for him to
conquer women that he tired of it. For some time, out of
sheer laziness, he even waited for women to throw themselves
at him. Women, yes, but little girls. . . The erection brought on
by Thérèse had literally terrified him and he almost ran away,
back to his house and his bed. What he felt came quickly and
violently — and he understood that he could never do without it
again. The mixture of fear and sexual pleasure contained a new
source of delight, whose existence he'd never even suspected
before: danger. His sex life had always been too easy for him
to really appreciate it. Thérèse, with her not-so-innocent kiss
of a little girl who asks too many questions, gave him a glimpse
of horizons streaked with the red of shame and the black of sin,

exciting him tremendously and gave macabre overtones to the
danger, making it an inviting secret ceremony ruled by guilt,
concealment and remorse. He regretted the incident, but how
he'd enjoyed it! When he finally came out of his torpor at almost
half-past five, he blew the whistle that Grampa Gariépy had lent
him with all his might. The peeved mother collected her twins;
the spinning little boy kicked at the whirligig; and Thérèse,
Philippe and Marcel slid one last time down the boards that had
been polished by the buttocks of generations of ill-fed children.
Philippe, who hadn't missed the fact that the attendant was no
longer looking their way, had stopped playing cripple and was
just beginning to enjoy the afternoon when he heard the whistle
blow. 'Just when I was starting to have some fun!' Thérèse
pulled up her little brother's trousers, which, in the course of
the day, had picked up certain suspect colours. 'Philippe, when
we leave the playground, you're going to have to cross your eyes
again — and your legs too!' And they walked past Gérard Bleau:
Thérèse, pink with joy and confusion; Philippe, limping more
than ever; Marcel, adorable and repulsive. Gérard's glance
followed Thérèse for several seconds and he began to feel the
same agitation, the same rush of adrenalin that shook him and
left him tense and wild with expectation. 'Gotta find out where
she lives. . .' He followed the three children and was the first
one to spot Gabriel crossing the street, gesticulating wildly and
running towards them. Gérard hid behind a tree. Suddenly,
he was overcome with remorse. 'God Almighty, am I going
to spend my whole life hiding behind trees?' But pleasure
overcame his remorse and Gérard Bleau, shaken by spasms,
pressed his forehead against the bark of the tree.

'You don't have to tell him about the mysteries of life! I've
already told him all that!' Victoire and Edouard saw Mercedes
and Richard coming towards them, hand in hand, the little
boy smiling at last, his back straight and eyes bright. Edouard
expected his mother to fling herself at the young woman, with
her claws out, calling her a wanton floozy, but Victoire merely

held out her hand to Richard. 'Did she do anything to you?'
'No, we just talked. I needed to talk.' 'To a stranger?' 'Yes.
What I had to say was too serious. I couldn't tell anybody in
the family.' Victoire turned her back to Mercedes and pulled
her grandson along by the hand. Edouard smiled at the young
woman. 'Thank you, Mademoiselle. . .' 'Mercedes.' 'Is this
your day off?' 'Yes. No. Yes.' They both burst out laughing and
Mercedes took Edouard's arm. 'I used to see you at the Penguin
a few years ago. . . but you wouldn't remember me. . . You
didn't pay much attention to the women.' 'You used to work
there?' 'You call that work? Fatso Petit wasn't a boss, she was
an army general! And I wasn't interested in marching in step.'
'So now you're. . . on your own?' 'Yeah. . . It isn't always a
picnic, but at least I've got my peace of mind.' Victoire was
leaning on Richard's shoulder. Richard stuck his hands in his
pockets. 'Did she tell you everything?' He suddenly blushed,
going with no gradation from white to crimson in less than five
seconds. 'You don't want to talk about it?' 'No.' 'Well, it's your
conscience. If you'd asked me. . .' That was what everyone in
this family always said when a child, an adolescent or even an
adult, spoke to someone else. But nothing was further from the
truth: Victoire would never have spoken of those things, not to
anyone. She had kept her own children completely ignorant of
the facts of life and she didn't regret it. (It was Paul, finally,
who had told Albertine of her 'conjugal duty'; and it was only
a week before Gabriel got married that he managed to find a
priest sufficiently versed to give him some information. As for
Edouard. . . from early childhood, experience had shown him
more than his mother would ever know.) Just then, the sound
of someone shouting made them all turn around and Philippe
burst out from behind a clump of bushes, pursued by his father,
about to explode. 'Don't ever give me a scare like that again,
you goddamn little monkey! I thought you were going to have
a fit and convulsions!' But Philippe was agile and he managed to
get away from his father, now panting like a seal. They stopped
directly in front of Victoire, as if they'd been caught out in the
middle of some dirty trick. Philippe hesitated for a moment,
then hid behind his grandmother. She eyed Gabriel, frowning.

'Drunk again!' 'It's Saturday!' Her brow smoothed out. 'Well, in that case. . .' Why not — a man who worked like a slave all week to feed his family was entitled to get drunk on Saturday. 'What're you doing in the park, Mama?' 'It's Saturday! You get drunk, I go for a walk!' She took her two grandsons by the hand and walked away. Philippe, who knew very well that he'd just escaped a well-deserved thrashing, made himself as small as he could. 'What monkey business have you been up to now?' He didn't answer and Victoire sighed. 'That's right, everybody stop talking to me! Cut me out of your lives, like some old dry branch, and leave me to die in my corner.' Gabriel followed them, his head hanging. 'He was pretending he was crippled, Mama, and I thought he was sick.' 'Shut up, you! I didn't ask you anything, you damn blabbermouth!' Béatrice, who was walking behind Gabriel with Thérèse and Marcel, threw herself into Mercedes' arms, crying. 'Where have you been, for God's sake?' 'I'll tell you everything later.' 'I looked for you all afternoon!' Betty looked at Edouard. 'Clients?' 'Of course not. Calm down, everything will work out fine. . .' 'What happened at the house?' Mercedes lowered her voice. 'Wait till we're alone.' Marcel held out his arms to his uncle Edouard who, making a face, lifted him in the air. 'If you were a little piggy, I'd say you smelled good, but you stink, goddamn it!' Thérèse was resting her head against Edouard's arm. 'And you there, in the clouds, you look like you're in love!' Thérèse looked at her uncle, shocked. And they all began to walk. A very strange procession emerged from the park. Leading it was a broken-down old woman dragging two little boys by the hand, the first, tall, pale, bony, with ears sticking out of his head, frequently running his hand over his trousers as if to erase some invisible stain; the second, short and chubby, trying to conceal a tic that made his left eye blink; followed by a clearly tipsy man, his hands in his pockets, his eyes to the ground, his back bent. Next came two very beautiful young women with their arms around each other's waists, the younger one leaning against the older one's shoulder, taking refuge in her sweet soapy odour; and finally, a fat man who drew up the rear, with a grubby little boy in his arms and a

too serious little girl clutching his jacket pocket. What made
the group so bizarre was the fact that no one was speaking;
everyone seemed lost in thought, almost unaware of the others'
presence. They walked slowly along Fabre Street, which was
completely empty. They could just as well have been returning
from a wedding where they'd enjoyed themselves too much, or
emerging unharmed from some cataclysm. Their features were
erased by fatigue, so that it looked as if they were coming from
nowhere, from no time; a procession with no destination or
meaning going down a deserted street that smelled of supper.
It was six o'clock and Montreal's one hundred church bells
proudly chimed the hour. A man was following them, far
behind, hesitant, confused, a wild look in his eyes. A fallen
angel trying to tag along in a parade from which he had been
banned. A moth attracted by a fatal flame. At the corner of
Marie-Anne, Mercedes seemed to shake off her torpor. 'We'll
leave you here. We can't go back to our apartment.' Victoire
spoke without turning around. 'Come home for supper with
us then. It'll be a treat for Albertine!' Mercedes turned to
Edouard, who burst out laughing. He nodded. 'Sure, come
on. Afterwards, we can go out.' Then, there was once again
silence. The sun was toying with the low branches of the trees;
a big ball of fire grazing the roofs of the houses. A feeble meow
that seemed to come from under a balcony a few houses from
Mont-Royal made Marcel start and then begin to squirm in his
uncle's arms. 'Plessis! Plessis! It's Plessis!' Edouard put him
down and the little boy rushed over to a fence, walked around
a huge dog that was licking its paw, and opened the gate. Marcel
knelt at the base of the balcony. 'Plessis, where are you?' He
spotted the cat under the stairs, covered with dried blood. Flies
were beginning to buzz around his wounds. Duplessis' heart
exploded with joy when he heard the boy and he stretched out
his neck, as if to hasten a caress that seemed slow in coming.
When the little boy's hand was on the cat's head, Godbout
leaped up and began to growl. Thérèse kicked him in the side.
'Don't bark at my little brother, you goddamn mutt!' Godbout
slunk away, whining, and disappeared into the lane. They had
all stopped to watch Marcel, who was on the verge of tears.

He picked up the cat gently, but Duplessis meowed in pain. 'So much suffering! So much suffering for a caress!' Ah! the smell! The little hands that didn't know how cruel they were! And the beloved head bending over his ruined eye! At last, Duplessis was happy. Marcel got up and walked away from the lawn. Edouard looked at Victoire, who didn't say a word. She hated the cat, but she knew that Marcel loved it and she didn't have the courage to separate them at a time like this. 'I want to bring him home. He's sick!' And Marcel took up the head of the procession, the dying Duplessis pressed against his heart. They walked the rest of the way in silence. They crossed Mont-Royal without looking to see if any cars or streetcars were coming. Victoire couldn't take her eyes off her grandson. 'When I die, he won't even notice. He's so scared of me, that child! But I've never had a knack for children — especially not for other people's. I'm always too hard on them. They never come and see me. Maybe they don't even like me.' She dropped Richard's hand, then Philippe's. The boys seemed to relax, somewhat relieved. Rose, Violette, Mauve, and their mother, Florence, were on their balcony, waiting for Marcel. Violette had come out on the balcony to tell the others that supper was ready, but her mother put a finger to her lips. 'Wait a bit, Violette.' She took out the woollen circle that her daughter had knitted by mistake and turned it around in her hands. 'They'll stop here.' The procession drew closer. Marcel stopped in front of Florence's house. He leaned against the fence and spoke in a broken voice. 'Madame, Plessis's very sick. Look after him.' 'Who are you talking to, Marcel?' Victoire came up to Marcel and bent anxiously over his shoulder. The little boy went on, paying no attention to his grandmother. 'Take good care of him. He's my friend!' He opened the gate and stepped onto the lawn. 'Don't, Marcel. There's nobody there!' But for a brief moment, Victoire thought that she saw a woman come down the front steps and move towards Marcel. Then the apparition vanished and Victoire cried out, hiding her face in her hands. 'It's crazy, dammit! Crazy! If you keep up this damn foolishness, I'll end up seeing things myself!' Florence smiled sadly at Marcel. 'Put the cat down.' Marcel placed him on the

cement. 'Come back tomorrow. I'll do what I can.' Duplessis
raised his head. 'Don't leave me, my love!' Marcel crouched
beside the cat and kissed his head softly. 'Go back with the
others, Marcel. Go and eat your supper.' Marcel smiled at the
four women and walked away. Victoire started climbing up
the stairs to their apartment The others followed. Marcel was
now crying uncontrollably. Gabriel took him in his arms. 'The
lady said Duplessis would be better tomorrow!' Gabriel kissed
Marcel on the neck. 'Yes, that's what the lady said.' Most
of all, he didn't want to contradict his nephew who seemed
so completely overwhelmed. Philippe shrugged. 'I must be
hearing things!' Florence waited until they'd all gone before
she bent over the cat. She was now holding Violette's woollen
circle. 'Violette, you'll have to fix this.' Violette ran down from
the balcony and picked up Duplessis. The four women walked
into the house leaving four empty chairs on the balcony.

When Josaphat-the-Violin arrived around a quarter to six,
Albertine had her head stuck in the oven of the coal stove where
she was basting a gigantic turkey whose skin was beginning
to turn beautifully golden. 'Oh, it's going to be a good little
bird!' She didn't hear the doorbell ring or the fat woman
shout: 'Bartine, the door!' Josaphat-the-Violin came into the
house, followed by his daughter, Laura, who was squeezing
her legs together, nearly writhing as she walked. 'Quick, Papa,
let me by! I can't stand it any more!' Laura ran across the
dining room without even glancing into her cousin's bedroom.
'Hello, auntie!' (She called Albertine and the fat woman 'auntie'
because of the difference in age, but also because she'd been
brought up in Saint-Jérôme and met the women only recently.
In addition, she called Victoire, 'Grandma,' though the old
woman was her aunt.) She jostled Albertine as she rushed
behind her on the way to the bathroom. Frightened, Albertine
screamed and fell to her knees, her head almost disappearing
inside the roasting pan. 'Hello, auntie! Sorry, I have to go!'
'Good Lord, you gave me a fright! Where were you? How'd

you get in?' Josaphat-the-Violin put his violin case and a big bag
of groceries on the kitchen table, then helped her up. 'Through
the door, Albertine, through the door!' They heard the fat
woman laugh. Albertine rubbed her knees. 'That's no daughter
you've got, it's a cyclone!' Without replying, Josaphat-the-
Violin pointed to the bag on the table. 'I brought you some
oranges.' Albertine stuck her nose in the bag and sniffed.
'What nice oranges! That will make Marcel happy!' She took
an orange from the bag and pressed it to her nose and mouth.
'Where do they get these oranges anyway, when there's a war
on?' 'Lordy, Bartine, they still grow on trees!' Josaphat-the-
Violin turned around and headed for the fat woman's bedroom.
'I haven't said hello yet. . .' The onset of Albertine's good
mood suddenly ended. 'So. . . he's off to pet his fat favourite
darling. . .' She heard loud kisses and the creak of springs as
the old man sat down at Gabriel's wife's bedside. 'That's right,
stay glued there while I break my neck making your supper!'
Her cousin flushed the toilet and came out of the bathroom,
laughing. 'Hope I didn't hurt you, auntie! But I didn't push
very hard. I think it was the surprise that turned your legs to
jelly.' Albertine was bent over again, pushing the pan back into
the oven. 'You're really putting on weight, Laura! If you keep
on, you'll soon be as fat as your aunt!' Albertine knew that
Laura couldn't bear any talk about her obesity. But she gave
as good as she got, and smiled maliciously at her aunt. Albertine
stood up and rubbed her back, then glanced at her cousin for
the first time. 'You're due the end of June, I suppose?' Laura
was sitting at one end of the kitchen table, playing with the
empty ashtray. 'Yup, same as my aunt!' Albertine tried to
bend backwards. 'Same as just about all the women on the
street! I've never seen so many women pregnant at the same
time!' 'It's normal, it's summer. . .' 'It isn't summer, it's
spring.' 'I read an article in Le Canada the other day, where
they said that just about everybody's born in the summer in
North America because the winters are so long. . .' 'And what
difference does that make?' 'Well, auntie, when the cold lasts
so long, sometimes you want to warm up a little. . . And when
you get warmed up, well, you know. . .' 'And they talk about

that in the papers! Now I've heard everything! It's bad enough
the women on the street don't even hide it when they're in the
family way, now the papers talk about when they make their
babies!' Expecting a baby was a somewhat shameful event
for the women in the city. They usually hid their big bellies
under corsets that suffocated them and very loose clothes that
disguised their silhouettes. Even the fat woman wore a corset
during her first pregnancies. And if a woman who was 'a little
too pregnant' walked down Mont-Royal, people looked away,
as if she were some obscene, shameful object; and there was
always some nervous Nelly or sanctimonious mealymouth to
point out: 'In the last month, women usually stay at home.'
And it was true. Rather than submit to the silent reproaches
that they could discern in every glance they met, women stayed
home for the last weeks of their pregnancy. In the end, they felt
a certain embarrassment at being misshapen and jostled about
by the bundle of energy, the powerful life preparing to leave
their bodies. Crushed by a monstrous religion that forbade any
means of contraception, a religion founded on men's selfishness
to serve the selfishness of men, men who held women in
contempt and were so afraid of them that they had created the
image of the Mother, the Virgin Mary, Mother of God, a virgin,
pure and intact, inhuman creature with no will and, most
important, no autonomy, who one day discovered that she was
pregnant without having wished it, through the workings of the
Holy Spirit (whom they dared to represent in the form of a bird!
The Mother of God impregnated by a bird!), and who delivered
without having to give birth, the ultimate insult to women's
bodies; oppressed by the dictates of priests as hollow as they
were cruel, in which high-flown, insulting, condescending
words like 'duty' and 'obligation' and 'obedience' predomi-
nated, French-Canadian women, particularly those who lived
in the cities, felt an unhealthy shame at being pregnant, they
who were not worthy (unlike that Other Woman) of bringing
a child into the world without a man, their owner and master,
who would have his way with them; women who had no right
to shirk their 'duty,' their 'obligation,' because they owed
'obedience' to the marvellous instrument of fate that had

been directly provided to them by the Will of God: their husbands. In a word, the Catholic religion denied the beauty of child-bearing and sentenced women *never* to be worthy, because the mother of their God, the consecrated image of Motherhood, had been only a temporary depository, which the Child neither entered nor left. Albertine lifted the cover of the cauldron of boiling soup and began to stir the steaming liquid energetically to give an impression of composure. 'If they keep that up, I'll stop buying the papers!' '*L'Oratoire?*' 'Even *L'Oratoire!*' She replaced the cover to the soup, making as much noise as possible. 'Help me set the table. I'm all by myself and I'm as lonely as can be.' Josaphat-the-Violin had taken his niece's hand in his big calloused carpenter's paws and he looked at her, smiling. 'Do any reading today?' 'No, uncle. I can't seem to concentrate.' 'Too much commotion in the house?' 'No, it isn't that. Everybody but Bartine went out. . . But. . . it's as if I'm not in the mood to read as much as I used to. The baby's moving a lot and I'm off in my daydreams.' 'Still Mexico?' 'No. More serious.' 'Mustn't do that. Acapulco has always helped you go on. . .' 'But I'll never see it! As long as I thought I'd get there some day, even though I knew I wouldn't, it was all right, but now. . .' The fat woman took her hand from her uncle's and fixed her hair which had fallen across her forehead. 'It isn't drying the way it should. . . I wish my dreams weren't so crazy! If I could only dream about going to somewhere accessible, it wouldn't be so bad! But, oh no! Acapulco!' 'It's your Indian blood that makes you want to travel. That's normal!' 'My Indian blood turned to water a long time ago.' 'This is the first time since December that I've seen you so down in the mouth. Something happen with Gabriel?' 'Of course not. . . I'd just like to get up, drag myself out on the balcony, sit and look at the spring sunshine, instead of watching its reflection in Madame Chagnon's window up on the third floor! I'm sick of dreaming about Acapulco when I can't even go outdoors and sit on the balcony!' 'Listen, listen. . . Tonight, after supper, Edouard and Gabriel and I, we'll try and take you out. . . It's warm enough. . . An hour or two of fresh spring air, that'll cheer you up!' This time, it was the fat woman who

took Josaphat-the-Violin's hand. 'Can I have chips and Coke?'
'Anything you want.' 'And will you play the "Meditation" from
Thaïs for me?' 'I'll try.'

'I never saw anybody gobble down their food so fast! Whenever
I come here, the food sticks in my throat and I nearly always
get sick!' 'Quit moaning and groaning, Mama, and dry the
dishes!' Germaine Lauzon and her mother, Rita Guérin, were
washing-up. At a quarter past six, the evening meal was over
and the dishes were already half done. In the early days of her
marriage, Germaine Lauzon had trouble getting used to the fact
that her husband ate whatever was put before him in about five
minutes flat, then asked for more between two loud belches and
two sips of beer, but she'd finally got accustomed to it and was
even beginning to take on her husband's rhythm, shovelling
down meat, vegetables and bread, as if each mouthful were her
last. The first time Rita Guérin came to eat at her daughter's,
she said: 'Poor Germaine, you got yourself a real pig for a
husband. You ought to feed him dishwater — he'd never notice
and think of the money you'd save!' But as the months passed,
she realized that her daughter was slowly being transformed
until she resembled her husband, so she said nothing more.
She simply watched the two of them, the corners of her mouth
betraying a slight expression of disgust. 'As long as they're
happy, it's none of my business. They'll produce more little
pigs and everybody'll be happy!' This was the first time in a
long while that Rita Guérin had allowed herself to make such
a remark. But the meal at which she'd just been present (she
couldn't say that she'd taken part, as she'd barely seen the
plates pass) had beaten all records for speed and piggishness —
and Rita Guérin thought that she could still hear her son-in-law,
mouth full of mashed potatoes and what seemed to be smashed
peas, ask: 'What's for dessert?' She almost told him the bread
pudding was hidden under the potatoes, but Ernest would
likely have believed her, so she held her tongue. Germaine put
her hands in the dishwater to stir up the suds, but the water

was too greasy and cold. The young woman sighed: 'You're exaggerating again, Mama! I've never seen you get sick here!' 'I hide it, little girl! So that you won't be ashamed! You ate so fast tonight, your dessert must have tasted like soup. I'm not kidding!' She laughed at her joke and put down the stack of plates she'd just dried. 'I exaggerate so much that I scare myself sometimes.' Germaine stuck her hands back into the dishwater and pulled a long face. 'Good thing you know you exaggerate. Otherwise, we'd have to keep reminding you and that would be a drag.' Rita Guérin replaced her wet teatowel with a clean one which she took from a drawer near the sink. 'You want me to stop?' 'Stop what?' 'Stop exaggerating!' 'Don't ever do that, Mama. I've got so used to dividing everything you say by ten, I'd get all mixed up if you ever stopped!' 'By ten! Now you're the one who's exaggerating, Germaine!' 'I am not! When we were having supper, how old did you say you felt?' 'Four hundred and sixty.' 'See?' 'That was a coincidence. . .' Pierrette, the youngest Guérin girl, who at eleven was too tall for her age and had a complex because her teeth were growing crooked, burst into the kitchen, horrified. 'Germaine, your husband's in the radio again!' Without even exchanging a glance, the three women rushed into the hall that led to the living room. 'Poor girl, your husband doesn't just eat fast. As soon as your back's turned, he's up to his old tricks again!' When they got to the living room, it was too late: the odour of electricity drifted through the room and some smoke was escaping from the radio. Ernest Lauzon, a sorry sight, screwdriver in hand, cleared his throat before he spoke: 'It isn't my fault! I didn't touch the wires! I just gave the valves a little tap to see if they were working!' Germaine Lauzon pulled the screwdriver from his hands. 'Good thing you put on your gloves, otherwise you'd look like a piece of toast! I can't leave you alone for two minutes! You'd blow up everything! I bet the power's off in the whole house and we'll have to go and buy fuses from Marie and they'll laugh in our faces again! This is the second time this week that you've blown the fuses. Do you think that's clever?' 'I'm telling you, it isn't my fault. . .' 'It's never your fault! I caught you up on the ladder Wednesday night digging around in the sockets in the attic and now you got the gall to tell me you never touched a thing — and if there wasn't any power in the house, it's because the fuses were too weak!' She rubbed her belly. The baby had just moved and her heart contracted with joy. 'If this keeps on, I'll have to ask the baby to bring you up!' Pierrette burst out laughing, followed by her mother, who put her hands in front of her mouth to hide her laughter. Ernest smiled. His finest smile. He knew that his wife couldn't resist his smile and he took full advantage of it very often, especially in delicate situations like this one. He held out his gloved hands to his wife. 'I like it when you chew me out like that! You're beautiful and you make me feel important.' He got up and took his wife in his arms. Rita Guérin's laughter stopped immediately. 'Pierrette, sweetheart, go and buy some fuses for your sister.' She followed her daughter onto the balcony and sat in the rocking chair. 'If they do it as fast as they eat, their nights must be long.' She hummed a song from her village, tapping her foot. Germaine was sitting beside the radio. 'That's a real disease you've got. I don't know what they call it, but if it has a name, they must be able to cure it! We're going to spend the rest of our lives just missing being burned to death!' Ernest crouched at his wife's feet and placed his head in her lap. 'I like electricity.' 'How come you aren't working in it then? It's not too late, you're only twenty-two!' 'I'm fine where I am! If I worked in electricity for my living, maybe I wouldn't like it so much. . .' Her husband's strange logic always amazed her. 'You mean, you couldn't spend your life doing something you like?' 'No, I just mean, a job's no fun, not even if you like it. . .' 'Where'd you dig up a crazy idea like that?' 'Have you got a job? No, eh? Well, shut up then! You don't know what you're talking about!' He sprang to his feet, irritated, and left the room, slamming the door behind him. Germaine was left standing there, holding the screwdriver. 'Now I suppose I'm the one that'll have to apologize again!'

It was a memorable meal. The atmosphere was like the eve of
an apocalypse, as if some final event or imminent catastrophe
were approaching in the shadows without deciding yet whether
or not to happen. The period before sitting down to eat had
been too quiet. When Albertine saw Mercedes and Béatrice
walk into the house, she thought she was dreaming, but she
restrained herself. She leaned against the wall in the hallway
with one hand over her heart. 'It isn't true! They couldn't do
that to me!' She stared at the two women without speaking to
them, as if they were in a store window or a stall. She was
well aware that Edouard was laughing to himself during the
introductions, which infuriated her. Victoire had closed herself
inside her room, where Josaphat-the-Violin came to join her, or
calm her rather, as she was crying and couldn't explain why.
Then Edouard, very pleased with himself, showed the two
hookers around the house, opening all the doors, describing
everything in a loud voice (very much the mistress of the house)
beneath his sister's murderous gaze. Gabriel dragged his long
face into his bedroom. As she did every Saturday when he
came home, more or less drunk, the fat woman waited for
him to speak to her before she spoke to him. Philippe ran
straight to the kitchen and began to hover around the stove,
playing the fool. Richard and Thérèse sat on the sofa reading
the paper. Marcel, for perhaps the first time in his life, went and
took refuge in Albertine's arms and she stood there completely
stunned. He clung to his mother's shoulder and his breathing
became spasmodic, as if he wanted to cry and couldn't. His
mother asked if he was sick. He said no, but Duplessis was,
and he was very upset. It was because of Marcel, in fact, that
Albertine didn't have a fit as she watched Edouard and the two
young women go from room to room, laughing, exclaiming or
apologizing when they disturbed someone. She didn't want to
know how or why these two creatures had turned up in her
domain, she just wanted them to disappear as fast as possible.
'Must be another one of Edouard's and Mama's little tricks! I
know those two! They'd do anything to drive me around the
bend! Me, serve those two supper? Not on your life! Anyway,
women like that don't eat, they drink!' Albertine sat in her

mother's rocking chair, which had the place of honour in the
dining room beside the radio. She rocked Marcel, with no great
hope of putting him to sleep. Suddenly, the little boy began
to tremble and his forehead became wet with sweat. 'Does
Mama's little angel want to go to sleep in my big bed?' Little
angel? She'd called him little angel! And without even noticing
it, her voice became soft and lilting. Thérèse looked down at
her mother and smiled. Albertine, aware of Thérèse's stare,
lowered her gaze. Marcel straightened up in his mother's
arms. 'Don't want to sleep. I want my supper. Tomorrow,
Plessis's going to be all better and Marcel wants to feel better
too.' 'Thérèse, Richard, get to the table! Fast!' Albertine lay
Marcel on the sofa. 'It won't be long. Mama's going to feed
you first.' Edouard, Mercedes and Béatrice had ended up in
the living room. Edouard did what he could to put the two
young women at ease. He looked like a fat Santa Claus, in
civvies on holiday in some hot country. 'I can't offer you a
drink, girls, because liquor isn't allowed in the house! By-law
six thousand and twenty-two. Not even beer! But we've got
cream soda and Coke by the gross, if you want some. Unless
you'd rather have a nice tall glass of chilled St Lawrence!'
The hackneyed old jokes only made Béatrice and Mercedes
more embarrassed, as they began to realize that no one but
Edouard was speaking to them and that they were, perhaps,
somewhat out of place in this house that smelled of soup
and roast turkey. For Béatrice, it smelled of Christmas and
that made her sad. Finally, Mercedes asked for a Coke and
Béatrice, a cream soda. When Edouard went into the kitchen,
the two friends tried to explain things to each other, but it
was too complicated: Mercedes still didn't know that the
three soldiers had wrecked the apartment; and Béatrice, in
her eagerness to say a great deal in a short time, explained
herself poorly and was growing impatient. So, when Edouard
came back with the soft drinks, he found the two women in
the midst of a heated argument, Betty, on the verge of tears,
and Mercedes, on the verge of exploding at her. Edouard put
the drinks on the coffee table. 'Listen, girls, if you've got
something to work out, I'll go and help my sister with the

supper. . . I'll call you when it's ready. . .' He withdrew, waving at them as though they were children. They were grateful to him for letting them sort out the day's events. Josaphat-the-Violin sat beside Victoire and saying nothing, waited for her to stop crying, his mere presence comforting his sister, and most important, pacifying her. Victoire blew her nose three or four times, then she described her vision to Josaphat-the-Violin who, to the old woman's great surprise, didn't laugh. He didn't even smile at her, but kept looking her straight in the eye as she tried to describe what she called 'the first signs of madness,' sometimes nodding encouragement, so attentive that he seemed hypnotized. 'There's nobody in that house! I know it! I must have been worn out, I don't know. . . Or maybe it's because Marcel thought he was talking with some woman. . . But I saw her, just for a second, you know. . . And I'm not crazy! Marcel. . . Sometimes he's funny. . . He says funny things and he does funny things. . . His mother doesn't notice. She doesn't look after him. . . But I watch him for days at a time, you know. I haven't got anything better to do, and I'm telling you, he's not like everybody else. Not by a long shot!' She stopped, as if she had been struck by a thought that surprised her. 'Come to think of it, he reminds me of you when you were little. . .' Victoire was eight years older than Josaphat-the-Violin and it was she, the big sister whose mother was too busy, who had brought him up, surrounding him with love and attention, singing as she changed his nappies and washing him three times a day in basins of warm water that soon became the great delight of young Josaphat. He had been a secretive child, excluding others from his games as well as from his affection, constructing an imaginary world where Victoire reigned and he was a toy in his sister's hands. All through his childhood, he worshipped Victoire, who returned his affection silently, an efficient little mother who quivered at her child's slightest surge of affection. They remained very close and a strange passion developed between them, from which sexuality was totally absent, but all the other components — jealousy, possessiveness, doubt, tears, secret joys, break-ups, reconciliations — were more deeply rooted than in any ordinary love and even more demanding, always leaving them gravitating between the two poles of the forbidden — guilt and remorse — and condemning them from puberty to love one another without ever touching, for, in their rural surroundings, sin was to be found far more readily on the surface of the body (the skin!) than in the labyrinth of the spirit. (Confessing an evil thought, even a criminal one, was a trifle, but admitting to a wicked touch!) Victoire married late, at twenty-five, and being separated from Josaphat (who already, at seventeen, was beginning to be called 'Violin,' because of his genius for learning to play in record time on the instrument that his father had made for him the most complicated jigs and the most daunting reels, giving them a transcendent interpretation, marking them with his personal stamp so that some became musical masterpieces, though still humble enough just to make people want to dance) had been equally excruciating for her when she left for Montreal (Montreal! City of the damned! Cursed city! City!) on the arm of a man that she didn't love and barely respected. As for her brother, who shouted when he learned that she was leaving: 'If you go away, Victoire, I'm hanging up my fiddle! I'm taking down my axe and I'm going up to the lumber camp for the rest of my days!' Josaphat-the-Violin did, in fact, hang up his fiddle after Victoire's departure, but almost three winters of being Josaphat-the-axe disgusted him, and rather than seek refuge in alcohol as so many lumberjacks secretly did, he came back from the logging camp one Monday afternoon in January and threw himself on his instrument as though it were his last hope, making the hearts of the village girls tremble with his tunes and dancers' feet beat with rhythms that were more mad than before. Josaphat-the-Violin wasn't married. No one knew if he'd ever known a woman and the women he had known (Rosette Blanchette, the mayor's wife, for instance, or Luce-Amanda Poitevin, the librarian, who for fifty years had ruled over one hundred and thirty-two books that were never borrowed, a donation from the Fathers of Sainte-Croix, useless like all their gifts, because most of them were incomplete, having left the printers' half-printed — hence, the good father's generosity) were all totally discreet, never admitting their fault (not even — especially not — to their priest, whom they'd stopped trusting, thanks to Josaphat for whom priests were a sadistic, degenerate lot) and concealing their happiness beneath perpetual smiles. Five or six of the village women, then, had kept the fiddler's mark imprinted on their faces throughout their lives and the five or six men to whom they were married had, throughout their lives, extolled and sung the praises and, even, paraded the unspeakable joy, the blazing happiness of which they were only victims, ridiculous, cuckolds, who, without knowing it, sported the biggest, the heaviest, the most comical horns in the Laurentians. Even Imelda Beausoleil, who had given him Laura in the early twenties, never said a word to a soul. She managed to conceal her pregnancy until the end and went down to Saint-Jérôme to give birth at one of her sisters', who swore on the Bible that she would without a word to anyone raise the little girl as though she were her own. When she came back to Duhamel, Imelda Beausoleil went to show Josaphat-the-Violin a photograph of Laura. 'There's your daughter. If you want her, she's at my sister's. If you don't want her, you're a son-of-a-bitch!' Josaphat-the-Violin immediately made the trip to Saint-Jérôme to embrace his daughter. He left her with Imelda's sister, where she grew up. When Laura married Pit Cadieux, a lad from Saint-Jérôme who was going to Montreal to try his luck in the kitchens of one of the big hotels, Josaphat took his daughter aside. 'I want to go to Montreal too, Laura. Let me come with you and Pit. I don't need much room. My two sisters are all I've got left and they're down there. . .' Imelda Beausoleil never saw her daughter again. She never even spoke of her. Perhaps, in the end, she even forgot her. And when Imelda Beausoleil died, Josaphat-the-Violin wept. When he arrived in Montreal, he found his passion for Victoire intact, inviolate, hard as a diamond, but much more shy. Victoire had opened her arms to him, calling him 'my precious little puppy,' as she had in the old days, or 'my little darling boy.' 'Yes, I thought about you when you used to come in and say the women next door were making their jam, and every time, even if there wasn't anybody in the house, it smelt of

jam. . .' Josaphat-the-Violin put one hand on his sister's knee.
'If you see that woman again. . . If you're still seeing things,
Victoire, tell me about it. . .' 'You'll put me in the nuthouse.'
She smiled, hoping that her smile would drive away her anxiety,
as if she'd just become aware of the absurdity of her vision. . .
'No, but if it starts again, we'll have to have a serious talk.
I've got some things to tell you. . . Now come and eat. You
mustn't keep the company waiting too long.' When Victoire
and Josaphat-the-Violin reached the dining room, everyone
was at the table (Mercedes and Béatrice had been seated on
either side of Edouard, who was puffed up with pleasure and
chuckling like a girl), but a strange silence hovered in the
room. Gabriel looked pleadingly at his mother. 'Mama, Bartine
won't serve the two — the two guests.' Albertine was, in fact,
standing in the kitchen doorway, ladle in hand, with a stubborn
expression on her face, an expression that made her look like
a pig. 'Stubborn as a mule! She only served Marcel.' Marcel
was eating his soup, paying no attention to what was going
on around him, concentrating on his soup spoon which he'd
learned to hold properly only a few months before. Mercedes
half rose. 'We don't want to make a fuss. . . If your daughter
doesn't want to feed us, it doesn't matter. We'll go somewhere
else. . .' 'You sit down! I invited the two of you and you're
going to eat! When Victoire invites people to eat, they eat!'
She walked around the table and stood before her daughter.
'You don't want to serve the visitors?' Albertine stood up to
her mother's look, but her voice was hoarse, as if some strong
emotion had stuck in her throat. 'Mama, you aren't going to
make me feed those two hussies! I've had to put up with enough
today, if you ask me! Please don't do that to me!' She held out
the ladle to her mother. 'Serve them yourself!' Victoire seized
the ladle with a firm, decided hand. 'It's about time somebody
asked me to do something around here! I'm starting to grow
roots in my rocking chair! But I'm warning you, if I serve the
visitors, I serve everybody!' 'You can't do that, Mama, your
leg!' 'My leg took me all the way to Lafontaine Park today,
I think it'll take me to the stove, goddammit! Go sit down
Bartine — and try and look like a human being, for the love

of God!' Edouard applauded and his mother turned around
and looked at him. 'And don't you go thinking that you look
like a rose in between two thorns, Edouard! You look more
like a toad in a field of daisies!' Josaphat-the-Violin burst out
laughing, followed by Gabriel — and even the fat woman, who
could hear everything from her bedroom. Edouard answered
his mother in the same tone of voice. 'And don't you go
thinking that you can serve us properly, Mama! A rickety
old woman wouldn't be my choice to serve the soup!' But
this time, no one laughed. And Josaphat-the-Violin's slap hit
Edouard in the midst of his triumph. 'Sometimes you're funny,
you big lump, but don't ever make fun of your mother when
I'm around!' Edouard got up, went around the table and took
the ladle from his mother. 'I'm sorry, Mama. Go and sit down,
I'll serve.' Victoire took back the spoon. 'Not on your life! If
you've never seen a rickety old woman on her toes, watch out
for your boots, little boy! I'll bet you your next pair of pants
that I won't spill a drop!' Mercedes and Betty applauded the
old woman, who made a little bow to them. 'Ladies, you're
about to taste the best soup in town! My daughter Albertine
made it, but the recipe comes from her old mother, me myself,
and in my day, I've known people that travelled all the way
from Duhamel just to taste it!' Josaphat-the-Violin raised his
hand. 'Me, for instance!' Victoire approached her brother and
put her hands on his shoulders. Her voice, softer now, became
caressing. 'Him, for instance.' And suddenly, everyone was
struck by the resemblance between them, even the children
who were silent as they looked at the superb picture they
formed, the two of them: a couple united by so much subtle
affection and so many tragic bonds that, in the end, they had
the same wrinkles, the same face. From that moment on, the
atmosphere relaxed somewhat. Victoire didn't spill a single
drop of soup ('Edouard! You owe me a pair of pants!') and they
all ate in silence, scraping the bottoms of their bowls with their
spoons and eating the last grain of barley. As Béatrice placed
her spoon in her empty bowl, she looked at Victoire. 'That's
the best soup I've ever eaten!' Victoire smiled. 'You'll have to
tell my daughter. She's the one that made it.' Béatrice took

her courage in both hands and spoke to Albertine. 'That's the best soup. . .' 'Okay, I heard you! You already said so!' And Albertine slurped her last spoonful.

In the last rays of the setting sun, Ti-Lou was dying. When she felt her heart beat faster and her vision begin to blur, she straightened up in bed and stretched one arm out towards the window. 'One last time. To see the sun set behind the chimneys one last time!' But a sudden dizzy spell pinned her to the pillows again. 'I took too much! I'm going too fast!' The bottle of Doctor Sanregret's drops lay empty in a corner of the bedroom. After emptying the contents into a very small amount of water, Ti-Lou had hurled the bottle with all her might against the wall that faced the window, but the bottle didn't break (it was mocking her, the crippled old lady thought). 'I don't want to go so fast! I don't want to die with the window shut!' And for almost ten minutes, she struggled, supporting herself, at first on one elbow and using her free arm to push with all her strength, then, gradually, unfolding the arm on which she was resting, until finally, she succeeded in sitting up in bed, her one leg half out of the covers. The bed pitched and tossed; the room sloped dangerously towards the right. 'If the whole house is leaning that way, I'll fall out the window and land on the fence!' Imagining her body pinned to the fence made her laugh. 'They'll think I broke a leg and they'll look all over the place for it, but they won't find a thing!' She was bent double laughing, tears streaming down her cheeks. 'Gotta keep up my strength. . .' She breathed deep, but her heart kept pounding wildly. The room was sloping more and more, so much so that she began to look for something to lean on. She turned over, brought her leg out from under the covers, and stood on the floor. 'My crutches. . .' Generally, Rose Ouimet left the crutches against the straight-back chair between the bed and the window, but this time they weren't there. Ti-Lou was panic-stricken as she leaned out of bed. 'They aren't there! I can't get up! I'm going to die in my bed, just like everybody else!' It was at this moment that the noise began. The house suddenly filled with clicking and whispers, with strident whistling and demented laughter. It was as if corpses were being dragged into the corridor or prisoners in chains were being shoved into the cellar. 'I'm imagining it! There's nobody in the house! My heart's beating too hard and my blood's circulating too fast. . . My brain needs air. . . *I* need air!' She leaned against the bedside table with her right hand and, with her left hand, she managed to draw the straight-back chair towards her and even turn it around so that she faced the window. Leaning on the back of the chair, Ti-Lou stood up on her one leg. She felt dizzy and her head spun, but she concentrated all the energy she had left in her arms and managed to stand. When the vertigo passed, she realized that the voices and noises had stopped. She sighed. 'I held them off!' She pushed the chair towards the window, hopping on her one leg, then began again, until the chair was leaning against the radiator. 'Have to walk around the chair. . .' Realizing that she'd never be able to hop around the chair, she pushed it furiously to the right. It swayed to one side, first falling onto the bedside table, then, after springing back, overturning the lamp that hadn't been used for years and that Ti-Lou had started to hate because it was so high that she couldn't switch it on. Then, the lamp crashed into the wall. The glass globe burst into a thousand pieces and a hail of sparks began to run along the electric wire. Ti-Lou balanced on her one leg for a moment, then fell forward. She stretched out her arms and managed to lean against the windowsill. 'I can't fall! This is my last chance!' She was half sitting on the radiator. She pressed her forehead against the window, closed her eyes and breathed slowly. 'All that fuss over a goddamn sunset!' She opened her eyes again. Blood coursed through the sky in long brilliant streaks. 'Five minutes and it'll be too late.' Gathering all the strength that she had left, Ti-Lou got up, bent down and opened the window in a single motion. She stood there, resting against the window frame, arms outspread. 'Ah! I'm going to go the way I lived! Upright, come what may!' Ti-Lou saw all the nights of her life again: the splendid ones, the ones that she

willingly talked about because they were flattering, when the
elite of Ottawa had crowded around her, along with visiting
dignitaries from countries that she'd never seen, but where
she'd imagined herself in black arms, or in the yellow or brown
or too white arms of one of its representatives whom she'd had
to call: 'Your Grace,' or: 'Your Highness,' or: 'Mr President,'
or simply: 'Comrade,' men who were always intelligent and
gallant, who showered her with presents as they told her that
she was Canada's finest jewel, the only pearl ever created in the
cold; and the far less glorious nights that she'd spent in hotel
rooms, in the arms of drunken officials with fetid breath, whose
requirements were as brusque as they were brief, who forgot
her as soon as their hunger was appeased, sometimes even going
so far as to show her to the door, calling her by the name of the
act they'd just done to her; all those nights that had ended with
humiliating ablutions; all the pale dawns, the hour of the wolf
— but not the wanton she-wolf — spent washing from her body
the traces of love (love?), the odour of the vomit of crowned
heads, and even the shit of the great of this world. Those nights,
those mornings so horrible that Ti-Lou sincerely believed she'd
dreamed them. She believed that they were nightmares sprung
from her own imagination; while the other dreams (a house of
her own and quail with grapes) remained the truth for her, the
only truth — the only acceptable bearable truth. Crucified at
her window, Ti-Lou saw once more the kings, the cardinals the
presidents, generals, admirals — but she saw them with their
clothes on. And when the last ray of light touched her brow,
she began to howl: this lonely, crippled she-wolf remembering,
before she died, all her progeny scattered to the four corners
of the forests, though she was well aware this progeny knew
nothing of her, that it denied her because she'd become useless
and would die with no one knowing anything about her, a
rotting carcass they would hasten to devour before it polluted
the surrounding air. The howl of the she-wolf of Ottawa rang
out like gunshot, rose up the maple tree in the yard and echoed
all over Plateau Mont-Royal — until Ti-Lou's despair entered
the houses, the churches, in the presbyteries where priests,
served by fat servants in love with them, placidly ate vegetable

stews or boiled chicken, their heads in their plates like horses at their troughs; it even scaled the steeple of Saint-Stanislas Church and made the great bell ring out once, dong! only once, one little ring for the dying she-wolf, who'd never be allowed inside the church on her final journey or be buried in consecrated ground, the bitch! Little Marcel looked up from his plate, while Josaphat-the-Violin got out of his chair and walked over to him. 'Plessis's gone!' Josaphat-the-Violin took him in his arms. 'No, not Plessis. Another animal. Come here, Marcel. Your uncle Josaphat's going to turn on the light in the moon.' And Josaphat-the-Violin went out on the back balcony, still holding Marcel in his arms. Rose, Violette, Mauve, and Florence, their mother, stopped eating too. Florence took the woollen ball from her pocket and looked at Violette. 'It wasn't Duplessis, Violette. You knitted somebody else's death.' Ti-Lou died upright, the way she had wanted.

When Josaphat-the-Violin had finished, he laid his instrument down on a chair on the balcony and took Marcel in his arms. 'Look how beautiful it is. She's going to climb up and up and up in the sky, and then she'll climb back down the other side so I can put her out. I have to wait till she comes back down, otherwise it's too high and she can't hear the music right.' 'You do that every single day?' 'Yup, every day. Ever since. . . well, for a long, long time. I'm the one that does the job now. The other guy, the one before me, he took off in a flying canoe and he's never been seen since. . .' 'A flying canoe?' 'I never told you about that?' 'No.' 'Well, well. You should've asked me. You want me to tell you now, right away?' 'Oh, yes!' 'All right. Now, listen carefully. . . Ah! It all happened a long time ago. . . such a long time ago. . . way before you were even born. . . I was just a little boy myself, hardly any older than Richard. I was living in the country. You know, the country. . . I've told you about it before. . . Out where there's not many houses and lots and lots of trees.' 'I know, Duhamel.' 'That's right. Anyhow, back then there weren't any cars, so to

get from Duhamel to Montreal, it took you two days. You had
to sleep over at Saint-Jérôme, and let me tell you, we thought
Saint-Jérôme was a pretty big place! Yup! It was quite a treat,
spending the night at the Hotel Lapointe! Anyhow, what I'm
working up to is to tell you that Duhamel was a good way
away and we didn't know a thing about Montreal. Didn't miss
it either. Anyway, one night I was taking a bucket of raspberries
over to my aunt Marguerite, my father's sister. She was so poor
that she fed her kids right off the table, without any dishes. So,
we chewed the fat a while and the time passed without us even
noticing it and night was falling before I decided to head back
home. It was August, I remember — and a real fine night it was!
I didn't have a buggy, nothing — I'd come with uncle Arthur,
aunt Marguerite's husband — and I was gonna have to walk
back home. A three mile walk in the dark! So, I went out on
the front balcony with my aunt, and she'd've been real glad to
have me stay over, but I never really liked the way it smelled
in that house, so I said no. . . You couldn't see six feet in front
of you! That's the truth! I was standing there on the doorstep
and my aunt was holding a lantern that shed a little light on
the floor and the posts that held up the roof of the balcony. . . .
But down at the bottom of the steps — nothing! I didn't want
to tell my aunt, but I was a little scared. . . I never liked the
dark. . . I'm no sissy, never have been, but all the same. . .
Like I said just now, I had a good three miles to go through
the woods, over a little road where it wasn't unheard of to run
into a bear in broad daylight. . . And I'll tell you straight out,
all alone there in the dark, the farthest I'd ever gone in the dark
like that was to the outhouse! Aunt Marguerite tells me: "I'd let
you have a lantern, Josaphat, but your uncle and your cousin
Manuel took two lanterns and I'll be needing this one when I
go and have a last look in the henhouse. . ." "I don't want any
lantern," I tell her, "I know my way home!" Then, to show her
that I wasn't afraid, I ran down the front steps and there I was,
in the dark. . . It was like falling into water. . . As soon as I left
my aunt's lantern behind, it started getting cold. . . not like in
the winter, no; in fact, it was blazing hot. . . It was as if. . . as
if, I felt cold inside. . . I couldn't see a thing in front of me; my

heart was ticking away like a busted watch. . . When I turned around, I saw aunt Marguerite waving at me. . . The lantern was throwing big shadows that went flying out all around. . . She looked like a ghost, goddamn it! I felt pretty small in my boots, let me tell you! Then, all of a sudden, she went back inside the house and there I was, all by myself. You know how quiet. . . how quiet it is in the country. . . How can I explain it?. . . When you're all by yourself in your room, lying on your back with all the lights out. . . it's the silence itself that scares you. . . You're scared of the silence. But when you're in the country, *inside* that silence, it isn't the silence that's scary then, it's the thousands and millions of little sounds that live in it. . . That's when you realize that there's really no such thing as silence. . . that there's always something to hear in the silence. . . I was. . . it was as if I was paralyzed there by the side of the road. Nothing in front of me, nothing behind, nothing alongside. . . And up over my head, no moon in the sky; the sky was empty. Empty! But in the midst of that emptiness, there were sounds. . . all around. . . noises. . . Old leaves crackling. . . little branches breaking. . . and. . . things crawling over the pine needles: the padded paws of animals that you hear because it's dark. . . An owl hoots and you think it's a ghost; a crazed bat that flies every which way instead of in a straight line! Ah! A little light. . . two, five, twenty, a hundred little lights! Fireflies on parade, going to look for the damned soul of a sinner to fetch him for his last journey! I sure wished I was somewhere else! Eventually, my eyes got used to the dark and I could see the road like a long yellow ribbon, a little paler than the surroundings. . . I took all the courage I had left (about enough to fill a thimble, I think) and I set off down that road, my head scrunched between my shoulders, my eyes as wide as soup plates, my heart changing place every two or three beats. . . What's that? A rat? A rabbit? A raccoon? A dog? A sheep? A wolf? A bear? What is it? I started to run. . . Another squadron of fireflies. . . Good God, was that somebody laughing? Eh? How far is it to the house? Dumbbell, you just left! I'm suffocating. . . Too bad, I'll stop! If they want to nab me, they'll nab me; at least I'll know who

I'm dealing with. . . Hey, what's that? I hear a sound behind
me, louder than the others. . . I look around and what I see is
a sort of white light moving along the road. . . Horses! It looks
like horses coming this way! Yes, that's what it is! I'm saved!
Maybe it's somebody I know! Maybe I'll be able to get into my
bed sooner!. . . Ah! What's that? Over there!. . . Horses. . .
White ones! Loose!. . . You won't believe me, Marcel, but
true as I'm standing here, I saw two, four, six, eight white
horses galloping down the road! Eight big white horses with
manes so long they looked like wings!. . . The horses seemed
to be running as if they were on their way somewhere very
important. . . They were whinnying like crazy. . . They came
closer and closer and their hooves made the road shake. I could
see them as if they'd been lit up by the moon. But there wasn't
any moon. Hide! But I was too scared to get down in the
ditch! They're coming closer! They're coming! They're. . .
so. . . beautiful! Haaaa! They streaked past me like bolts of
lightning, galloping and whinnying, their ears in the wind, their
nostrils all foamy, their eyes wild. . . You'd almost think they
went right through me! My hair was standing up on my head!
I had goose pimples! . . . I wanted to piss and I was pretty
close to doing the other thing too. . . The horses had taken
the road that curved in front of me. Then they disappeared,
as if there was nothing after that curve. I was paralyzed in
the middle of the road; I couldn't move; I was too scared
of what I might see after that curve in the road. . . And I
couldn't move backwards either. I was sitting in the middle
of the road and I started howling like a kid. (I was a kid,
but I never used to howl like one. I was too proud.) Seeing
things like that in the middle of the night, when you're all by
yourself in the middle of the mountains, it's pretty scary. . .
You start wondering if maybe you're on your way downhill
and at the bottom of the hill, the asylum's waiting for you. . .
Especially because my mother always told me that I dreamed
too much and some day all that dreaming was going to play a
trick on me. . . So, there it was, for Christ's sake! If I'd had my
fiddle with me at least. . . You know, sometimes music. . . But
that's something you'll understand later. . . So, what I did, my

boy, was pick myself up and just keep going. . . And there was nothing beyond the bend in the road. Walk, walk, walk. . . no news from the horses. I ended up thinking that I'd really been dreaming, and then, I started whistling to forget about it all. When all of a sudden, I hear a terrible uproar back behind the mountain. . . There was such a commotion, child, it was as if half a dozen thunderclouds were clashing. . . Then, I heard a kind of whinny, far, far away, on the other side of the mountain. . . More than one. . . as if there were horses moaning somewhere the far side of the country. . . Then, when I looked up, I saw a sort of greyish-yellow light shining on the trees on the mountain. . . "Is our place on fire?" And then. . . I saw. . . the eight big horses coming out from behind the mountain. . . and rising up to the sky, whinnying and pawing the ground! They were pulling on chains and they seemed to be straining like I've never seen animals strain before in my life! As if they were pulling on the heaviest thing in the world. The chains dug into their skin and there was blood running all down their hides. . . I could see their bleeding sores and their wild eyes. The eyes of animals that have gone crazy, that don't know why they hurt so much! And then. . . at the very end of the last chain. . . you could see a red ball. The moon! They were pulling the moon up from behind the mountain! It was big — nearly as big as the mountain, I'm telling you — and red! You know, like the full moon in August that's so scary. . . The horses' blood was running onto the moon and the moon was dripping like an orange. . . Then, as soon as the moon was on top of the mountain, and nice and round, the chains came apart and those eight horses ran off in eight different directions, like a compass card. The full moon never looked so much like a big wicked eye. I started to cry, yelling, I didn't want the moon, that it was a beautiful full moon, but that was no reason to make the poor animals suffer like that. . . It wasn't dark any more; it was nearly as bright as those nights in winter when the snow gives off its own light. . . I got back on the road again. . . It was as if I'd been hit over the head. I felt as if the moon was watching me. She was up there on my left as I walked, and she was looking at me. . . You'd have thought somebody'd fired

off a cannon in the sky and made a big red hole. . . But. . .
I wasn't quite so scared now, because I could see up ahead of
me. . . I'd almost made it back home when, off in the distance,
I heard a sort of music, like a bunch of drunks singing a sad
song. I looked behind me on the road. . . nothing. But the
song was coming closer. When it was so close that, ordinarily,
I'd have seen the singers, my heart was in my mouth again. . .
White horses a while back; now, invisible men. . . I don't know
why, but I looked up. . . maybe to check if the moon was still
there (I was pretty close to thinking it was the moon that was
singing) and then. . . I saw a bark canoe come out from behind
the mountain, with eight guys paddling through the sky and
singing as they went. . . A fiery red bark canoe with seams that
looked like stars. . . They were singing at the tops of their lungs
and they were drinking from bottles of caribou. . . Then, all of
a sudden, the canoe stopped just above me and I recognized
those eight men singing themselves hoarse: there was Willy,
Ti-Pet Turgeon's boy; there was Gaspar Petit — I'd seen him
the night before. He had double pneumonia and he had the gall
to be wandering around the sky in his pyjamas; there was big
Laurent Doyon, the priest's hard-hearted brother, who worked
as beadle from time to time, but only when it suited him; there
was Georges-Albert Pratte, the village barber, who also worked
as a dentist and according to my mother, got drunk on eau
de Cologne, but maybe that's just gossip; there was Rosaire
Rouleau, too, the beggar, who we hadn't laid eyes on for a
good long while, who we thought might be dead; and the
Patenaude twins, Twin and Twin — one Twin, with his blind
eye; the other Twin, with a stump for an arm; and last of all,
there was Teddy Bear Brown, the only Anglo that we'd ever
seen in the village, who always claimed he was the one that
turned on the light in the moon. . . Every day, at the end of
the afternoon, he'd disappear, and when he came back, there
was the moon, pale or shining bright, full or as thin as a slice
of lemon, depending on what day of the month it was. . . All
eight of them were as drunk as skunks and they were having
so much fun in that canoe that they seemed about to fall out of
it. Georges-Albert Pratte, who was a kind of relative, because

he was married to my mother's brother-in-law's sister, leaned out of his canoe and yelled at me: "Hey, Josaphat. We're on our way to Saint-Jérôme to see fat Minoune! Want to come along?" Then, he started laughing himself silly. . . You see, fat Minoune — well, I was still a little young to be going to see her. . . But that's something you'll learn about later. . . Anyhow, the whole bunch of them were having fun, that's for sure! Then, Teddy Bear Brown leaned over the canoe and shouted at me with his squarehead accent: "Hey there, Josaphat! You want my job, old buddy? I'm sick of lighting that old moon. If you want the job now, it's yours. You and your fiddle. . . It'll be better because I had to bark and, you know, at my age, it's a bit ridiculous, you know. . . You want it? *Oui?* Okay. You start tomorrow. I'm on my way to Saint-Jérôme to see fat Minoune and if you never see me again, think about me when you play your tunes to light up my old friend." The loud vulgar laughing started up again, and the canoe shot off, heading for the moon, nearly capsizing at every stroke of the paddle. Then I realized that if the horses had suffered so much that night, it was because that asshole Teddy Bear Brown hadn't done his job! So I told myself that I, Josaphat-the-Violin. . . I'd be faithful to that moon for the rest of my life, and never again, as long as I lived, would those horses have to pull the moon out from the side of the mountain. . . And ever since, every day, my fiddle's climbed up in the sky, and the moon can come out in peace.' Marcel had fallen asleep, overcome with happiness and fear, his head filled with horses, moons, bark canoes and lanterns shaped like fiddles. When he was quite certain that the little boy wasn't listening any more, Josaphat-the-Violin finished his story. 'And some day, when I'm too old, some fine afternoon I'll come and see you and I'll say: "Marcel, I'm tired." I hope you'll understand and that you'll respect the moon as long as you live. Because the moon's the only thing in the world you can be sure about.' From her dining room window on the ground floor, Florence had been listening to Josaphat-the-Violin tell his story. When he finished, he bowed gallantly to her and she responded with a smile of complicity.

Laura ate her supper with the fat woman. When she saw the
house suddenly filling up, she took refuge with her cousin
on the pretext of a dizzy spell. 'Can I stay with you a while,
auntie? I feel sick when there's too many people around. . .
Does that ever happen to you?' The fat woman gave her the
ghost of a smile. 'There's never a lot of people coming to see
me all at once, you know. . .' 'I'm sorry, you're right, you
can't move and the room isn't all that big.' 'Sit down, Laura.
You're supposed to be feeling dizzy.' Laura sat on the bed,
legs together, arms folded across her bosom. 'And relax. . .
I'm not surprised you feel sick, you're wound up tighter than
the strings on your father's fiddle!' Laura unfolded her arms,
but her legs remained firmly stuck together. 'Laura, really!
Let yourself go! Lie down on the bed. . .' 'Come on. I'm
not that sick. . .' 'Will you listen to me, Laura Cadieux?
If you want to eat like a civilized person, you're going to
have to rest a little first. . .' Laura lay on the bed, but still
she seemed ill at ease. 'Did you and your father walk here?'
'Yes.' 'You shouldn't walk too much in your condition. . .'
'No, that isn't what's wrong. I like walking. And it's good
for me. . . No, I know why I'm not feeling good. . . I eat
too much. That's what it is. There's a reason why I'm so
fat! If you could see how much I eat in a day, auntie, you
wouldn't believe it!' The fat woman burst out laughing. 'Do
you realize who you're talking to? I haven't got a reputation
for living on lettuce, you know. . .' Laura raised her head
somewhat as she answered her cousin. 'It's different for you.
I've seen pictures of you when you were my age. At least you
weren't fat when you were twenty-two. . . But look at me. . .
If I keep putting on weight like this, what'll I look like when
I'm forty?' Laura's voice broke and her eyes began to moisten.
She lay her head on the pillow. 'That's what happens when you
marry a man whose crazy on cooking!' The fat woman looked
at Laura a long time before answering. 'You don't have to
eat everything he cooks, you know. . .' 'But I like eating!
And everything Pit makes is so good!' Pit Cadieux, Laura's
husband, worked as an assistant cook at the Windsor Hotel,
one of the great hotels of Montreal, and his culinary talents,

especially at sauces, which he never spoiled and which he
prepared with unusual skill, were beginning to draw attention
from the chef, for whom he was truly a blessing, right up to
the management, who were delighted that the reputation of
their dining room was growing from week to week. People
were even starting to come to the Windsor Hotel just for the
sauces of Chef Vaillancourt, who was careful not to admit that
his great speciality was, in fact, the work of some third kitchen
boy he'd discovered by chance one day when everything was
going wrong and he'd finally been obliged to ask the staff:
'Does anybody here know how to make a *sauce béarnaise*? I
haven't got time and there's a bunch of fucking Frenchmen
out there that won't eat their fucking steaks without it!' Pit
Cadieux timidly raised his hand. 'I'm good at sauces. I like to
make them.' Without really knowing why, Chef Vaillancourt
trusted the young man who was fat and nearly bald and who,
he'd noticed some time before, did whatever he was asked with
love. Pit's *sauce béarnaise* turned out to be far superior to Chef
Vaillancourt's. The Frenchmen were overwhelmed and insisted
on shaking the hand of Chef Vaillancourt. He went along with
the ceremony and came back to the kitchen delighted. 'Do
your sauces always turn out that good?' 'Every time.' 'Okay.
Whenever I need one, I'll ask you. Where do you come
from anyway?' 'Saint-Jérôme.' 'Where'd you work before?'
'The Hôtel Lapointe.' Chef Vaillancourt nearly choked. 'You
mean, you learned how to make *sauce béarnaise* at the Hôtel
Lapointe in Saint-Jérôme?' 'Hell, no! You eat worse than the
devil there! I learned out of books. I'd try the sauces out at
home.' It was Laura, in fact, who'd been the guinea pig for
Pit's experiments ever since they met. Every Saturday before
they got married, instead of taking his girlfriend to a restaurant
and wasting money on frightful hot chicken sandwiches or
club sandwiches thrown together from the week's leftovers,
Pit would spend hours with his cookbooks, then go off to do
his shopping with Laura on his arm. He bought everything
himself. He trusted no one, especially not Laura, who he
knew was a little too thrifty and had a tendency not to buy
the finest ingredients. Afterwards, he spent the afternoon in

the kitchen, happily trumpeting the songs of Fernandel, while Laura went to the movies with her girlfriends, or watched him work, fascinated. And when it was time to eat. . . bliss. Laura and Pit looked at one another as they ate, smiling, throwing kisses. Laura would say, 'It's so good!' And Pit would answer: 'Shut up and eat!' After supper, they went for long walks around Saint-Jérôme and people who met them would nudge each other. 'If you ask me, they've just committed a sin, those two. . . Or they're getting ready to.' But the only sins Pit and Laura committed at the time were of a sort that would have greatly disappointed the curious. And since their marriage, it was even worse. Their cravings for food had multiplied tenfold and they ate at every hour of the day — before *and* after making love, and sometimes even in bed. As soon as he'd become the master saucemaker at the Windsor Hotel, a sort of frenzy had taken hold of Pit Cadieux and, at home, he began to try out every sort of sauce imaginable, from the simplest to the most complicated, dreaming of seeing his greatest successes on the menu. And Laura, who was already plump, started to get dangerously fat. When she complained about her obesity to her husband, he shrugged or kissed her neck, saying: 'I like you fat. There's more of you to love. And I hope the little one that you've got in the oven isn't going to look like a skeleton either!' Sometimes late at night, Pit would bring home cakes made with almond paste, Laura's favourite, and they would ceremoniously sit in the dining room and savour them. A little piece of cake to finish off a little glass of milk. Then, a little glass of milk to finish off a little piece of cake. Afterwards, obviously, they slept badly, but as Pit Cadieux, *chef saucier* incognito of the Windsor Hotel in Montreal, put it so well: 'If you miss a night's sleep, you can always catch up on it; but if you miss a meal, it's a waste!' The fat woman wiped her sweat-covered face with a damp washcloth. 'If you're that crazy about eating, don't complain!' When Gabriel came into the bedroom without saying hello to his wife or to Laura, whom he hadn't seen for months, the latter, feeling that she was in the way, struggled up from the bed, but the fat woman gestured to her not to

leave the room. So Laura stayed at her cousin's side while
Gabriel lay down beside her, turning his back to them. The
two women remained silent for several minutes. Laura sensed
that her cousin wouldn't open her mouth until her husband
decided if he was going to talk, or until he started snoring.
But after a while, Gabriel sighed, and when he spoke, his
voice seemed faint and weary. 'Sorry I didn't say anything
right away. . . I'm a little bit drunk. And I'm really down
in the dumps.' Laura and the fat woman exchanged a glance,
frowning. 'I'll take a little nap for half an hour, then I'll
feel better. Bonjour, Laura. Everything all right? How about
Pit?' And almost immediately, Gabriel fell asleep. All the
time that she'd been lying in her cousin's bed, Laura had
felt the need to confide in her: the words rose in her throat,
confidences she'd held back for too long, doubts she didn't
understand, that struck her more and more frequently, even
when she was eating, doubts about Pit and herself. There
were questions, too, that had been forming in her head for
some time and which she couldn't answer; they nearly came
tumbling out, like a plea, but Gabriel's arrival intimidated the
young woman, who immediately began to babble the sort of
trivia that fills meaningless conversations between people with
nothing to say to one another. She no longer felt like confiding
because there was a man sleeping behind her and men were
wet blankets when it came to confidences. Only once had she
tried talking to Pit about her doubts. Her husband stopped
her cold with a gesture and silenced her questions. 'If you
start asking questions, we'll never get out of the woods! Do
like me, throw yourself into your work and stop thinking!'
And though she loved her Pit — she was sure of that — the
growing importance of cooking in her husband's life made her
feel uncomfortable. In a way, she was jealous of her husband's
work. She had no idea how to combat this state of affairs, the
reasons for which she hadn't figured out. Was she annoyed at
Pit because he was the reason that she was getting so fat so
fast? Or was she just annoyed at how he made a living? But
if Pit had been a shoemaker, she'd still have eaten as much,
because she had a natural penchant for eating well. Perhaps

the fat woman couldn't answer all these questions, but just talking to someone about them would be an immense relief for Laura. Instead, though, she heard herself asking her cousin if she needed anything, or whether or not it would bother her if she had a cigarette before supper — and she heard the fat woman reply, 'No, I don't need anything.' And, 'Yes, it'd bother me if you smoke, because it's bad for your health and the baby's too.' The fat woman, for her part, was aware all this time that Laura wanted to talk, but she hadn't dared to ask any questions, telling herself that if the need was there, everything would come out by itself. While the fat woman waited, she kept the conversation going, occasionally casting a glance at her cousin that might have suggested a question, but which Laura interpreted as an encouragement to gossip. And when Edouard, shouting at the top of his lungs, 'Dinner's ready, ladies!' waddled through the house, trying out some ridiculous dance steps, Gabriel woke with a start, stretched like a cat sluggish with sleep, and walked out of the bedroom, rubbing his eyes. Then, Laura was even more embarrassed to be there, an involuntary witness to a silent domestic scene. Her cousin patted her hand. 'Don't worry, Laura. We'll talk to each other eventually, my husband and I. . .' 'You're lucky. . . I can't talk to Pit. The only thing he cares about is what's on his plate.' But Laura said no more, thinking this wasn't the moment to bother her cousin with problems that didn't concern her. So, the two women ate in silence, laughing when they overheard something funny from the dining room and never looking at one another, because obese people don't watch one another eat. When the meal was over, they heard, through the open window, Josaphat-the-Violin telling Marcel the story of how the moon got its fire. The fat woman wept uncontrollably. Gabriel had often told her that he'd grown up under the spell of his uncle Josaphat's legends and every time she heard the old man tell one of his stories, with their mixture of true and false, of humdrum country life and its astonishing need for illusions and the marvellous, her heart began to beat faster, and she would be carried away with joy in the playground stall or in the land of nuns' farts where you got the giggles and lost

your memory. As for Laura, she envied Marcel; she envied
his innocence, his great naïveté, and his touching credulity.
'I believed it too, just like him! I wanted so badly for it to
be true! If it were true, it would give us all a reason for going
on!' After Josaphat's story, the fat woman put her plate on the
bed, beside Laura. 'Do you ever talk to your father? He knows
a lot about things, you know. . .' 'My father? He's a poet, my
father. . . He never has his feet on the ground. He says that he
can light up the moon, but he walks down the street with his
fly undone! How can you talk to a man like that? He makes
up legends for himself; I make up problems.' And suddenly,
so easily it seemed almost ridiculous, Laura began to talk.
Everything came out at once, the way that she'd felt it was
beginning earlier; and as she spoke, she could see her problems
flying away from her like birds escaping from a cage. 'It feels
good to talk, auntie! It really helps!' 'That's as it should be.'

'There's still time to get there before the show starts. . .' 'I
said no, Mastaï! And I don't want to hear another word about
it! Next time, you'll think twice before you talk! It's fine to
pull my sister's leg a little, but you didn't have to make her
suffer that much!' 'Gaby, it was just a joke.' 'I know it was
just a joke! That's what makes it so awful! You never want
to hurt anybody, but you always go too far, so this time, I'm
going to teach you a lesson. . .' 'If you cut me off, you'll be
cutting yourself off too!' 'That's exactly it — and I hope
you'll feel twice as guilty.' Mastaï Jodoin took the theatre
tickets from his pocket and put them on the table. 'Two
and a half bucks shot to hell! Maybe we can give them to
somebody. . .' 'Who? The show starts in half an hour. . . .
They'd have to break their necks to get there. . . . No, no.
Throw them out.' Gabrielle Jodoin came out of the bathroom
where she'd just made herself beautiful again. She and Mastaï
had been talking through the closed door while she gave her
hair a final brushing. She rumpled her husband's hair and
screwed up her face in distaste. 'You aren't even changed!'

Gabrielle was truly ravishing in her flowered dress and Mastaï
felt his anger melt like snow in the sun. 'We're only going to
your sister's, Gaby. . . And anyhow, I'm not dirty!' His voice
was softer now and Gabrielle was aware of it. She held back the
smile that was already beginning to turn up her lips. 'Put on a
shirt at least. . . I'm not crazy about seeing you cross the street
in your undershirt.' As soon as he set foot in the house, Mastaï
had the unfortunate habit of parading about in his underwear
— and Gabrielle hadn't yet managed to cure him of this defect,
which she and her sisters considered outrageous, but which
their mother, Rita Guérin, thought was funny. She often said
that her son-in-law resembled a big baby looking all over for
his mother and never finding her. No one really understood
this image, but Rita Guérin seemed to find it most amusing.
When Mastaï put on his clean shirt, Gabrielle undertook to fix
his hair with her hairbrush, something her husband particularly
enjoyed. He sat on a kitchen chair, squeezing his wife between
his legs and moaning with joy. He wrapped his arms around
Gabrielle's big belly and assumed his little boy's voice, a voice
that made Gabrielle laugh so much — thanks to which he
could get anything he wanted from her. 'Your big honeybear
all forgiven?' 'You look too damn swell, Mastaï. I'd have to be
blind in both eyes if I really wanted to be pissed off at you!'
Mastaï raised his head and rested his chin against his wife's
belly. 'Want me to call a taxi? It wouldn't take us more than
fifteen minutes to get there. . .' Gabrielle bopped him on the
head with her hairbrush and he howled, more from surprise
than pain. 'You think I'm a nincompoop, Mastaï Jodoin? I told
you I forgave you, but I never said I'd forgotten everything!
So get La Poune and Juliette Pétrie out of your head, because
it won't do any good!' Everything happened so abruptly that
Gabrielle had no time to react. Mastaï literally leaped on the
telephone and dialled a number. 'For the love of God, what
are you doing?' 'Calling a taxi! Maybe you don't want to go
to the theatre, but I do!' He gave the address and hung up,
grabbed the two tickets which were still on the kitchen table
and headed for the door. 'Go play cards with your mother and
your sisters, if you want. I'll ask Germaine's husband to come

and see La Poune with me!' Gabrielle ran after him. They
crossed the street behind one another — Gabrielle holding her
belly with both hands, and Mastaï waving the tickets in his right
hand. 'If you do that, you'll be sorry, my little man!' Mastaï
stopped at the bottom of the outside staircase that went up to
Germaine's apartment. He turned around and faced his wife.
'Will you stop treating me like a child? And stop punishing
me like a baby when I do something you don't like! I'm not a
child, Gabrielle Jodoin, and you won't get me to do something
by taking away my candy! My mother tried that trick when
I was little and you can see where it got her! I bought these
tickets because I knew it'd make us both happy! And I don't
see any reason why I shouldn't enjoy myself! Okay, so I didn't
treat your thin-skinned little sister with kid gloves, but that's
no reason to turn it into a three-act tragedy! I'll tell her I'm
sorry and then we'll forget the whole business! I'll bet that
she's already forgotten all about it! Sometimes your sister "The
Actress" is a hell of a lot less dramatic than you are!' Gabrielle
sat on the steps, her head down. Her husband sat down beside
her. 'Here comes the taxi. Are you coming with me or should I
take Ernest?' Gabrielle put one hand on Mastaï's knee. 'Go with
Ernest. I see what you mean, but I'm not in the mood to go out
any more.' Mastaï sprang to his feet, furious, and climbed the
stairs four at a time. He walked into his sister-in-law's house
without knocking. Gabrielle folded her arms on her knees and
lay her head on them. 'How do you expect me to have any
fun when you get me all worked up like that?' Rose Ouimet
and her husband, Roland, were walking slowly down the street
towards Germaine Lauzon's house. Despite the heat, Rose
Ouimet was wearing a roomy wool coat over her dress, probably
to conceal her pregnancy. She jumped at the sight of her sister
Gabrielle sitting on the stairs. 'Good Lord, something's wrong
with her!' Roland Ouimet raised his eyes to Heaven. His wife's
family was grounds for wailing and the gnashing of teeth,
Roland Ouimet knew only too well. After all, he had married
the most dramatic daughter in the family, Rose, who saw
tragedies everywhere, revelling in them constantly, watering
them copiously with her tears and never doing anything to

settle them. He spoke so softly that his wife didn't hear him. 'Jesus Christ, another drama! You must be proud of yourself!' Just then, a taxi stopped in front of Germaine's house. Mastaï and Ernest came out on the second-floor balcony, waving their arms. Rose walked faster, leaving her husband behind her. 'Just what's going on here?' When she reached the stairs where her sister was prostrate, her two brothers-in-law were coming down the steps. Mastaï walked past Gabrielle without a word and ensconced himself in the taxi, followed by Ernest Lauzon, who didn't seem to have the slightest notion of what was happening to him. Germaine Lauzon, Rita Guérin and Pierrette Guérin, in turn, came out on the balcony. Mastaï Jodoin slammed the taxi door shut and shouted: 'Bye, everybody, have a nice time!' The taxi drove away. Slowly, Gabrielle got to her feet and climbed up a few steps. Rose Ouimet followed her, almost in tears. 'Good Lord, what'd he do to you now?' 'They're all alike, the sons of bitches, every last one of them!' Roland Ouimet had remained at the foot of the stairs, watching the two women climb the stairs. He spoke to his mother-in-law, who was waiting for her daughters on the balcony. 'They gone for the night?' Rita Guérin shrugged. 'What do *you* think? Did they look like they were going to buy an ice-cream cone, numbskull?' Roland stepped back a few paces. 'So, I'll be the only man here tonight! I can't stand playing cards with a bunch of women! Play with yourselves, I'm going to the tavern!' As his wife watched him with contempt, he began to walk along Mont-Royal. When her two daughters reached the balcony, Rita Guérin took Gabrielle in her arms. 'Instead of playing cards tonight, we'll sit out on the balcony. It's warm enough. . . Pierrette, bring out the chairs. Your sisters mustn't strain themselves.' Gabrielle blew her nose noisily into the handkerchief that her mother offered her. When she'd finished drying her eyes, she sighed deeply. 'The worst of it is that he's right, curse him!'

Léopold Brassard walked into the living room without making a sound. The room was plunged in darkness. Guessing at his wife's silhouette, Léopold approached the window, his hands in his pockets, embarrassed. Immediately after supper, without a word, Marie-Louise had gone back to the living room, to her kingdom, and attached herself to her window, without even thinking of switching on the lamps. Marie-Louise didn't hear her husband come in and she started a little when he spoke. 'How come you're sitting in the dark like that?' Is there anything worth looking at in here?' 'Is there anything worth looking at outside?' She buried her head a little deeper in the lace curtain. 'It doesn't bother me, what's outside. It's more interesting.' Léopold put his hand on his wife's shoulder. 'Did the baby kick today?' Marie-Louise freed herself, as if some disgusting animal had touched her. 'Please keep your hands to yourself, Léopold! You smell of the printshop.' She brought her hand to her mouth. 'Why not come right out with it and say I make you sick?' 'Yes, Léopold, you make me sick.' 'See how silly you are. . . I was coming to get you so we could go out and sit on the balcony. . . Everybody else is out on their balcony to celebrate the arrival of spring. . . We're the only ones shut up inside — as usual.' 'Maybe they've got something to celebrate. We haven't.' 'Please, Marie-Louise. It's just as dark on the balcony and it's cooler. . . In your condition. . .' 'What do you know about my condition?' 'Not much maybe, but I know if a woman shuts herself up in the dark, in her living room, it's because she's got something to hide!' Marie-Louise jerked her head towards her husband. 'You said it! I've got something to hide all right!' She got up slowly, leaning on the back of her chair. 'This!' Laughter burst out on one of the balconies across from them, but Marie-Louise and Léopold didn't look towards the window. They were lost in their mutual hatred, looking into one another's eyes, almost hypnotized. Mercedes and Béatrice were coming down the stairs of the house across the street. They were followed by Edouard, who was singing at the top of his lungs 'Some Day My Prince Will Come,' and throwing kisses, left and right. On the balcony, Thérèse, Richard and Philippe were laughing like lunatics. Very slowly,

Léopold looked away from his wife's face in order to glance out
the window. He managed to smile. 'Some people know how
to have fun.' Marie-Louise clicked her tongue four or five
times. 'That's right! Go down the stairs singing "Some Day
My Prince Will Come" and I'll laugh.' Léopold walked out of
the living room, his heels clattering on the linoleum. He took
a folding chair from behind the door in the hallway and put it
on the balcony, beneath the amused gaze of the fat man who
had stopped singing as soon as he saw him come out of the
house. Edouard bent over his two new friends. 'Sweet Jesus,
girls, the rats are coming out of their holes! The plague can't
be far behind!' Mercedes and Béatrice hid behind their hands
and laughed. Léopold, smiling at the sight of his neighbours
in such a merry mood, took out his tobacco pouch and pipe.
'I wonder what the hell he said to make them laugh like that?'
Mercedes, Béatrice and Edouard were now sitting on the steps
like children. Béatrice seemed impatient. 'That taxi's taking
its sweet time. . .' 'Cool it, Betty, the night's still young. . .'
Edouard took the girls by the shoulders. 'Betty's like me, she
likes them young!' Thérèse and the boys had come out to
join their elders on the steps. She dislodged her uncle and
sat between Mercedes and Béatrice. 'I'd like to know how
come you were laughing your heads off just now.' Edouard
tapped her shoulder lightly. 'You're too young, Thérèse, you
wouldn't understand.' Visibly angry, Thérèse leaped to her
feet and stood with her fists against her hips. 'I understand
a lot more than you think, aunt Edouard!' Edouard collapsed
on the steps with laughter, while the two women nudged
each other, snickering. Thérèse, who had thought that her
reply was insulting, even though she didn't understand all the
implications, was taken aback. 'They're such dummies tonight!
They'll laugh at anything!' Before sitting down again, she held
her hands round her mouth to form a megaphone. 'I kissed
a man on the mouth this afternoon!' Her words didn't have
the expected effect. Béatrice had just sprung to her feet, her
nerves on edge. 'There it is! There it is!' She was pointing at
a taxi. 'I hope we won't be too late.' Edouard waved both arms
to attract the taxi-driver's attention, as the driver checked the

house members. 'Anyhow, girls, Juliette Pétrie and La Poune
never come on before the middle of the show. . . They're the
stars, you see, so they fix it so people have to wait for them!'
As the taxi drove off, Thérèse heard Mercedes say to Edouard,
'That niece of yours is going to be a real beauty.' Thérèse smiled
with satisfaction. She couldn't hear her uncle's reply. It would
have pleased her less. 'She'll be a beauty all right, but if you ask
me, she's going to be a goddamn monster.' The taxi turned west
on Gilford and disappeared with squealing tyres. Edouard was
leading Mercedes and Béatrice towards a destiny that none of
them could guess at: a twenty-year reign of feasts and splendour
for Béatrice, who until the early sixties would be the darling
of Montreal's night-owls, the prostitute draped in more jewels
and compliments than any other in the city's history, always
demanding and sometimes perverse, voluptuous when fashion
demanded it, and thin as a rake the rest of the time, a second
Ti-Lou, but without the accent and, more important, without
her pretensions. (Béatrice was quick to realize that, though
they paid better, the high and mighty didn't fuck too often
— and she quickly began to specialize in businessmen who
were less glamorous, but hornier.) Sometimes she was rich
enough to give away her dresses after wearing them only once
(one day she happened upon a biography of Marie-Antoinette
and decided to copy her, instead of watching her outfits wilt
in her wardrobe); sometimes she was as poor as the bums in
Dominion Square, for whom she felt much affection, and who
returned it, though they concealed it cleverly as they waited for
the next windfall, which, in time, would descend on them; and
for Mercedes, there would be an ephemeral but dazzling career
as a singer, unfortunately cut short in the middle of the 1950s,
by an automobile accident that cost her her life. Back-stage at
the Théâtre National where Edouard had an entrée, thanks to
a tap-dancer recently hired by La Poune, Fine Dumas was
waiting for them, a self-styled impresario for touring dancers,
but in fact, an unscrupulous procuress and supplier of fresh
talent to all the whorehouses in Quebec, from the sleaziest to
the fanciest, from the most discreet to the most garish. Fine
Dumas would appreciate immediately the considerable value

of the merchandise that Edouard was innocently bringing her, and she was to take over the two friends, turning them into the crowned heads of Montreal nights. And so it was that three plucked soldiers and a walk through Lafontaine Park would supply Montreal with ten years of love songs and twenty years of furtive but dazzling loves. Léopold watched the scene as he pulled voluptuously on his pipe. The good smell of tobacco that made him feel so secure gradually enveloped him, and he felt himself becoming light. A few minutes later, the door opened discreetly behind him. He heard the door open, but he didn't turn around. Marie-Louise spoke in a very low voice, as if she were telling him a secret. Or a confession. 'Go and get the rocking chair, Léopold. It's too hot inside.' On the other side of the street, Philippe, who was intently picking his nose, asked Thérèse a question that made the little girl blush. 'Thérèse, did you really kiss a man on the mouth this afternoon?'

Albertine, Josaphat-the-Violin and Laura were washing the dishes as Victoire listened to the news on the radio. Albertine seemed exhausted and large drops of sweat were running down her face. 'You could have left the dishes till tomorrow, Bartine. . .' 'Tomorrow. . . Don't make me laugh! Tomorrow I have to start all over again. If I don't do the dishes at night, I have to get up early tomorrow and do them.' 'How come the children don't give you a hand? Thérèse is big enough. . .' 'She's big enough, all right, but she is not keen, as you can well imagine! Not very often, anyway. I always feel as if she's judging me, so there's times when I'd just as soon she wasn't around.' 'You should stop thinking that everybody's judging you, Bartine.' 'I'd think it even if it wasn't true! Do you think I couldn't see all of you at suppertime? Eh? I didn't want to serve those two floozies out of principle but all I got for my trouble was stupid jokes and mean cracks. I got laughed at because I've got principles! Let me tell you, I'm starting to ask myself a hell of a lot of questions! If it's got to the point where you have to invite floozies for a meal to get some respect in your

own house, I'd like to know what happens next!' Furiously,
Albertine emptied the kettle that was full of hot water into
the now tepid dishwater. 'Don't scald yourself now! That
isn't necessary!' 'And all those stupid ideas that you're filling
Marcel's head with. . . . Just now, I heard you tell him that
story about turning on the light in the moon. I ask you, does
that make any sense? The child's four years old, don't forget,
and he believes everything you tell him. Last Saturday, you told
him that story of yours about the nuns' farts that make people
lose their memories, and Sunday morning, he started telling me
that he didn't know where his shoes were because a nun's fart
had hit him during the night. Four years old, I tell you, and
he's making fun of me already!' 'If you had more of a sense of
humour, Bartine. . .' 'A sense of humour! Hocus-pocus that
you can't make head or tail of that turns our kids into liars!
Life's tough enough without them making up things on top of
everything else!' Josaphat-the-Violin decided to stop arguing
with his niece. Albertine turned to Laura, who hadn't said
a word since the conversation began. 'And how about you,
Laura? How can you tell when your father's stringing you a
line and when he's telling the truth?' Laura stopped drying the
dishes for a moment. She seemed lost in thought. When she
did speak, it was with conviction — and her reply required no
response. 'I don't really care. In fact, I think sometimes it even
helps me get on with my life, the way he spins his yarns.'
Albertine plunged her hands into the boiling water. 'Okay. I
get it. I'm the one that's crazy. Go ahead and dream, the
whole bunch of you. One of these days, you'll tell me you'd
have been better off with your two feet on the ground like
me.' Josaphat-the-Violin and Laura looked at one another and
shrugged. In the dining room, Victoire had her ear pressed to
the radio, as she did every evening, but she wasn't listening.
The long walk that afternoon had tired her far more than she
was willing to admit, and her heart was beating a little too
fast for her liking. 'Goddamn potato! It's going to blow up on
me!' She took the shawl that was always draped on the back
of her rocking chair and shivered as she wrapped it around
her shoulders. 'I shouldn't have served the supper either. . .

I'm too goddamn proud!' The presence of the two fancy women in the house had had a predictable effect: Albertine was furious, but Victoire wasn't able to derive the slightest pleasure from that fact. Usually, making her daughter angry was one of her greatest delights (it was her way of reminding Albertine that she still existed, even though she was kept away from everything that went on in the house because of her age and her infirmity), but at supper tonight, perhaps for the very first time, Victoire had felt some pity for poor Albertine as she contemplated Mercedes and Béatrice with such horror and disgust that it seemed as though she might be sick in her plate at any moment. 'I'm getting old too fast. Getting soft. There's no reason to feel sorry for Bartine. She goes looking for trouble!' Marcel, who had been sleeping on his sofa for a good half-hour, stirred in his sleep and uttered a few incomprehensible words, among which Victoire thought that she could recognize 'moon' and 'horsey.' Her vision from the afternoon came back to her. She didn't want to think about it any more. Ever. Josaphat-the-Violin had half-comforted her by making her feel that she wasn't crazy. . . but the old woman on the balcony seemed so gentle. . . and she looked at Marcel so tenderly. . . And that family resemblance! . . . 'I'm overtired, that's all! Instead of seeing things like that, I just won't go out! Ever again!' And suddenly, she was filled with all the dread of that possibility — until it submerged her and she brought her hand to her heart, thinking that she was going to die. 'No! No! I don't want to stay cooped up in here! I don't want to!' Gabriel was sitting at his wife's feet. He told her about his afternoon: the incident with Willy Ouelette, the too many beers, his doubts about the war, his flight, and finally, his meeting with Béatrice. The fat woman listened to everything, stroking his head. When he finished, she spoke to him softly, almost as if she were speaking to a child, emphasizing certain words by pressing her fingers against her husband's temples or his neck, waving away his doubts as much with her hands as with her voice, slowly comforting this soul that she knew to be weak, but whom she loved so much, concealing her own problems, her own fears, in order to tend to his. At last, he fell asleep, his head on the fat woman's lap. Then she was silent and she turned her face towards the moon that had moved into her corner of the sky. Her breathing was spasmodic, as though sobs were trying to come out of her throat. She rested her head against the back of her chair. 'Acapulco!' The child in her belly kicked so hard that she couldn't help crying out in pain. Gabriel awoke with a start.

Catholic church marginalizes role of pregnancy.

Objects to appearance

Pierrette Guérin was still out of breath. She'd come running down the street to announce her good news to her best friend, Thérèse, but to her great surprise, Thérèse didn't seem at all excited. On the contrary, she frowned and grimaced in distaste. 'How come you're carrying on like that, Thérèse? I give you some good news, but you look as if I'd just slapped your face!' 'I don't know if your news is all that good, Pierrette. . .' 'Oh, everybody knows you've got straight teeth and everybody thinks you're beautiful! But if you had big spaces in between your teeth like me, you'd be singing another tune!' Thérèse and Pierrette were sitting at the foot of the stairs. Pierrette was fiddling with the hem of her dress. Richard and Philippe, who didn't like Pierrette very much, had disappeared as she approached and gone up to sit in the big chairs on the balcony before the grown-ups came outside and took them away. 'Listen, Pierrette, I think a plate's disgusting. Can you see yourself stuck for the rest of your life with this thing in your mouth that's too big for you? That you have to take out of your mouth and clean and. . . yuck! Just thinking about it gives me the creeps.' Pierrette stopped playing with the hem of her dress and now she was looking at her friend with pleading eyes. She would have liked a word of encouragement, an affirmative nod, a friendly pat, but instead, Thérèse was doing everything possible to discourage her. 'But Thérèse, at least I'll have straight teeth!' Thérèse got up, turned her back to her friend and climbed up a few steps before replying. 'Anyhow, do whatever you like, because I don't want a friend with false teeth that could fall out anytime that she sticks in a glass of water beside her bed when she goes to sleep at night!' Thérèse had often seen her grandmother's false teeth in a glass of water that Victoire kept on her bedside table, and she imagined that everyone who wore dentures was obliged to take them out in order to sleep. Abandoning her friend with no remorse, Thérèse went to join the boys on the balcony. Philippe was rocking a little too hard in his father's chair, and sometimes, the back struck against the brick wall with a thud, while Richard was falling asleep in his grandmother's folding chair. 'What's she up to, your pal Pierrette? Did she bite you with her crooked teeth?' 'Don't worry, Flip, pretty soon, she won't be able to bite!' Pierrette was going home, her head drooping, when she met the dog. It was a huge yellow beast, flabby and ugly; it was following a trail with determination, sniffing the sidewalk lustfully, as though about to eat it, furiously sniffing the air when he smelled an odour different from the one he was pursuing, then letting out a little moan of satisfaction when he smelled it again. Pierrette, her hands behind her back, cautiously approached the yellow dog. 'You're a big doggy! And real ugly too! You looking for something to eat? There's a little girl over there on the second floor. . . I wouldn't mind if you took a couple of bites out of her. . . She's pretty skinny, but you'd be doing me a favour!' Pierrette had come a little too close to the dog, who suddenly began barking wildly. Five seconds later, Pierrette was running up the stairs of her sister Germaine's house, throwing herself into her mother's arms, sobbing. Rita Guérin put down her Coke on the floor of the balcony. 'Well, another tragedy, eh? Was that you the dog was barking at? Yes? Well, that's just too bad! How many times have we told you not to get too close to dogs you don't know? And don't wipe your nose on my dress like that! I just washed it!' Rita Guérin held out her handkerchief to Pierrette, who blew her nose loudly. 'I saw you gabbing with your great friend Thérèse just now. . . I hope you didn't go and tell her that I promised you a set of dentures. Because when I told you that just now, it was only to get you off my back. You're getting on my nerves, you and those damn teeth of yours! You're only eleven years old, Pierrette. Your teeth've got all the time in the world to straighten out. . . I wouldn't get your teeth pulled at your age, it'd be criminal! Now don't go telling anybody that I said that or else they'll think I'm crazy! Wait till you're seventeen, like everybody else!' As soon as Pierrette disappeared, the dog continued on its way. The track it was following stopped abruptly in front of a wrought-iron fence that smelled of fresh paint. The dog walked back and forth in front of the fence three or four times to be sure there were no gaps that he could slip through, then he flattened himself in front of the fence gate, his head on his front paws in a gesture of supplication. He began to moan like a puppy that has lost its mother. His act was pure hypocrisy. While he seemed on the outside to be pleading and pitiful, ideas of carnage and murder were seething in his head. 'Come out, you goddamn cat! Come out, if you aren't too yellow! Instead of staying inside there, being fussed over like some lily-livered coward, try and show me how brave you are, so I can put out your other eye and then jump on your throat and finish you off! I have to finish you off! I have to make sure you're dead! Otherwise, knowing you, you could get better in no time and come back and shit all over me. I gave up my territory tonight so I could come and settle things with you once and for all! But it's worth it! I won't be safe till I'm sure you're off in cat heaven or maybe cat hell, where mice and dogs are allowed to chase you and kill you and eat you up and then start all over again, for ever and ever!' Philippe was leaning over the balcony railing. 'Look, Thérèse, that damn dog from this afternoon followed us all the way home.' But Thérèse wasn't listening. For several minutes she'd been watching a shadow slumped on one of the staircases on the other side of the street. At first she thought it was Monsieur Brassard or Monsieur Poitevin, but Monsieur Brassard was up on his balcony smoking his pipe and Monsieur Poitevin had been in the hospital for weeks. Then, a gesture that the shadow made, the way the man ran his hand through his hair, made Thérèse's heart leap. 'It's him! He followed me all the way home!' A mixture of sensual pleasure and fear ran through her body and she began

to tremble. 'My Lord, what'll I do? I have to tell somebody. . .
No. . . no. . . There's no danger. . . and it's exciting. . . He
liked it when I kissed him and he wants more. . . He wants me
to do it again! Well, he'll just have to wait, goddamn him, if he
thinks I'm going to jump on his neck like that. . . Sure, he's
handsome. . . But I can be independent when I want!' Thérèse
began to laugh softly and Philippe looked at her, amazed. 'You
think it's funny, him following us all the way home?' Thérèse
smothered her laughter. 'Did you see him too?' 'Can't you hear
him howling? But I know what he wants. He's waiting for his
victim so he can kill him.' Thérèse, panic-stricken, ran into
the house. On the staircase across the street, Gérard Bleau was
weeping.

all characters looking to set out

Around nine o'clock that evening, Josaphat and Gabriel helped
the fat woman out onto the balcony. It wasn't nearly as
complicated as they'd expected. The fat woman managed to
get out of her chair, and then, by putting an arm around each
of the men's shoulders, she walked slowly across the bedroom,
taking small steps, supported more by her will than by her
legs. She stopped for a moment in the dining room in front
of Marcel's sofa, where the little boy was asleep with his fists
closed, and smiled at her mother-in-law, who was beginning to
drift off to sleep in her rocking chair. 'I'm going out to sit on
the balcony and I'm so glad!' Victoire belched, coughed and
cleared her throat. 'I do believe I was having a snooze there. . .
I'd better go to bed, I think. . . You ought to spend the night
out there, if it isn't too chilly. . . Cover yourself up well and
breathe deep. It'll do you good!' Josaphat, Gabriel and the fat
woman began to make their way slowly down the corridor. The
fat woman felt as if she were dreaming. Often in her sleep, she
had seen herself get up and walk — or float, rather — through
the house, going into all the rooms to check that nothing had
changed and kissing every member of the family, as if they
were all her children. This time, though, she wasn't dreaming,
and yet, the same sensation of lightness supported her on her

long walk to the balcony. Everything in the house was smaller than she remembered, though. The rooms, the furniture; even the huge furnace that sat imposingly in the corridor between Victoire's room and Edouard's. The ceilings were lower too. 'Maybe it's because I've got so fat. . .' Philippe and Thérèse came to meet her and they encouraged her as much as they could. 'Keep going, auntie. You'll see. It's worth it. It's so beautiful outside. . .' 'Want me to help you, Mama? Is there anything I can do for you?' Albertine followed behind, grumbling: 'What are you doing, going outside like that? In your nightgown! And in your condition! What will people think? They'll be calling us gypsies!' Victoire followed on the fat woman's heels, pushing her daughter from the back. 'Bartine! Leave her alone! I'd rather be called a gypsy than find her in her bedroom tomorrow morning dead of boredom!' Laura Cadieux brought up the rear, holding her belly with both hands. When they finally reached the door to the balcony, the fat woman asked for a few moments' respite. 'Let me catch my breath. It's been so long since I've taken a step. . .' She stood there, clutching her husband's and her uncle's neck, but stretching her head so that she could look outside. She was so eager that her heart leaped. 'It's beautiful. . . the leaves haven't started to grow yet, but it won't be long now. . . It smells of April and May, all at once!' Inside her, the baby moved again. 'It won't be long now, angel. It won't be long. Mama's finished her walk and now you can see how good it is to breathe the fresh air!' She advanced a few paces and stepped onto the balcony. Richard woke with a start and cried out in delight when he saw his mother there. He got up and huddled against her belly. 'Come, sit down, Mama. . . You feeling all right? You sure?' They sat the fat woman down in Gabriel's big rocking chair. 'Everything all right?' 'You comfortable there?' 'You need anything?' 'I'll get you a pillow.' 'A nice cold soft drink would taste good, don't you think?' Even Albertine was leaning over her. 'I bought some spruce beer this afternoon. . .' When everything was silent again, and the fat woman was able to contemplate the street as much as she liked, steep herself in the images and sensations of the early spring night, scrutinize the smallest shadowy corners, recognizing, in spite of the darkness, the faces of all the neighbours watching her from their balconies, breathe deep the promises of May, and what still remained of April, time was suspended and nothing moved. Then, very softly, as if he were afraid of breaking the spell, Josaphat-the-Violin offered to play a tune on his fiddle. Around him, the faces all lit up. 'Now what should I play for you? "Humoresque" or the "Meditation" from *Thaïs*? Or maybe you'd like a jig or a reel. . .' 'I asked for the "Meditation" from *Thaïs* this afternoon uncle. That's what I'd like. . .' Philippe ran to get his uncle's fiddle. And the 'Meditation' from *Thaïs* rose above the street perhaps a little wobbly, but played with such sincerity that even the wrong notes transported the soul and chased sorrow away in concentric waves. Then, Josaphat played 'Humoresque,' which he played better, and after that his country sorcerer's repertoire, which in just one evening, can make you forget all the miseries on this earth and all the unhappiness in the world. Victoire even started tapping her foot as she used to do when she was young; and Gabriel warbled along, as his father had taught him to do. Albertine went inside and awakened Marcel, who thought he was dreaming, and expected that, at any moment, Duplessis would jump up on his lap, telling him in his pussycat's language: 'I'm back! I'm back! And I'm more marvellous than ever!' Thérèse, Richard and Philippe, the first city generation, for whom music was something that came out of the radio, not from the hands, feet and mouth of people they knew, were fascinated, and, transported by the sight: their grandmother, tapping her foot, and their great-uncle, the balcony magician. The fat woman herself launched into a song as she did in the days when all the street would listen to her sing when she made her red ketchup and green preserves in the fall. On the other side of the street, without realizing it, Marie-Louise Brassard put her hand over her husband's hand. 'It reminds me of back home! I don't feel as if I'm in a cage any more!' Rita Guérin and her three pregnant daughters came down from their balcony, followed by Pierrette, and sat on the steps. Claire Lemieux, abandoning

her fat white whale of a husband to his beer and potato chips,
came and joined them. Marie-Sylvia put the little sign that read:
'Closed until 7 tomorrow morning' in her window and walked
across the street in her Saturday dress, its freshness now gone.
And suddenly, after 'Heure Exquise,' which everyone sang
in chorus, swaying from left to right, the fat woman leaned
over the balcony railing and said: 'Come on up! Come on!
Come up and have a chat!' She looked, in turn, at Germaine
Lauzon, Rose Ouimet, Gabrielle Jodoin, Claire Lemieux and
even Marie-Louise Brassard, who hadn't left her own balcony.
'I'm going to have a baby too, just like the rest of you. . .
Come on. Let's talk about it.' The three Guérin sisters were
the first to make up their minds, followed closely by Claire
Lemieux. The last to move was Marie-Louise Brassard, who
indicated at first that she didn't want to leave her balcony,
even getting up to go into the house. But when the fat woman
spoke directly to her ('Come on, Madame Brassard. You too.
We don't know each other yet.'), she was obliged to obey. All
the same, when she crossed the street, she tried to conceal her
pregnancy with a sweater draped over her arm. The others left
the balcony discreetly, making way for the pregnant women.
The fat woman's family disappeared into the house, and soon
you could hear Josaphat's fiddle playing in the dining room.
Marie-Sylvia went down Fabre Street murmuring: 'Duplessis!
Duplessis!' looking under balconies and behind fences for her
cat; and Rita Guérin went back to her own balcony, dragging
Pierrette behind her. Godbout and Gérard Bleau hadn't stirred.
Then, from the balcony came laughter, whispers and shouts
that were held back by hands placed over mouths. There were
seven women. Six were in their early twenties and didn't know
what was in store for them, while the seventh, who could have
been their mother, explained it all to them.

Rose, Violette and Mauve were knitting. Their balcony was
plunged in darkness, but their hands automatically carried
out the correct movements, the right rhythm. In her lap,

Florence, their mother, was holding a sick cat whom she'd finally managed to lull to sleep. She smiled as she listened to the seven pregnant women above her. Godbout suspected that something was up. He searched the darkness in vain. Despite that damned smell of cat that clung to the night air, the balcony remained empty, mocking him.

marginalization of males

3 fates

smelling cat,
    cant see it

cat can see ladies
ladies here
3 ladies want to get all
    ladies out together

gesture

men are
gone.
cat is left
+ in touch
w/ myth